I0710480

Books by Tina Folsom

Scanguards Vampires

Samson's Lovely Mortal (#1)

Amaury's Hellion (#2)

Gabriel's Mate (#3)

Yvette's Haven (#4)

Zane's Redemption (#5)

Quinn's Undying Rose (#6)

Oliver's Hunger (#7)

Thomas's Choice (#8)

Silent Bite (#8 1/2)

Cain's Identity (#9)

Luther's Return (#10)

Mortal Wish (# 1/2)

Blake's Pursuit (#11)

Fateful Reunion (#11 1/2)

John's Yearning (#12)

A Taste of Greek (#3)

A Hush of Greek (#4)

Venice Vampyr

Wicked Lover (#1)

Final Affair (#2)

Sinful Treasure (#3)

Sensual Danger (#4)

Thriller: Eyewitness

Code Name Stargate

Ace on the Run (#1)

Fox in plain Sight (#2)

Yankee in the Wind (#3)

Tiger on the Prowl (#4)

Hawk on the Hunt (#5)

The Hamptons Bachelor Club

Accidental Escort (#1)

Accidental Truth (#2)

Vanessa's Bravery

Scanguards Vampires #18

Tina Folsom

1

Vanessa Giles got out of her beat-up Volkswagen Jetta and locked it when the high-pitched sound of a woman's screams reached her ears. Somebody was in trouble.

Fuck!

She'd already checked in with the homeless and the sex workers in SOMA, which had taken her a good three hours. Luckily, everyone seemed to be doing as well as could be expected. She'd encouraged one of the homeless men she'd encountered to visit a free medical clinic the next day to make sure his cough didn't turn into something worse. Two of the sex workers plying their trade on the streets south of Market were overdue for their medical exams, and Vanessa made sure they knew that they had an appointment to see their doctor this week.

This was her job at Scanguards, the security company her entire family worked for. Officially, she carried the fancy title of Community Outreach Manager, but what the job really boiled down to was being a social worker taking care of the vulnerable population in San Francisco: the homeless, the mentally ill, the drug users, and the sex workers. She made sure that they weren't being mistreated and went to the city's free clinic when they were sick or injured. A chunk of the mayor's budget went to Scanguards for those services. Just as a part of the police department's budget went to Scanguards to deal with any preternatural or vampire-related crimes committed in the city.

Both her brothers, Ryder and Ethan, worked as bodyguards and investigators at Scanguards, while her father, Gabriel, was the second-in-command, and her mother, Maya, ran a small medical facility in the bowels of the Scanguards headquarters building in the Mission.

Vanessa sprinted in the direction of the scream. She was approaching the border between Chinatown and Nob Hill. She ran at a fast clip, her vampire senses alert. She was used to patrolling the city at night and felt no fear. Any man attempting to attack her would find out very quickly—and very painfully—that she wasn't somebody to trifle with. She might look barely twenty, slender, and vulnerable, but beneath the façade of a helpless woman lay the speed and strength of a vampire. Not only that, like her brothers, she'd undergone the bodyguard training at Scanguards, and was versed in several disciplines of hand-to-hand combat. A human had no chance against her. And the man currently attacking a woman —as much as she could deduce from the sounds drifting to her—would feel her wrath.

At the next corner, she turned and could finally see what was happening in a dark alley. She hadn't been wrong about a woman being attacked, though she had been wrong about *who* was assaulting her.

Shit!

The blood was the first thing she smelled. It overpowered the foul smells coming from a dumpster and the sewer grids running along the middle of the cobblestone road. The aura identifying the attacker as a vampire registered only a split-second later. He pressed a woman with long red hair against the wall of a building, while she hit her fist against him, desperately trying to fight him off, but the vampire already had his fangs in her neck.

In a millisecond, Vanessa assessed the situation. She had to stop the vampire, before he did irreparable damage to his victim. But killing another being had never been her first choice when trying to stop an assailant. Nor was it Scanguards' preferred modus operandi. It would be sufficient to apprehend him so he could be transferred to the vampire council who would determine his punishment.

Vanessa charged toward the assailant, planning to pull him away from his victim before he even knew what was happening, but the clickety-clack of her boot heels warned the vampire of her approach. He whipped his head to the side, growling, his eyes red like beacons, his fangs dripping with blood, while he was still holding on to the woman.

"Pick on people your own size!" Vanessa spat.

For a fraction of a second the vampire seemed to be stunned as if he didn't know that she was a vampire too, albeit a vampire hybrid, half vampire, half human.

Vanessa lunged at him, trying to kick him away from his victim, but the rogue grabbed the woman and tossed her toward Vanessa. His aim was off, and the woman landed on the dirty and smelly cobblestones a couple of feet to Vanessa's left.

Before she could ascertain the condition of the woman, the rogue vampire jumped toward her and punched her in the side, making her stumble. She caught herself quickly, still surprised at the vampire's quick reaction. Knowing she had to subdue him quickly because the victim on the ground was still bleeding profusely, she turned on her own axis, using the centrifugal force to kick her boot into his midsection. With a dull thud, the impact catapulted the aggressor against the opposite wall.

"Fucking bitch!"

Fury now spewed from the vampire as he came toward her again.

"Haven't had enough, have you?" she taunted him.

He rushed her like a crazed animal. What he lacked in finesse and style, he made up for with brute determination. He punched her with such force that she was lifted off her feet and crashed against the wall.

Ignoring the pain the impact had caused her, she pushed herself away from the building. Now he'd really pissed her off. Glad that she was wearing her leather gloves, she pulled her silver knife from the inside pocket of her jacket. She charged in the rogue's direction, wielding the deadly knife, though she intended to merely injure him before she could handcuff him with the silver cuffs in her pocket.

Something flashed in the rogue's eyes when he saw the knife, and he backed away, his back hitting the dumpster. Now she had him, and he knew it. The dumpster and the wall prevented him from escaping.

"You're gonna pay for this, bastard," she

warned and lunged, when she stumbled in mid-stride as if being pulled back by an invisible force.

"Fuck!" She couldn't move her left foot.

A quick glance to the ground showed her what had happened. The heel of her boot was stuck in a sewer grid.

The vampire saw it too. A gleeful grin spread on his face. "Bad luck, huh, bitch?"

Vanessa wiggled her boot, trying to free herself, but the rogue was already on the move, heading for the exit of the alley by the time she managed to free her heel.

A moan came from the injured woman on the ground. The smell of human blood was more intense now, and she realized that the woman would be bleeding out if she didn't help her now. She glanced back at the rogue.

He was already at the end of the alley, where he looked over his shoulder, laughing as if he understood her predicament. She could run after him and catch him, but by then the bleeding woman would be dead. She had no choice but to tend to the victim.

"Ginger, it's Vanessa. I've got you."

Ginger was one of the sex workers she saw regularly, and she was a good person—though she had a drug problem, which unfortunately made her take more risks than she should. But this wasn't Ginger's fault. The vampire who'd attacked her was a rogue, and he had to be stopped.

"Vanessa? Thank God." Her voice was weak.

Vanessa crouched down next to Ginger and pressed a hand on the deep wound the vampire had left in her neck. He'd taken chunks of skin and flesh out, attesting either to his brutality and callousness, or to his inexperience. She instantly recognized the grave error she'd made. Had she snuck up on the vampire without announcing herself, and staked him instantly, Ginger's injuries would have been less severe. But by being careless, she'd startled him and probably caused him to rip flesh and skin from Ginger's neck by not retracting his fangs first.

Guilt charged through her. But to kill somebody was a step she'd never taken—never had to—and hoped never would. Either way, Ginger was in bad shape. She needed help right now.

"Press your hand on here," Vanessa said, taking Ginger's hand. "Press really hard, and just close your eyes, okay? I'll give you something that'll help you."

When Ginger closed her eyes, Vanessa bit into her own wrist, before holding it over Ginger's lips so the blood dripped into her mouth. "Swallow."

Ginger swallowed dutifully, but continued to moan from the pain the rogue had inflicted. As Vanessa ran her eyes over her now, she discovered the claw marks the assailant had left on her breasts. Her skimpy top was ripped, and blood seeped from the gashes.

After a few moments, Vanessa lifted her wrist from over Ginger's mouth and licked over the incisions. The tiny holes her fangs had left closed instantly, healed by her saliva. She wished she could heal Ginger just as quickly, but her injuries were too deep. The drops of vampire blood Vanessa had given her would help her hold on until they could reach a safe place.

"We've gotta go," Vanessa said and lifted Ginger up, sliding one arm around the woman's waist, while placing Ginger's arm on her uninjured side across her shoulders so she could support Ginger's weight. "Just keep pressing on that neck wound, okay?"

Ginger mumbled something incoherent. Vanessa dragged her out of the alley, heading uphill. The closest safe place was only a few blocks away. As long as Ginger could hold on for five more minutes, she would make it.

2

Cole Whitlock looked at the boxes that still sat unopened in one corner of the Russian Hill condo that he'd moved into only a week earlier. How long he would live in San Francisco, he didn't really know yet. He never lived anywhere for too long. He needed the constant change of scenery to add excitement to his life that he couldn't find in other pursuits. His company, an internet startup that had turned online advertising on its head, ran pretty much without him, affording him to live wherever he wanted. This time, his choice was San Francisco, but he hadn't picked it for its architectural beauty, its history, or European flair.

He was finally ready to face his demons so he wouldn't meet with the same fate as his father: spiraling down into a deep depression from where he'd only seen one way to escape. By committing suicide. Trent Whitlock had been a lonely man but a good father, who'd done everything in his power to make life easier for his only son.

Cole felt his heart beat faster at the memory of finding his father dead in his home. Cole had been a junior at college, and deep down he'd always known that one day his father wouldn't be able to hold on to this life any longer. Cole had been dealt the same shitty hand, but he was determined to find a different solution to his problem. He wouldn't give up. He would keep fighting.

He opened his father's old journal where he'd recorded everything he'd attempted in order to alleviate his condition... and things he wanted to try but hadn't accomplished before his death. The notes, which included names and numbers of doctors, charlatans, faith healers, and other dubious individuals didn't make much sense to Cole, but he had nothing to lose at this point. With his company secure, he had the money and time to pursue what his father had given up on.

He'd found the San Francisco phone number in his father's journal quite a while ago, but hadn't called it yet. There was no name associated with it, and when he'd used a reverse phone lookup tool, he'd discovered that the number was unlisted.

"It's now or never," he mumbled under his breath and dialed. He put his cell phone on speaker mode and heard it ring.

It kept ringing, and Cole felt his hope evaporate with every second.

"Dr. Drake's office," a woman answered breathlessly. "Darn it! Get him outta here!"

Her last words sounded muffled, and he assumed she'd put her hand over the receiver to address somebody in the room.

"Hello? Who's calling?"

"Uhm, yes," Cole muttered so she wouldn't hang up. He had to think quickly. He hadn't expected to reach a doctor's office at this time of night. After all, it was well past 9 o'clock. He didn't really know what he'd expected. A private home maybe?

"Sir?"

"Yes, this is Cole Whitlock. I'd like to make an appointment with Dr. Drake."

"He's all booked up tonight."

"How about tomorrow during the day?"

There was a noticeable pause, and the woman's voice suddenly changed from saccharin-sweet to icy-cold. "You must have the wrong number."

"No, no. I've got the right number. It was given to me by my father." That wasn't the absolute truth, but it was the gist of it. "I really need to see Dr. Drake."

"We don't take any new patients at the moment," she said, her voice hesitant.

"Miss, please," he beseeched her, letting his charm flow into his voice. He knew he had a voice any radio personality would be envious of, and he had no scruples using the few advantages he'd been given in life. "You sound very busy. And working so hard at night must really take a toll. Can't be easy to deal with difficult patients."

His last insinuation was an educated guess. Her curse earlier was most likely directed at an unruly patient.

"You have no idea!" she agreed with a huff, but her voice began to change. "Sometimes, I really don't know why I'm still working here."

"I'm sure the place would fall apart without you," Cole said as sweetly as he could without sounding sarcastic. "But there are people who need you."

"You're right. I wish all patients were so considerate."

He smiled to himself. She was on his side. Now he had a chance to get to see the doctor.

"You said that tonight he's all booked. Do you have any openings in the next few days at all? I don't care what time, if only you could squeeze me in."

He heard the faint tapping of fingers on a computer keyboard. "Oh, actually, looks like we had a cancellation. We have availability tomorrow at 8:15pm."

Did this doctor see all his patients in the middle of the night? Maybe this guy was a charlatan who wanted to fly under the radar. He probably didn't even have a medical license. But who was he to judge? He had to find out why his father had Dr. Drake's number in his journal. Maybe the guy knew something that none of the other medical professionals Cole had consulted knew. It was worth a try. All he had to lose was a few hours of sleep.

"Eight fifteen tomorrow night? That's perfect. I don't think I have your address."

"I'll text it to you. Is this a good number for you?"

"Yes, this is my cell. Perfect."

"Enjoy your night, Mr. Whitlock. We'll see you tomorrow."

"Thank you, uhm, Miss...?"

"Please call me Marilyn," she said, her voice suddenly sounding like a kitten.

"Thank you, Marilyn. Have a good night."

He disconnected the call, and about thirty seconds later, he received a text with the doctor's office address. He tapped on it to see where in San Francisco it was located.

"Nob Hill." It wasn't far from his condo.

Cole let out a breath of relief. One hurdle was past him. What he needed now was something to relax him, or he'd explode with nervous energy. He wouldn't be able to sleep right now. He wanted company, female company.

He scrolled through his address book. The high-class establishment he'd frequented in Chicago had recommended a similar place in San Francisco. A place where as long as a man paid the right price, he wouldn't be turned away. And money was no object for him. His misgivings about having to pay for physical pleasures had long ago vanished. It was the best approach to deal with his need for sex, and it guaranteed him relief, which visiting a nightclub to pick up a woman didn't.

Cole stopped scrolling. He read the note he'd made. *Vera's, the sign says Executive Services.* The address was noted below it. He tapped on it. It was right at the border of Nob Hill and Chinatown. He put his cell phone in his pocket and walked into the bedroom, where he glanced into the full-length mirror. He wore casual but expensive pants, and a shirt that hugged his broad chest. He was neither overdressed nor underdressed for a visit to a brothel. All he needed was his wallet and his jacket. He slipped into his jacket, placed his wallet in the inside pocket and marched to the door. From a hook near it, he snatched his keys, and left his condo.

When he reached the underground garage of the small condo building, he walked past his Land Rover and straight to his Aston Martin and clicked the remote. He didn't drive it very often, since it was really meant for a smaller man, not one who was 6'3" and looked more like a bodybuilder than a computer whiz. Working out and bulking up had been a survival mechanism for so long that it was second nature by now. He wasn't the little kid anymore that had been every schoolyard bully's prime target. He'd learned to defend himself, and he didn't take shit from anyone anymore. Nobody could hurt him anymore, because he didn't let them get close enough to inflict pain.

But tonight wasn't about pain. It was

about pleasure, and he was determined to take what he needed so desperately. It had been a while since he'd touched a woman, and ever since he'd arrived in San Francisco, he'd felt his need for sex rise faster and higher than anywhere else. And tonight, it wasn't just the need to decompress before his appointment with Dr. Drake that sent him to a brothel, but a little voice inside him that kept nudging him to seek his pleasure in the arms of a woman and forget everything else for a couple of hours.

And that was exactly what he would do tonight.

3

"Bring her in here," Vera ordered, ushering Vanessa to a room at the end of the corridor, past the opulent staircase that led to the upper floors of the Queen Anne mansion that had once belonged to a railroad baron.

Vera held the door open, and Vanessa carried the unconscious Ginger into the room and placed her on the bed. "She lost consciousness a couple of minutes ago."

Vanessa continued pressing her hand over the gash on her neck to stop the blood loss. Ginger looked white as a sheet already, and she hoped that she wasn't too late.

"What happened?" Vera asked while she grabbed a towel from the ensuite bathroom, folded it, and pressed it over Vanessa's hand. "I'll put pressure on it."

Vanessa removed her hand, extended her fangs and bit into her wrist. With her other hand she pried Ginger's mouth open and let the blood from her wrist drip into the injured woman's mouth.

"She was attacked by a vampire."

"Did you get a good look at him?"

"A brief one, but I didn't recognize him. He's not one of us."

"Out-of-towner?"

"I assume so." Vanessa pressed her ear to Ginger's chest to listen for a heartbeat. It was so faint that even her sensitive vampire hearing barely picked it up. "Her heart's still beating." She looked up, her wrist still bleeding into Ginger's mouth. "She's got a chest injury too."

"I can heal that," Vera offered, motioning to the towel.

With one hand, Vanessa pressed the towel to Ginger's neck, so Vera could remove hers. She watched as Vera's hands transformed into claws, and she ripped her top to shreds to remove it. There were four long cuts across one breast and down to her abdomen, claw marks. Blood seeped from the wounds, and together with the blood that drenched Ginger's clothes and the towel, the small room was filled with its metallic scent. Vanessa couldn't help her fangs from extending, even though she had no intention of drinking Ginger's blood.

Vera's fangs were peeking past her lips too, but Vanessa knew she could trust the petite Asian woman with the porcelain face and the long black hair. She'd been a vampire for a long time, and she had her needs under control. It was a godsend that Vera's brothel was close by, sitting on the top of Nob Hill not far from the famous Fairmont Hotel.

Vera lowered her face to Ginger's breast and began to lick over the wounds, depositing saliva onto the cuts. A vampire's saliva had healing properties that could mend a human's skin without leaving any scars. The wounds on the woman's torso were shallow enough for the saliva to work. Unfortunately, the wound on Ginger's neck was too deep to heal by licking it. The vampire blood Vanessa gave her would heal her from the inside.

Vanessa felt her head spin suddenly, and realized that she couldn't give Ginger any more of her own blood. She removed her wrist and licked it to close the puncture wounds. At the same time, she felt heat crawl up her spine and engulf her head.

Fuck! She didn't need this right now, but she knew there was no stopping what always started like a fever. She closed her eyes, trying to push down her rising needs.

"You all right?" Vera suddenly asked, her hand on Vanessa's shoulder.

"Just a little faint and hot." She pulled her cell from her pocket, while still applying pressure to Ginger's neck. "I need to call HQ. Tell them what happened."

"I'll take over," Vera said, nodding toward Ginger's neck.

Grateful for the help, Vanessa tapped on the main number of Scanguards' headquarters. She rose from the bed and walked toward the ensuite bathroom, where she had to brace herself for a moment in order not to lose her balance.

"Vanessa, what's up?" It was Benjamin, one of Amaury's twin sons who was on duty at the central command center that triaged all incoming emergencies and vampire-related incidents.

"One of my girls was savagely attacked by a vampire," Vanessa said. She knew every single woman who plied her trade on the streets of San Francisco, and she considered them her girls to protect.

"Fuck! How is she? Is she alive?"

"Barely. I'm with her at Vera's. She's got a pulse, and I gave her blood."

"Good. I'll put the ambulance on standby."

"Thanks, I'll let you know when to send it."

"Who's the vamp?"

"No idea. Never saw him before. He must be new in town."

"Okay, describe him."

"About five foot nine, mouse-brown short hair, not sure about the eye color—they were red the entire time I saw him." She heard Benjamin tapping away on a computer keyboard.

"Where did it happen?"

"On Waverly Place, between Sacramento and Clay. He escaped down Clay Street, probably headed toward the waterfront. But

I couldn't follow him. Ginger would have bled out."

"You did the right thing," Benjamin assured her quickly. "We've got this. I'll send patrols out to look for him. Did you see him well enough to help us with a sketch?"

"Yeah, I can do that. But I need to stay with Ginger until she's more stable. She's still unconscious."

"Good. Stay there. When she comes to, ask her where he grabbed her before they went into the alley; maybe a traffic cam caught him. And then you know what to do. I don't need to tell you—"

"I know. I'll wipe her memory. See you later."

Vanessa disconnected the call and shoved the cell phone back in her pocket. In the bathroom mirror she caught a glimpse of herself. Her face was blood-smeared, one side of her jacket and T-shirt drenched in Ginger's blood. She was surprised that nobody had stopped her and called the police when she'd brought Ginger here, walking a good four blocks mostly uphill. Without her vampire strength, she would have never made it. But now, even she felt drained. One reason was the fact that she'd fed Ginger her blood. She looked over her shoulder back at Vera.

"Do you have bottled blood here?"

Vera nodded. "In my apartment upstairs. I'll get you some. And some clean clothes too. You can't go outside like that, or you'll draw the wrong kind of attention."

"Thanks, Vera."

"Why don't you take a shower, get the blood off you?" She motioned to Ginger. "She'll be out for a while. And I'll be back in five minutes."

Vera left the room, and Vanessa studied Ginger. She appeared peaceful now. She snatched a clean washcloth from the bathroom, let warm water run over it, and then used it to clean the injured woman's face and torso. The cuts on her torso were already closing, and no more blood seeped from them. Vera's saliva had done a good job.

Vanessa carefully wiped crusted blood off Ginger's face, before gently cleaning her neck around the area where the vampire had fed from her. The wound looked as if the vampire hadn't known what to do. There were several incisions and tear marks as if he'd had trouble latching on to her.

What the vampire had done to Ginger was barbaric. She understood that vampires needed to feed directly from humans if they didn't have access to bottled blood like everybody associated with Scanguards. But a vampire's bite didn't have to hurt, and it certainly didn't have to leave such life-threatening injuries. On the contrary, a vampire's bite could be sensual and bring pleasure to the human host, not just the vampire. So why had this vampire acted so cruelly?

By the time Vera was back with a bottle

of human blood and clean clothes, the wound on Ginger's neck wasn't bleeding anymore. But it would take a couple of days to heal. Vanessa took the bottle of human blood and unscrewed the top. She took a deep gulp from it, letting the cold liquid coat her parched throat and revive her tired senses.

"I'll have Ginger transported to Scanguards' med center a bit later," Vanessa said. "Mom can take care of her there." She set the bottle back to her lips and knocked back more of the delicious liquid.

"She's no bother here, if that's your concern," Vera offered.

"That's very kind of you, Vera. But you're doing so much already. Scanguards is best equipped for this. She needs to be monitored for a few days. We'll move her in a few hours. I'll arrange it a bit later."

Vera nodded. Then her forehead creased, and she stretched her arm out to touch

Vanessa's cheek. "You're burning up, Nessie, is it your time?"

She knew what Vera was referring to. "No, it's not."

A few times a year, she went into heat like a feline, because she wasn't just a vampire hybrid, she'd inherited the satyr gene from her parents. It was the gene that equipped her father and her two brothers with a second cock, and sent her mother and herself into sexual heat several times a year. Without sex, the heat would rise to a high fever that was unbearable. But this wasn't her time. She wasn't due to go into heat for another month.

"But it looks like it," Vera said, concern coloring her voice. She took the empty bottle from Vanessa's hand.

"It feels like it too." She looked toward the bathroom, feeling as if she was dying of thirst. "I need a cold shower."

4

Despite the cold shower and the fresh clothes, Vanessa still didn't feel any better an hour after she'd brought Ginger to Vera's. On the contrary: she felt like it was getting worse, and the feverish feeling turned into a full-blown attack. She was going into heat, and there was no rhyme or reason to it. She'd always known what she would have to deal with all her life. Her mother had prepared her for it, and drilled it into her to find a man to have sex with as soon as she could when her cycle began, or the pain would become too unbearable, and she would lose control. And once that happened, she could easily hurt a human even though she didn't want to.

Sex had always been a subject openly discussed in the home she still shared with her parents, Maya and Gabriel, and her brother Ethan. Ryder had moved out four years earlier, when he'd mated with Scarlet, a human woman who'd also inherited the satyr gene. Her mother had told her that nobody would judge her if she had sex with a hundred guys as long as she would take care of herself. Ryder had frequented Vera's brothel before he'd met Scarlet. That was the reason Vera knew all about satyrs, and how vital it was to not ignore the satyr's needs for too long.

Dressed in the tight leather skirt Vera had given her, her own black boots, and one of Vera's frilly tops that showed way too much cleavage, Vanessa cast another look at Ginger sleeping peacefully. Her breathing had normalized, and her heartbeat was getting stronger. She would make it. While she felt a twinge of guilt that she wasn't staying with Ginger to watch her, Vanessa couldn't wait any longer. She had to go somewhere to find a man to have sex with. Vera would understand.

Vanessa stepped into the hallway and shut the door behind her. As she walked toward the foyer, coming around the stairs, she heard Vera speaking to a man.

"...a recommendation from Chicago," the man said, the deep timbre of his voice beckoning her like a lure enticing a fish to bite the hook.

A pleasant shiver ran down her spine as she entered the foyer and spied Vera in conversation with a tall stranger. A flame shot through her core, scorching her from the inside. The man was human, an incredibly well-built human with a tall frame, broad shoulders, and muscular arms, and a butt filling out his pants perfectly.

"Whatever your tastes, I have ladies who can satisfy them. What in particular are you looking for tonight, Mr. Whitlock?" Vera asked.

The man suddenly looked over his shoulder, maybe alerted to her approach by the clacking of her heels on the stone floor. He pivoted fully, his chin dropping, his eyes drinking her in, his body motionless as if frozen in time.

His eyes were milk-chocolate brown, his lips full and plump, his nose straight. His hair was black and just the right length to run her fingers through. As she walked closer, she could smell his clean scent, the aroma of a pure virile man. Everything female inside her responded to him. She wanted this stranger. He was perfect.

He suddenly looked away from her and addressed Vera. "I want her."

"But, Vanessa isn't—"

Vanessa lifted her hand to interrupt her. "No problem, Vera." She bridged the last few yards between them with determined strides, until she stood only a couple of feet from the stranger. "I'm available."

"Uhm, Vanessa, may I have a word with you?" Vera nodded to the man she'd called Mr. Whitlock. "Just a moment, please."

Vera took her arm and they walked far enough away so the stranger wouldn't be able to overhear them.

"He's a new client. This is his first time here. I know literally nothing about him. It's too risky," Vera warned.

"I want him. I need this. I'm going into heat, and I don't know why. Even if I go to a club right now, by the time I get there and pick up a guy, I might already be too far gone. Vera, he's human. I'm stronger than him. He's not gonna be able to hurt me."

Vera scrutinized her for a couple of seconds, before nodding. "Fine. If it will help."

"It will."

"Take room twenty-three. I'll send him up in ten minutes."

"Thank you, Vera, you're the best."

As they returned to the stranger, Vanessa noticed the worry lines on his forehead. She smiled at him. "Mr. Whitlock, I'll be waiting in room twenty-three for you."

While she turned toward the stairs, he called to her, "Please call me Cole."

She cast a smile over her shoulder at him, before she ascended the stairs, feeling his eyes on her back.

"Mr. Whitlock, let's settle the financial aspect of your booking," Vera said.

5

Cole handed Vera his credit card, but he didn't even listen to her telling him how much she would charge him for spending time with the most enchanting creature he'd ever laid eyes on. The moment he'd heard footsteps behind him when he'd been talking to Vera at the reception desk, he'd sensed something surging through him, something he'd never felt before. He'd been compelled to turn around, and he felt instantly drawn to the beautiful long-legged brunette who approached. The second he'd looked into her green eyes, he'd realized that she was a dream come true. Her graceful movements made him imagine how she'd writhe against him when they made love, her long legs wrapped around his hips as he thrust into her again and again.

He'd turned rock-hard in a millisecond, and every sane thought had deserted him just by gazing at her. He was surprised that he'd been able to utter a phrase at all, because the woman Vera had called Vanessa made urgent desire surge inside him, reducing him to nothing more than a beast wanting to mate. It was an odd thought, primal and raw. As if he wasn't a sophisticated, educated man, but merely an animal dressed in fine clothes, unable to hide his base needs.

Cole waited impatiently as Vera processed the credit card transaction and explained the house rules to him, though he didn't absorb a single word as if she spoke a foreign tongue. His brain couldn't process the words. They didn't matter anyway. He was familiar with house rules in establishments like this. Besides, he played by his own rules.

"You may enter now," Vera instructed from behind him.

Cole blinked and realized that he was standing in front of room twenty-three. He had no recollection of walking up the stairs, too absorbed in the anticipation of touching a woman so beautiful, so perfect that she could only be a figment of his imagination. Fuck! He hoped this wasn't an elaborate dream he'd concocted.

He heard Vera's footsteps retreating, and took a deep breath. Cole felt his heart thunder in his chest so loud he was certain everybody in the building could hear it.

His hand trembling, he knocked at the door.

"Come in."

Cole opened the door and entered the

room, then pulled the door shut behind him and locked it. The only lights illuminating the comfortably furnished room with the king-size bed were small lamps on the nightstands. They threw a warm glow over the room and the woman who lay on top of the sheets, propped up with pillows against the headboard.

Vanessa had changed out of her skirt and blouse, and now wore a revealing red negligee with tiny black ribbons tied into bows to hold the garment together in the front. Her olive skin glistened, and her chest rose and fell with every breath, the almost transparent garment revealing firm breasts topped with hard nipples.

"Hi, Cole," she murmured in a husky voice, while her eyes roamed his body.

Her sensual voice sank deep into him, stoking the flame inside him to a roaring wildfire that—if not contained—would incinerate the entire city.

"Vanessa." He shrugged out of his jacket

and tossed it on a chair, then approached the bed, stopping at its edge.

"What would you like tonight, Cole?"

He swallowed hard, wondering if she would agree to his wish. "There's something I'd like that I know isn't customary in establishments like this."

She raised an inquiring eyebrow. "And what is that?"

"I want to kiss you on the lips, and I'm willing to pay ex—"

Vanessa shook her head, interrupting him, and shifted, until she kneeled on the bed, only inches from him. "No need to pay extra. I was hoping you would want to kiss me."

The disappointment that had tried to rise when she'd shaken her head was instantly squashed by her words. Relief and delight spread in his chest. "I would have paid anything for a kiss from you."

She lifted her hand to his face, sliding her index finger over his bottom lip. "And I would have never accepted it. I should be paying you."

A surprised chuckle tore from his throat. "Then how about we call it even, and do what we both want to do?"

"That's a good idea."

"I have another good idea," he added. "How about you pretend you're my girlfriend, and you're madly in love with me?"

Something golden flickered in her irises. "Yes, madly in love. I can do that as long as you can pretend that you're madly in love with me. Can you do that, Cole?"

"Oh, that won't be a problem." No problem at all. Because already now, he could imagine how easy it would be to fall in love with a woman like Vanessa.

Cole put one arm around her waist and pulled her closer to him. With his other hand, he brushed her hair back behind her shoulder, revealing her graceful neck.

"Kiss me," she whispered. "Kiss me as if I were yours."

Cole slanted his lips over hers and kissed her, while he slid his hand to the back of her head. Her lips yielded to his demand, and she parted them and welcomed him. He tasted her fresh breath, which reminded him of a meadow of wild flowers, the sun shining brightly. In his mind, a picture of innocence bloomed, even though he knew that the woman in his arms was anything but innocent. She was an experienced seductress, but the way she welcomed him, the way she kissed him back, didn't conjure up the image of a woman who was being paid for physical pleasure, but that of a lover who truly saw him and accepted him. It was more than he'd expected.

Without haste, Cole explored her mouth, dueled with her responsive tongue, and pulled her body closer to his, so her breasts were crushed against his chest. She felt hot in his arms, or maybe it was he who was hot, because Vanessa's response to his kiss was more passionate than he'd hoped. He didn't care that she did this for money, and because he'd asked her to pretend she loved him, because all he wanted right now was to feel, not to think; to enjoy, not to question his fate. To lose himself in the arms of this beautiful woman and bathe in her tenderness and passion.

Vanessa's hands were on him, eagerly opening the buttons of his shirt, while he touched her through the thin fabric of her gown. He wanted to take his time, but already now, he could barely control himself. All he wanted was to find out what her naked skin would feel like pressed to his. He didn't protest when she rid him of his shirt, but when she put her hands on the waistband of his pants, he grabbed her wrists and stopped her.

She ripped her lips from his. "Let me touch you."

As much as he wanted just that, he couldn't allow it, or their passionate encounter would come to an abrupt end. "I wanna caress you first."

He let go of her hands.

"Then touch me," she whispered.

Still standing at the edge of the bed, he lifted her into his arms, allowing her to unfurl her legs, before he placed her down on the sheets. With her legs spread, she pulled him to her, and he braced himself over her.

"You're so beautiful," he murmured and reached for the top bow of her negligee. He undid the tie and brushed the fabric to the sides, revealing the top of her breasts, leaving her nipples covered by the thin fabric but not hidden from his view.

He brushed his fingertips along her cleavage, caressing her heated skin along the natural curve of her breasts, before he slid his fingers beneath the fabric to touch her nipples.

A sharp inhale pushed Vanessa's chest toward him, and a soft moan rolled over her lips. He glanced at her face, and noticed that she'd pulled her lower lip between her teeth as if trying to stop herself from crying out. Pleased with her reaction, Cole dipped his head to one breast, and licked over the hard nipple, leaving the fabric damp and fully transparent, before doing the same to the other nipple.

Vanessa gripped his hips, trying to pull him closer, her pelvis tilting up, looking for friction. If he rubbed his rock-hard erection against her now, he'd come in no time, even with two layers of clothing between them. He had no choice but to resist.

"Patience."

Cole untied the second bow, then the third, and pulled the negligee open. Again, he dipped his head to her breasts, and this time he licked over the smooth skin, while he captured her other breast in his palm, kneading it gently. He sucked her hard nipple into his mouth, loving the responsiveness of her firm flesh and the softness of her skin.

Her hands were on him now, stroking his shoulders, caressing the sensitive spot on his nape, while she thrust her breasts deeper into his mouth.

"Please, yes!" Her words were barely audible, her speech almost slurred as if she was drunk on the passion they shared.

He sucked her nipple harder, and she suddenly grabbed his hair and pulled his head up. Her eyes pinned him. "Bite me, Cole, please!"

"Bite you?"

"My breasts. Please..." she begged and dropped her hold on his hair.

Surprised by her demand, he lowered his lips back to her breast, and sucked the nipple into his mouth.

"Please..."

Gently, he brushed his teeth against her skin, pressing softly.

A gasp issued from her throat, then a

moan. He felt her pelvis tilt up toward him, and let one hand slide down to her hip.

"Let me feel you, Cole," she murmured. "Your cock. I want you inside me."

"Not yet."

Cole brought his hand to the apex of her thighs and dipped between them. She was hot and wet, and he bathed his fingers in the dew that was seeping from her. While he lifted his head from her breast and shifted to the other one to suck it into his mouth, he stroked along her pussy and explored her. He moved his dew-covered fingers farther up again, until he could rub them over her clit. She moaned and writhed beneath him, and he gently bit into her other breast. As she moaned with pleasure, he thrust one finger into her tight channel, while he rubbed his thumb over her clit.

Cole lifted his head from Vanessa's breasts and looked at her face. She met his gaze, her eyes shimmering golden in the low light of the bedside lamps, her face flushed, and a sheen of perspiration on her skin.

"Kiss me, baby," he demanded. "And I'll make you come as often as you want to."

There was no hesitation when she put her hand on his nape and drew his head to her so she could press her lips to his. She kissed him with such fervor that it felt as if she was imprisoning him. It was a prison he had no intention of escaping from. While he kissed her back and allowed himself to be carried away in this beautiful fantasy where he was a normal man with a loving girlfriend and a normal life, he caressed her pussy until he felt her climax with his finger inside her, her interior muscles clenching around him.

When Vanessa relaxed in his arms, and suddenly put her hands on his waistband, clearly with the intent to undress him, he knew he had to stop her before it was too late, before this wonderful experience would end on a sour note.

He peeled himself out of her arms and got out of bed.

"Cole?"

"Excuse me for a moment." Quickly, he snatched his shirt, and charged into the ensuite bathroom, closing and locking the door behind him.

6

Vanessa exhaled a long breath, her entire body still humming with pleasure. It took her a few moments to come down from her high and the feverish daze she'd been in before Cole had made her climax, but now she was fully aware of everything around her. Or everything that wasn't there: Cole. He'd practically stormed into the bathroom as if a swarm of hornets were chasing him. What had happened? One moment he'd kissed her and pleasured her with his talented fingers, the next he'd swatted her hands away when she'd tried to unzip his pants, and peeled himself out of her arms.

Why hadn't he fucked her? She knew he would have been perfectly capable of it. After all, the package in his pants had been hard to overlook. She knew he'd been aroused, and in the brief second she'd felt his erection rub against her, she'd noticed just how big he was.

Vanessa sat up and looked toward the closed door of the ensuite bathroom, her ears perking up. She could hear what he was doing in there. Her sensitive vampire senses confirmed it: Cole was masturbating. It felt like a slap in the face. She'd offered herself more than willingly, hell, she'd begged him for his cock. He'd paid for it, and dearly she imagined, knowing that nothing at Vera's was cheap. Was that perhaps the problem? Because he thought her to be a sex worker? But that made no sense either. He'd pleasured her like she was a goddess.

Everything in her mind began to spin.

Had she done something wrong? The thought made her shiver. Had the fact that she'd wanted to feel his teeth in her breasts disgusted him? She'd never had anyone do that to her. But when Cole had sucked her with such passion, she hadn't been able to stop herself from demanding he bite her. She felt cold all of a sudden and pulled the negligee around her to cover her nakedness, though it did nothing to warm her.

The faucet was running in the ensuite bathroom, and when the sound stopped, the door opened, and Cole came back into the room, now fully dressed except for his jacket. Her gaze dropped to his pants, and she noticed that his erection was gone. He'd found release at his own hand.

Vanessa opened her mouth, but she couldn't find the right words to ask him why he didn't want to fuck her. It would make her sound needy.

Cole approached and sat down on the edge of the bed, leaning closer. He put his hand under her chin and looked into her eyes. "I want to see you again."

His request stunned her. For a second, she remained silent, then she collected all her courage, and said, "But you didn't even f—"

He put a finger over her lips to stop her. "I like to take things slowly... to prolong the pleasure." He leaned closer and brushed his lips over hers, giving her a featherlight kiss. "You know how to make a man feel wanted. It feels good to be with you."

"But I was the one who had all the pleasure..."

He drowned out her words with another kiss, this time a deeper one, while he placed his hand on her breast, caressing her nipple. When he severed the kiss, he pressed his forehead to hers.

"Don't you have a wife or a girlfriend? Somebody who looks like you must have all kinds of women vying for your attention. And once they find out what a skillful lover you are…"

"Wives and girlfriends are complicated. I'd rather be with somebody like you. With somebody who knows what a man wants, and doesn't play games."

"Oh." Did this mean that he wouldn't have touched her if he knew that she wasn't a sex worker? That was odd to say the least. And confusing as hell.

"Now, tell me, Vanessa, shall we repeat this another night?"

Vanessa lifted her head and gazed into his eyes. There was something intriguing about this man. She couldn't figure out what it was. All she knew was that she wanted to be with him. He'd appeased her senses when she'd gone into heat, satisfying the satyr in her, and at the same time, he'd made her feel cherished, precious even.

"Yes. I'd like that. But you should call me directly. I'm happy to come to your place."

Because she didn't want to cheapen their next rendezvous by it taking place in a brothel. And she couldn't take him to her home, where her parents and her brother might hear them.

"You don't want to go through Vera's?"

"No."

"That's fine by me. I can pay you in cash, if you prefer that."

She sighed. She should tell him right now that she wasn't a sex worker, but maybe it would be best to discuss this the next time they met and find out why he didn't want a girlfriend or wife. Maybe there was a simple reason, and she could alleviate his concerns when she knew more about him. But for now, she had to continue to pretend she was a sex worker.

"Let's not talk about money."

Vanessa leaned in and kissed him, pulling him closer so her breasts touched his chest. Another flame of desire shot through her, but the knowledge that she would see Cole again helped her tamp down her need for now.

"Let me give you my number," she murmured.

He pulled a cell phone from his pocket and unlocked it. She watched him as he scrolled to his address book and handed it to her. "Here, program it in."

She typed in her cell number and handed him the phone back.

He tapped on the number, and her cell phone rang from inside the closet where she'd put her own clothes.

"Now you have my number too," he said with a smile.

"Aren't you worried that I could stalk you?"

He grinned, and it made him look younger and carefree. "I should be so lucky." He pressed a kiss to her forehead and rose.

She watched him take his jacket and leave the room. Vanessa dropped back into the sheets, and stared up at the ceiling. What had just happened? Had she dreamed all this in her feverish state? Because men who came to a brothel to pleasure a woman they thought to be a sex worker without fucking her didn't exist. Nor did they give out their cell phone numbers willingly. What was Cole's game? And more importantly: was she willing to play along?

An hour later, the Scanguards-owned ambulance drove into the parking garage at Scanguards HQ, and stopped in front of the elevators.

"Thanks, Nicholas," Vanessa said to the driver, and opened up the double doors in the back.

"I'll help you," Nicholas offered and killed the engine.

Vanessa jumped out of the back, and

with Nicholas's help she lifted the gurney with Ginger out of it. Nicholas closed the ambulance doors, while Vanessa rolled the gurney toward the elevator. The doors opened before she could press the button and Maya, her mother, dressed in a white doctor's coat appeared. There was blood all over her scrubs.

"Hey, Nessie, how is she doing?" Maya looked at Ginger, checking her pupils and her pulse while Vanessa rolled her into the elevator.

"She's getting stronger. I gave her as much blood as I could," Vanessa replied.

Nicholas approached, ready to join them.

"Nicholas?" Maya said, lifting her hand.

"Yeah?"

"We just had another emergency call come in. You'll have to head out again right away," Maya said.

A ping came from Nicholas's pocket.

"That'll be the location," Maya said,

before she pressed the button of the medical floor, and Nicholas turned on his heel and headed back to the ambulance.

There was a moment of silence, when the elevator doors closed. Vanessa gestured to the blood on her mother's clothes. "What happened?"

"The attack on Ginger wasn't the only one tonight. We got another human downstairs, a tourist. She was attacked near the baseball stadium. Sebastian and Adam brought her in."

"Damn it! I shouldn't have let him get away." Guilt surged through her.

Maya put her hand on Vanessa's arm. "Don't. We don't think—" She stopped herself and then looked straight at her. A concerned look crossed her mother's face. "Are you okay? You feel feverish. Are you going into heat?"

"I'm all right, Mom. It's already over. I took care of it."

Her forehead furrowed. "But it shouldn't

be your time."

Vanessa shrugged. "I know. It just suddenly happened when I brought Ginger to Vera's to administer first aid."

"That's odd."

"Don't worry, Mom, I'm fine. What were you gonna say about the other attack?"

"Oh, we don't think it was the same guy. The timeline doesn't fit."

"You're saying there is more than one rogue in the city?"

Maya nodded. "Benjamin thinks so."

The elevator doors opened, and they rolled the gurney along the hallway and through the next double doors into Scanguards' mini medical center. The large room with the nurses' station in the middle and treatment cubicles around its perimeter was as well-equipped as a trauma center in any major hospital.

Buffy, the young black human woman, whose stepfather was a vampire, was already expecting them. She'd been training with Maya for several years now and was well-versed in emergency medicine when it came to vampire-inflicted injuries.

"Over here," Buffy said and pointed to one of the treatment areas she'd prepared.

"Nessie, go see Benjamin. He needs more info on the rogue you encountered," Maya said.

Vanessa glanced at Ginger. Her neck injury still looked bad, but she and Vera had managed to stop the bleeding. Now it was simply a matter of time until she healed.

"Don't wipe her memory yet. Maybe she can describe her attacker better than I can, and give us information as to where he picked her up," she said. "Just keep her calm when she comes to."

"Don't worry, Nessie, we'll take good care of her."

With a nod at her mother and Buffy, Vanessa pivoted and left the medical center.

She almost collided with Rose, a full-blooded vampire like her mother, who looked barely over twenty, even though she was over two-hundred years old.

"Hey, Nessie," she said. "I figured I'd help your mother with the injured victims."

"She'll appreciate it, I'm sure." Vanessa gave her a quick smile, then hurried to the elevators.

When she entered the command center on the ground floor of the building, Vanessa was surprised to find it teeming with her colleagues. Even her father, Gabriel, was present, as was Samson, the owner of the company. Everybody was talking loudly over each other, and she heard bits of conversations she realized were all centered around several vampire attacks on civilians.

She spotted Benjamin near the command desk, and he waved for her to approach.

"Hey," Vanessa greeted him. "Sorry it took a while to come back here. I had to make sure that Ginger was stable first." The fact that this wasn't the only reason why she hadn't rushed back to HQ immediately after the attack, she kept to herself. There was no need to go into detail.

"You're here now. I've arranged for a sketch artist," Benjamin said. "But first, everybody needs to be brought up to speed." A phone rang at the command desk, and Benjamin tapped on it to reply. Simultaneously, the monitor on the wall above the computer console showed a familiar face.

"Quiet everybody. Patrick is checking in," Benjamin announced.

The room quieted down, and Patrick, Samson's youngest son, spoke to them via video link. Behind him was a dark street. "Hey, no sign of the rogue. He got away," Patrick said, his face and shirt full of blood.

"And the human?" Samson asked, walking closer to the console.

"I managed to stem the bleeding for now, but she's in bad shape. How far out is the ambulance?"

Benjamin looked at a smaller monitor on the console. "Ninety seconds."

"Good," Patrick said. "Send a few people to the Inner Sunset. Maybe we can pick up his scent. I think he headed toward Golden Gate Park."

"Can you tell us anything about him? Looks? Height? Clothing?" Samson asked.

"All I could see was that he's blond and average height."

Vanessa leaned closer to the microphone. "The one I intercepted had brown hair. And he was at the edge of Chinatown. He looked confused when he saw me."

Samson turned to her. "What do you mean by confused?"

Vanessa contemplated her next words for a second. "As if he didn't know that I was a vampire hybrid. It seemed to take a moment until it sank in."

Samson exchanged a look with Gabriel,

who was now standing next to him. "Newly turned?"

Gabriel grimaced. "Possibly."

Vanessa put a hand on her father's forearm. "That might explain why his bite wasn't clean. He made several attempts at Ginger's neck, until he finally latched on to feed from her. And when he heard me coming, he ripped her flesh savagely."

"Fuck!" Samson cursed, and the others in the room let out similar curses.

Then he looked back at his son on the monitor. "Patrick, stay put until Nicholas arrives with the ambulance. I'll have three guys meet you out there to look for the rogue." He turned to Benjamin. "Send Zane, Adam, and Damian to Patrick's location. Vanessa, once you've sat down with the sketch artist, take Quinn, Lydia, and Sebastian to the location where the sex worker was attacked." Then he looked at Gabriel. "Where was the third attack of the woman who's already down in the med center?"

"Near the baseball park. I'll go there." Gabriel turned around to the others in the room and pointed at several of them. "Blake, Oliver, you guys are with me."

Samson nodded, then pushed a button on the console. Thomas's face appeared on the screen next to Patrick's live stream. "Thomas, you and Eddie work on getting drones in the air. Top priorities are the three attack areas: Chinatown, Inner Sunset, and the ballpark. Once they're up, have your team control the drones and survey the areas. In the meantime, you and Eddie need to check every CCTV camera in the city. We need to know where those bastards came from and where they disappeared to. Questions anybody?"

There were no questions.

"I'll be in a roaming unit with Ryder and Ethan. We'll be covering the northern part of the city. Amaury will take John and Cooper and cover the southern part of town. Deirdre, Brandon, and Yvette will be on standby at HQ." He turned to Benjamin. "Where are Luther, Haven, and Roxanne?"

"At the prison in Grass Valley. For a security upgrade," Benjamin replied.

"Call them, and ask them to come back tonight. We'll need every man and woman. And make sure that Charles and Wesley are ready to jump in if we need witchcraft."

"You've got it."

"Okay, everybody. Let's roll out."

As people cleared the command center, Gabriel took Vanessa's arm and leaned in. "Your mother said you went into heat."

Vanessa let out a sigh. "Of course she did. Sometimes that telepathic bond between blood-bonded mates can be downright annoying."

"She's just concerned about you because it's not your time."

"I know that, but I'm fine."

"Are you sure you wanna go back out there tonight? The others can cover for you."

"The sex workers are my responsibility. I can do this, Dad, really. I'm totally fine."

"If you say so."

"I do."

He cleared his throat. "So you, uhm, took care of it?"

She rolled her eyes. "Yes. End of discussion." She brushed past him and headed for the door.

There were moments when she wished that nobody knew what she was going through when she went into heat. But there were very few things she could keep from her parents or anybody else at Scanguards. It was truly a big family where everybody knew everybody else's business. Keeping things a secret was difficult.

But just this once she wanted to keep her experience with Cole a secret. She didn't want to share any of it with anybody. Because what she'd felt when she'd been in his arms was different from any of her other sexual encounters, and not just because he hadn't even fucked her. She'd felt cherished and adored. Cradled by his big body, everything in her world had suddenly felt right. As if everything in her life was finally falling into place. With Cole in the center of it all.

7

Cole hadn't been able to sleep right away after coming back from the brothel. His encounter with Vanessa had churned up all kinds of long repressed desires. He hadn't acted the way he normally did when he slept with prostitutes. In general, he fucked them and got the pleasure he paid for. So why had he been unable to do the same with Vanessa? Sure, she was beautiful, more so than the other women he'd fucked. But there was something else about her. A vulnerability and mysteriousness that drew him to her like a moth to the flame. As if she'd put chains around him to imprison him. One look into her green eyes, and he'd become her captive.

The decision not to fuck her had been an automatic one, because once he did, it would be over. And that was a prospect he didn't relish. He wanted to seduce her slowly, to pleasure her, so maybe in this crazy dream of his, Vanessa would accept him for what he was and look past the ugliness he kept hidden. Yes, he could admit it to himself: he wanted the prostitute he'd just met to show him love and affection and mean it. How fucked up was that?

When he'd finally fallen asleep, he'd been plagued with dreams about her, dreams of a life he would never have. After waking around noon, he'd spent the afternoon and early evening walking aimlessly around the city, killing time until his appointment with Dr. Drake. He could only hope that the doctor had a solution to his problem, or he would be out of options.

After nightfall, he decided to walk to Dr. Drake's practice. It wasn't far, and considering how hard it had been to find a parking spot the night before, he didn't think it wise to take the car. By the time he reached the street where Dr. Drake's practice was located, a thick fog had descended on the city, giving it a spooky atmosphere. There was a chill in the air, and he realized he should have worn a thicker jacket. But it was too late to turn around now. He'd already reached his destination: a large Edwardian mansion with an iron gate in front.

He touched the gate and read the plaque on it: *Dr. E. Drake, Psychiatrist, By appointment only.*

Cole hesitated, his hope deflating. This was probably a dead end. If Drake was a psychiatrist, then he'd probably treated his father for depression—and failed. Though why his father had seen a psychiatrist in San Francisco when he'd lived in Philadelphia most of his life, puzzled him. He sighed. He was already here, and he had an appointment. What did he have to lose by talking to Drake? Just a few minutes of his time, and whatever fee the good doctor charged for the consultation.

Determined to get this over with, Cole pushed the gate open and followed the sign that led along the house to a tradesmen entrance where a light flickered over an unassuming door. He pressed the door handle down and pushed it open. Bright light greeted him, and he entered and closed the door behind him.

He stood in a reception area with a few seats and a vending machine, a fake Ficus tree, and a counter with a large computer and a busty blonde sitting behind it. The woman who looked to be in her early thirties lifted her gaze and stared at him, a frown forming on her face.

"Sir, what are you—"

"I'm Cole Whitlock. We spoke yesterday?" he introduced himself, approaching her.

"Oh," she said, her plump lips forming a perfect circle, while she rose, her ample cleavage suddenly in his direct line of sight.

Despite that fact, nothing stirred in his groin. The oversexed blonde didn't even remotely arouse him.

"You're his 8:15?"

"Yes, I know I'm a few minutes early. I can wait." He was about to turn toward the seating area, when she stopped him.

"Just a moment," she said quickly and picked up the phone then pressed a button. "Dr. Drake, your 8:15 is here. But, uhm, maybe you should... uhm... he's a new client. A civilian." There was a short pause. "Yes, of course."

Civilian? What did she mean by it? Was Dr. Drake only seeing members of the military? Perhaps he specialized in post-traumatic stress disorder.

The receptionist placed the receiver back on the cradle. "May I ask how you heard about Dr. Drake?"

"Well, it's a long story. Maybe I could talk to him myself." He tilted his head to the door that he assumed was the doctor's office.

"Are you here on a recommendation by somebody? Another patient maybe?" she asked, her voice more insistent now.

Surprised she was giving him the third degree, he found it best to not let her know that he didn't really know why his father had Dr. Drake's number in his journal. "Yes, you could say that. My father was a patient. He passed away..."

"Oh, my condolences, Mr. Whitlock. Just a moment, please."

She picked the phone up again and pressed the same button as before. "Dr.

Drake. He's here on a recommendation by a former patient. Yes."

When she disconnected the call, she pointed to the door. "He will see you now."

With a nod at her, Cole strode to the door, knocked briefly, and entered. Inside the large room the décor was very different from the airy, bright reception area. There was a large desk with an office chair, the only two items in the room that didn't look out of place. Everything else did: the murals that made the room look like a crypt, the oddly shaped black sofa with red velvet cushions that made it look like a coffin from the set of a cheap Dracula movie. Not to speak of the coffee table whose legs looked like wooden stakes. The armchairs opposite the sofa looked just as inappropriate as everything else in the room. One thing was instantly clear: Dr. Drake had horrible taste in furniture.

"Mr. Whitlock, please take a seat."

Drake was a tall, lanky man who looked

to be in his early forties—too young for having treated his father, who'd died seventeen years ago. Drake would have been in his early twenties and undoubtedly still in medical school, rather than running his own practice.

"You are Dr. Drake?" Cole managed to ask.

"The one and only," he replied. "Is there a problem?"

"Actually, you're too young to be the man I was looking for. No offense."

"None taken." He pointed to the armchair. "Now you have my attention. Who did you think I was?"

Drake sat down on the sofa, a tablet in his hand, and Cole took a seat in the armchair.

"My father, Trent Whitlock, came to see you, but his visit lies at least eighteen to twenty years in the past."

"Why's that? The timing, I mean?"

"Because he committed suicide seventeen years ago."

"Oh, I see. Hmm." He tapped on his iPad. "Trent Whitlock, you said?" He scrolled through something on the tablet, then nodded to himself. "Hmm, yes, interesting case."

"Are you saying you treated him?"

Drake gave him a non-committal smile. "Yes, and no. He came to this practice thirty-eight years ago..."

"That must have been just after I was born." Cole shook his head. "And you would have been a toddler at best."

"True. But he didn't come to see me. He came to see my father." He pointed to the tablet. "I recently digitized all his patient notes."

Excited that he hadn't been too far off the mark, Cole leaned forward. "So you know what he came to see your father about."

Drake nodded. "Indeed. An unusual case

to say the least. I didn't have any answers for your father back then."

"You? But you weren't his doctor."

"I mean, my father," he corrected himself hastily. "My father didn't have any solution to his problem. He couldn't help him. It saddens me to hear that your father took his own life."

"It was too much for him. He held on until I was almost through university and was able to look out for myself." At least that was how it had felt. His father had been a good parent, always protective and understanding. Cole lifted his eyes to look straight at Drake. "I suffer from the same condition as my father."

Drake nodded slowly. "That was to be expected. It's genetic. We know that now."

Cole drew in a big breath. "I guessed as much. So there's no cure, I assume."

Drake shook his head.

Disappointed, Cole rose. "I'm sorry to have wasted your time."

Drake rose too. "Don't go. There's something you need to know about your and your father's condition. There's no cure because it's a condition that needs no cure. Only a change."

"I don't understand. It has caused me more than my fair share of heartbreak and loneliness." He pointed to the tablet in Drake's hand. "You've read your father's notes. You should understand."

Drake put a hand on Cole's forearm, his grip surprisingly strong. "I know somebody who can explain everything you need to know about your condition and what it really means. It's not my place to do so."

"Who?"

"A man who has the same, shall we call it genetic mutation?" Drake shrugged. "Meet with him, and he'll put all your worries to rest. He leads a very happy life. A fulfilled life with his family. Trust me on this."

Drake's blue eyes bored into him, and Cole felt almost as if he stood under hypnosis, the urge to nod and agree with him unrelenting.

"Okay, I'll meet with him."

"Good. I'll contact him right now. My assistant Marilyn has your phone number?"

Cole nodded.

"I'll text you with the details of how and where he will meet you. Be prepared that it may be late at night. He keeps unusual hours."

"Like yourself, I guess?" Cole felt compelled to comment.

"Something like that."

Cole left the odd medical office and stepped out into the cool night air. He was conflicted. On the one hand, he was disappointed that there was no cure, on the other hand, a glimpse of hope dared raise its head: if there was another man who'd learned how to deal with his predicament and live a happy life, then maybe there was hope for him too.

Alone with his thoughts, Cole turned

onto the street that led to his condo. In the few days since he'd moved here, he'd grown to love the neighborhood, where every block revealed another vantage point from which to gaze upon the city lights. There was something calming about that.

A sound from behind him suddenly made him spin around, and he instinctively adopted a fighting stance. It had been a while since he'd gotten jumped—since high school to be exact, because since then he'd started working out rigorously to pack muscle onto his tall frame. Nobody had dared jump him since. Until tonight.

It took Cole a second to see the person who'd approached him with such stealth. Stunned disbelief paralyzed him for a short moment. It turned out that a moment was all the man attacking him needed to tackle him and fling him against the wall of the closest building.

Fuck!

8

Vanessa was on her way from her parent's house to meet with Lydia to start patrolling. Samson had ordered that nobody was allowed to patrol alone. She felt warm in the car, and with the air conditioning in the old clunker currently not working, she rolled down the windows to let the foggy night air cool her.

She felt feverish again, but she hadn't mentioned it to her parents. Her father would have pulled her off patrol-duty and demanded she go to a bar or club to take care of her sexual needs. But she wasn't in the mood for anonymous sex. Instead, she wanted to see Cole again. Maybe she would text him later to see if he was free. What exactly she would say to him, she wasn't quite sure. After all, he thought she was a sex worker, and since when did sex workers call their clients to arrange for a rendezvous? She would have to come clean. But would he judge her then for pretending to be something she was not? The whole situation was too complicated to deal with this instant. She needed to keep a clear head while patrolling.

At the next stop sign, the engine sputtered, and Vanessa let out a groan. "Damn car."

She kicked the gas pedal down harder, and the sputtering stopped, and the car moved again.

Her sensitive ears suddenly picked up a scream. She stepped on the brake, and stopped the car. She turned off the engine, and jumped out of the car, slamming the door shut, not bothering to lock it. Vanessa dashed into the direction of the scream, crossing the street then turning a corner, when she saw what was happening.

A vampire had a human man in his grip: a large, muscular man, who was trying to fend off his attacker rather admirably. But despite his large frame he had no chance against the smaller, skinny vampire. Vanessa could smell the human blood. There was something familiar in its aroma, something that made her charge toward the vampire. When she was only a couple of yards away from him, she finally recognized the man in the clutches of the rogue vampire: Cole. In a fraction of a second, she assessed the situation: the vampire's fangs were lodged in Cole's neck, and if she tried to pry him off his victim, he would tear Cole's carotid artery right out, killing him within seconds. She'd seen what had nearly happened with Ginger, and couldn't take that risk. She wouldn't make the same mistake this time.

Vanessa reached into her inside pocket, retrieved her weapon and in the same movement flung herself onto the vampire, slamming the wooden stake into his back, right between the ribs that protected his heart. For a split second, she feared she'd missed her target, but then the vampire turned into dust in front of her eyes. Several items clattered to the ground amid the ash: keys, a wallet, and a cell phone. Vanessa collided with Cole, blood spurting from his neck wound, drenching her face.

"Cole! Are you all right?"

She scrutinized his face and neck. He appeared dazed and confused. But she could feel his strong heartbeat, and knew he would be fine. But she needed to take advantage of the situation so she could close his wound and prevent more blood loss.

"It's all right, Cole. It's Vanessa, I'm here

now," she murmured and wrapped her arms around him as if she were merely hugging him, though she had an alternative agenda.

"Vanessa?" His voice was but a faint whisper.

He was clearly in shock. His blood was assaulting her senses now, and her hunger for it rose, but she pushed it down. She pressed her face in the crook of his neck, and licked over the puncture wounds the vampire had left. She recognized immediately that the vampire had left more than two punctures. He'd made multiple attempts at sinking his fangs into Cole.

Vanessa lapped up the blood seeping from the wound as she licked over the incisions, depositing her saliva on his skin so it could mend, when she suddenly felt Cole's knees buckle. Fuck! How much blood had the rogue taken? It would be best to bring Cole to Scanguards' medical center like the other human victims.

"You need a doctor," she said, lifting her

face from his neck, while supporting his weight.

Cole was conscious, but seemed disoriented. "No doctor. No hospital. Please." He stretched his arm toward the street behind her. "Home. Next block, number 2453, top floor."

"Lean against the wall," she demanded, making sure he was stable, before she bent down and retrieved the vampire's belongings, and shoved them into her jacket pocket.

"I can walk," Cole claimed as he pushed away from the wall and took a step.

He collapsed, and would have hit his head on the ground, had Vanessa not caught him. It took a few moments before she could hoist him over her shoulder, and carry him to the next block. He was a heavy guy, and had she been a human, she wouldn't have been able to carry him even one foot, but her vampire strength helped her bring him to the building he'd indicated.

She propped him up against the wall, and searched his pockets until she found his keys and was able to unlock the door. Luckily, the three-story building had an elevator, saving her from carrying him up to the third floor.

Arriving at the top floor, she unlocked the door to his condo and dragged him inside. It was dark, and she searched for the light switch and found it easily. Warm light illuminated the foyer that opened up to a large living area with a modern kitchen on one side, and floor-to-ceiling windows with a view of the bay on the other.

Vanessa laid Cole down on the sofa. He was still unconscious, and she knew she had to use this opportunity to heal him quickly before he came to and realized what she was doing, and therefore what she was: the same kind of creature that had attacked him savagely.

She managed to get him out of his windbreaker so she could inspect if he had other wounds. Like she'd suspected, he had several cuts on his arms and torso from trying to fight off the attacker. She would deal with those injuries later. But first, she had to make him drink her blood. It would help him heal from the inside. She checked his face again, making sure he was still out, then bit into her own wrist, before she held it over his mouth.

While the blood dripped into his mouth, Vanessa watched his face. With her free hand, she combed through his black hair and stroked along his strong chin. Her gaze drifted back to the spot where the rogue had driven his fangs into Cole, and her heart beat angrily at this violation. If anybody fed from Cole, then it would be her, not some violent predator who'd only inflict horror upon his victim. Had she had the occasion to bite Cole, she would have introduced him to the sensuality and tenderness of the bite. She would have made love to him while biting him to heighten their pleasure and deepen their connection. But now, after this horrific attack, how could she ever even contemplate telling him what she was, and what she wanted from him?

It struck her right then: although she knew next to nothing about Cole, and even though he'd paid for sex with her, she wanted him with an urgency that could only be attributed to the fact that she was going into heat again. As if Cole was the one to cause that biological change in her, as if she was responding to his presence. Just like the night before.

Vanessa removed her wrist from his mouth and licked over the incisions to close them instantly. As quickly and as gently as she could, she peeled his white shirt away from his chest injuries. The shirt was damaged anyway, so she simply ripped it apart so she could access the wounds on his torso and arms better.

Vanessa marveled at Cole's well-defined muscles. He wasn't a rich lay-about, that much was clear, but she knew he was rich. For starters, he'd paid a fortune at Vera's without blinking, and his condo with the almost 180-degree view of the city and the bay had to be in the four-to-five-million-dollar range. The furniture was classy, but simple. And it looked like he'd just moved here. Several moving boxes with the logo of a cross-country moving company stood in one corner, waiting to be unpacked.

She looked back at Cole's muscular torso. To maintain such muscle mass, he had to work out almost daily. And it had probably saved his life, because had he not been able to fend off the vampire for as long as he had, she would have come too late, and the rogue would have sucked him dry. She still shuddered at that thought.

Drawn to the blood covering the cuts the vampire's claws had left, she bent over his torso and licked over the long, thin cuts, lapping up the blood, while her saliva started to repair his skin. She stopped just short of completely healing the wounds, or he would become suspicious about why his injuries were gone. The cuts on his forearms were more superficial, and she dared lick over them only once to start the healing process.

Vanessa inspected his neck. There were indeed several puncture wounds, larger than they had to be if the vampire had known what he was doing. More and more she felt that the attacker from the previous night and the one tonight were both inexperienced, which pointed to them being newly-turned.

With Cole's immediate needs taken care of, Vanessa padded to a door on the other side of the kitchen. It was a bedroom. A king-size bed stood against the wall facing a floor-to-ceiling window, a weight bench in front of it. To one side was a walk-in closet, to the other another door. It led into the ensuite bathroom. She closed the door and took out her cell phone, calling Scanguards

HQ. She put the call on speaker phone, before she took a small towel, ran water over it and started to clean the blood off her face and neck.

"Vanessa, what's up?" Benjamin asked.

"There was another attack, this time on the border of Nob Hill and Russian Hill. I'll text you the location in a minute. Different vampire than I saw last night."

"Did he get away?"

"No. I had to stake him or he would have killed his victim."

"Damn!" Benjamin cursed.

"I know. But I have his keys, wallet, and phone. I'll bring it to HQ shortly. Thomas and Eddie can work with that to figure out who he was. And another thing."

"What else?"

"I think both vampires were newly turned. The injuries they left when they fed from their victims are messy. They have no clue what they're doing."

"I was afraid of that." Benjamin sighed.

"I'll send the ambulance to your location to pick up the victim."

"Don't. He's healing. He doesn't need to come in."

"You sure?"

"I'm sure."

"Okay then, but make sure you wipe his memory before you leave."

"I'm not an amateur, Benji."

Before Benjamin could say anything else, she disconnected the call. She looked into the mirror. Her face and neck were clean, but her top had blood splatter on it. She could grab a change of clothes at headquarters when she delivered the dead vampire's belongings to Thomas and Eddie. Every employee had a locker with spare clothes and any other essentials at Scanguards.

But what would she do with Cole? Did she really want to wipe his memory? Was it fair to leave him so exposed? She couldn't just let him think that he would be safe out there just because he was big and worked out. His attacker hadn't been taller than 5'10" and weighed at least seventy pounds less than Cole. Cole would have assumed he could defeat such a man easily. But at the same time, if she didn't wipe his memory of the attack, he would associate vampires only with violence and horror. Where would that leave her? How would she tell him that she was a vampire too? Would he see the difference? Would he understand that not all vampires were bad?

She stared into the mirror, looking for answers to her questions, but there was no magical genie that doled out answers, only her own reflection showing how conflicted she was.

A sound from somewhere else in the condo drifted to her, alerting her that Cole was up.

9

Cole sensed a soft surface at his back and felt disoriented. This wasn't the cold, hard wall he'd been pressed against by an attacker smaller, yet stronger, than him. Where the fuck was he? He opened his eyes, and for a moment everything was spinning around him. He wasn't standing anymore. He was lying on something soft. It took a moment for his eyes to adjust, and for him to realize that he was in the living room of his own condo, stretched out on the couch. Had he had a nightmare?

He lifted his torso, trying to sit up, when pain seared through him.

"What the fuck?" he groaned, and glanced down at himself.

His shirt was in tatters, and there was blood on the fabric and his skin. Like a headrush, everything came back to him. He'd been attacked by a monster that shouldn't exist. A monster that had driven its sharp fangs into his neck with the intent to suck the living daylights out of him. He touched his neck, feeling the broken skin.

"He got you pretty good."

At the familiar voice, he whirled his head toward the door to his bedroom. Vanessa, dressed in a leather jacket, tight jeans, and long black boots walked toward him, a towel in her hand. The top she wore beneath the open jacket was blood-stained.

"Vanessa, oh my God, you're hurt," he said, shooting up from the couch way too fast.

He swayed, the room moving beneath

his feet as if he were in the middle of an earthquake this city was famous for. Vanessa rushed toward him and steadied him, putting an arm around him.

"I'm not hurt, but you are. Let me see to your wounds," she said, while she eased him back on the couch.

She sat down next to him and wiped the damp towel over his torso in gentle movements.

"You came to my rescue." He shook his head, not understanding exactly how she'd fought off the attacker. All he remembered was a cloud of dust or ash, and then Vanessa's face right in front of him. "How did you..." He furrowed his forehead, another memory surfacing now. "When you ran toward me, I saw something in your hand."

"It was a scary situation. You're in shock."

Of course he was in shock, but that didn't change what he'd experienced. "I was attacked by a vampire. I felt his fangs in my neck." It sounded ridiculous in his own ears, but just to make sure he wasn't hallucinating, he touched the neck wound the vampire had left.

For a few seconds, it looked like Vanessa wanted to deny it, but then she seemed to decide against it and nodded.

"There's so much blood." He pointed to his shirt and then to her top. "Are you sure you're not injured?"

"I'm sure."

"Then whose blood is that?"

"Yours. It transferred to me when I helped you get home."

"I don't remember how I got home."

"You were in and out."

His forehead furrowed. "You could have never gotten me home if I was out. I'm too heavy for you."

"You were on your feet, it wasn't that hard. You just don't remember because you were in shock."

That didn't make any sense, but he didn't

press the issue any further. He had other questions.

"You killed him, and he just turned to dust."

"Is that a complaint?" Vanessa asked, still dabbing the damp towel at his wounds to clean them, before she proceeded to his forearm that he'd used to fend off the attacker. With little success.

Cole took Vanessa's wrist, stopping her from tending to him. "Tell me what happened. Why were you there? And how did you know what to do?"

Vanessa dropped the towel on the coffee table and turned back to him.

"I was on my way to work when I heard a scream. So I ran to investigate. I realized it was you. So, of course, I helped you."

What she was telling him sounded like a very sanitized version of the event that had scared the hell out of him. "You put yourself in danger. For me? You should have run away."

"Then you'd be dead now."

Hearing the words made the whole situation truly sink in. He'd escaped death tonight. And no other than a beautiful prostitute was his savior.

"I'm sorry, I don't mean to be ungrateful. I am... immensely grateful for what you've done. But I just don't understand how. I mean, I'm much stronger than you, and I couldn't fight that monster off. And you managed to kill him." He ran a hand through his hair, shaking his head. The more he thought about it, the crazier it all sounded.

Vanessa made a dismissive gesture. "I had the right weapon."

"Wooden stake?" he guessed.

"Just like in the movies." Then she pointed to his injuries. "How's the pain?"

Cole sat still for a moment, scanning his body with his mind to see where he felt pain, but to his surprise he only felt a dull ache, no worse than if he'd cut himself while chopping vegetables for his dinner.

"Actually, it doesn't hurt as badly anymore. But with all that blood, I mean, the injuries should have been much deeper."

Cole inspected the cuts on his arm, and realized that they seemed only superficial, and no more blood was seeping from them. The cuts on his torso looked a little deeper, but they too had closed and were healing.

He gave Vanessa a quizzical look. "How long exactly was I out?"

"Maybe a half hour. And now that I've cleaned the blood off, it looks like your injuries aren't as bad as I first thought."

He had to agree with her, even though it had felt like the bastard was sucking the life right out of him. But if his injuries were only superficial, then... "Why did I pass out? Trust me, I've had worse injuries and stayed conscious the entire time."

Vanessa leaned in. "Probably the shock."

Her voice was a mere whisper, and he allowed it to seep into him. His injuries were suddenly forgotten, and he was fully aware of Vanessa's body. Just like the night before, he was drawn to her as if she were a strong magnet, and he a small nail, because the power was all hers. He'd never met a woman who had such a strong effect on him. As if he was in her thrall.

"Vanessa, I owe you my life."

Cole leaned closer and lifted his hand to her face, his fingers gently tracing her jaw line and cheek bones. "If you allow me, I'd like to buy an hour of your time so I can thank you properly."

A breath of air rushed from her mouth as her lips parted. "How?"

"By giving you the pleasure you deserve."

Something in her eyes flickered golden as if fireworks exploded in her irises. "Like last night?"

"More intimate than last night."

"I don't think it can get any more intimate..."

He laughed softly, brushed his lips over her cheek, and brought his mouth to her ear. "This time I want to lick you until you come."

Vanessa gasped, and the sound sank deep into him, filling him with satisfaction that he could surprise the woman he had no defenses against.

"Why don't you let me undress you?"

He reached for her leather jacket and helped her out of it. She assisted willingly, and he pulled her face to his. "Now be a good girl, and pretend you're madly in love with me."

"Cole," she murmured. "Why do you want me to pretend?"

"Because I want to pretend that I love you too."

Though right now he wasn't sure whether he had to pretend at all. It took no effort to think that he could be in love with Vanessa. No effort at all. It came naturally to him. He could imagine all kinds of things when he was with her. As if her nearness ignited a flame inside him, a flame that showed him that he was capable of deep emotions that had nothing to do with his need for sex. He understood that both needs, the one for sex and the one for love could be separate, but they merged into one when Vanessa was in his arms. He wanted her to give him both, though he knew he had to content himself with the fact that her love was only pretend. But he could block that out, forget that this was only pretense, and find out what it felt like to have his need for sex and for love satisfied at the same time.

Cole slanted his lips over hers, exerting a tiny bit of pressure, and Vanessa instantly responded to his demand, allowing him entry. Her lips tasted so familiar, and his body responded to her taste by sending blood to his groin, filling his cock and turning it as hard as a rock. Arousal charged through him, and every cell in his body seemed to come alive. His blood pulsed excitedly in his veins, while his heart drummed in a rapid tempo as if it needed to get somewhere in a hurry.

His kiss became more urgent from one second to the next, while he took Vanessa's top and pulled it over her head, interrupting the kiss for it. When he gazed into her eyes, he saw a golden shimmer around her irises as if a fire was burning there.

"You're beautiful," he whispered and let his gaze drift lower to where a white lace bra covered her breasts, her nipples hard and visible through the thin fabric. "And your tits, they're perfect." He kneaded her firm flesh through the bra, before she reached behind her back and opened the clasp.

"Thank you." He pulled the straps down her arms and freed her from it.

Like two ripe pieces of fruit, her breasts fell into his palms, filling them. He caressed them while he pressed his lips back onto hers and kissed her with the passion that was overflowing in him. There was so much he wanted to do with this woman, so much he wanted to experience with her.

Impatiently, he opened the button of her jeans and pulled the zipper down, then grabbed the garment by the waistband. Vanessa helped him and shimmied out of the jeans, her white panties getting caught in the action, and sliding down with her pants.

Before he could free her of her jeans, he helped her get rid of her boots. Finally, she was naked. He shrugged off the tattered shirt, shucked his shoes and pressed Vanessa down onto the sofa so she lay flat on it, spread out like a sumptuous buffet meant only for him. He swept a long gaze over her flawless body before he pressed her thighs apart and slipped in the space he'd created for himself.

Vanessa watched him, her lips parted, holding her breath, when he slowly dipped his head to her pussy without breaking eye contact. He pressed his mouth to her pussy and inhaled her female scent, before he spread her wider so he could see her pink flesh covered in dew. He licked over her cleft, tasting her for the first time, and his entire body erupted in flames.

"Oh, baby," he uttered. "I'm gonna love doing this."

10

For the second time in as many nights, Vanessa was in Cole's arms, with him pleasuring her, and she felt a little twinge of guilt. She knew that Cole would feel aroused because—without his knowledge—she'd given him her blood to drink. Vampire blood was a strong aphrodisiac for any human, and for a man like Cole, who was clearly already attracted to her, the effect was even stronger. She should have never let it get this far.

She should have wiped his memory of

the vampire and everything that he'd seen including that she'd saved his life, but she couldn't do it. All she'd managed to do was to take some of the horror of the attack from his mind. And even that she hadn't done for his benefit but for hers. So he wouldn't grill her any longer on the details of what had happened and why she knew about vampires. All this because, again, she was going into heat, and she knew instinctively that Cole was the only man who could satisfy her inner satyr's desires.

Damn, she was turning into a selfish woman, manipulating him by calming his fears. Fears that could have stopped his arousal from rising to a level where he really had no choice but to sleep with her. He didn't have any free will at this point—he was driven by an overwhelming desire for sex.

"Cole, please, you don't have to..."

A strong flicking motion of his tongue against her clit made her gasp.

He lifted his head. "You don't like it?" There was a smirk on his face, confirming that he was aware of the effect he had on her.

"I love it, but I don't deserve this. You're not getting anything out of this."

A chuckle rolled off his lips, and he winked at her. "Trust me when I tell you that I get a whole lot out of this."

"You're crazy."

Without another word, Cole dipped his head to her pussy again and licked her. Unable to resist his tender ministrations, she relaxed back into the cushions, and allowed her body to simply react.

Cole didn't act like other humans. Any other man would be fucking her right now, pounding his cock into her in the search for satisfaction. Yet Cole still restrained himself by pleasuring her instead. The more she got to know him, the more mysterious he became.

"Who are you?" she murmured to herself.

He mumbled something against her tender flesh without stopping what he was doing. With his fingers, he laid bare her center of pleasure, and with his tongue he beat her clit into submission. She felt like a woman in need, a woman who would do anything to get that need satisfied. Her body was heating from the inside, and she welcomed the sheen of perspiration covering her skin like a protective layer.

Soft moans and sighs bounced off the walls of Cole's condo, but they didn't all originate from her. Cole moaned softly too, and she could feel his body move against the sofa, as if he was rubbing his groin against the cushion for relief.

Vanessa shoved her hands into his hair, touching his scalp, caressing his nape, making him shudder.

"Please fuck me," she begged. "Please, Cole. I want you inside me."

Instead of rising to undress, Cole remained where he was, and penetrated her with his finger. She welcomed the invasion, and her muscles clamped around his digit, trying to imprison him there. But he withdrew his finger, only to thrust back into her with two.

She gasped in surprise, her muscles tensing. "Cole! So close."

As if he knew exactly what she needed, he flicked his tongue over her clit in quick succession while increasing the pressure. In the same rhythm, he thrust his fingers into her over and over again. Everything inside her lit up like a wildfire, and she climaxed so hard she felt delirious. She barely realized that Cole had stopped his movements and finally scooted up to her. He drew her into his arms, pulling her up so she was draped over his naked chest. She could hear his heart thunder as if he was the one who'd climaxed, not she. With one arm he held her to him, with his other hand, he tipped her chin up to make her look at him.

"It's wonderful to see you like this," he

said, his eyes dark as if a storm was raging in them.

She let her hand glide down to his pants and felt his erection through the fabric. "Let me do the same to you."

Before she could squeeze him, he snatched her wrist and pulled her hand back up to place it on his chest. "Later. I just want to enjoy holding you in my arms for a little while."

She propped her head up on his chest. "If you're trying to be mysterious, you're doing a good job."

"You think I'm mysterious?"

"Yes. You said last night that you don't have a girlfriend or a wife. Why is that?"

He pursed his lips. "Relationships are complicated. You never really know a person. It inevitably leads to disappointment."

"That's not true for all romantic relationships." In fact, she knew dozens of happy couples in her extended Scanguards family.

"Let's just say it's hard for me to open up to women."

"It sounds a little like you're opening up to me right now," she teased him.

He tapped her nose with his index finger. "That's because I'm paying you to listen."

She dropped her lids, avoiding his gaze. Was he saying that he could be honest and open with her, because she wasn't girlfriend or wife material? Would he treat her differently if he knew that she wasn't a sex worker?

"Did I say something wrong?"

She quickly shook her head and looked at him. "No, it just made me think."

"About what?"

"Why you feel you can't open up to other women, I mean women you date."

"I don't date."

"You know what I mean," she pressed.

Cole let out a breath. "I don't want you to

get the wrong idea. I am the way I am, and I can't change that. And the few women I've been with didn't like what they saw. They judged me. And I don't like being judged for something that I can't change."

She heard the pain in his words and instantly regretted having asked the question. "I'm sorry. I didn't mean to pry and dig up old wounds."

He put his fingers under her chin and tipped it up, drawing her closer. "That's why I like being with you. You understand me. You know what it's like to be judged." He gave her a featherlight kiss on the lips.

She nudged closer to intensify the kiss, and Cole wrapped his arms around her and responded to her just as passionately as he'd pleasured her. Vanessa shifted on top of him, and found herself with her legs to either side of his hips, and the apex of her thighs aligned with his groin. Cole slid one hand down to her ass, pressing her to him while he moved his hips to rub himself against her center.

Excitement flooded her. He would finally fuck her. She moved to the side a little so she could get to the closure of his pants, but before she could, he stopped her and severed the kiss.

He breathed as if he'd been running a sprint, and she felt his heart thunder just as fast.

"You're a very seductive woman." He brushed a strand of hair from her face.

It looked like he wanted to say something else, but then a cell phone rang, and he looked in the direction of the sound.

"It's not mine."

Vanessa recognized the ringtone and sat up. "It's mine." She jumped off him and reached for her purse to pull out her cell. The name on the display confirmed who she'd guessed was calling. She turned to Cole. "I'm sorry, work."

She answered the call. "Lydia?"

"Where the hell are you? Are you okay? Did you run into any trouble?" Lydia's words came as if shot out of a pistol.

She cast a sideways glance at Cole, who'd sat up and was watching her.

"I'm all right. But there was an attack. I had to help out. Can you take Quinn instead? I'm gonna have to go by the office first."

"Yeah, I can do that. What happened?"

"I'll fill you in later. Thanks, Lydia."

Vanessa disconnected the call, and cast Cole a regretful look. "I'm sorry. I have to go to work." She reached for her clothes, when Cole rose and pulled her to him. "Stay here. I'll pay you for the whole night."

"I—"

As much as she wanted to stay, she couldn't. She had to get the dead vampire's belongings to HQ so they could identify him. And right now, she didn't have the time to explain to Cole that she wasn't a sex worker, because it wasn't a one-sentence explanation. They would have to have that conversation later when she wasn't pressed for time. She'd already spent too much time here.

"Can we talk later?" she asked. "I just have to do this one thing."

He looked dejected. "Fine. We'll talk some other time."

Even though she heard in his tone that he was rebuilding the shield around him that he'd started to lower earlier, she couldn't say anything that would change the current situation.

She had responsibilities. And if she didn't act according to them, people could die. It wasn't something she wanted to have on her conscience.

11

Cole watched Vanessa dress in a hurry. He could still taste her on his tongue, and it drove him insane with lust. He wanted more of her. It felt as if he was slowly getting addicted to her. He couldn't recall ever feeling anything like that for any of the other prostitutes he'd slept with in the last two decades. There was a self-confidence around her that only accentuated her beauty. She was strong, both in body and in mind. She struck him as a determined woman who could get anything she wanted. So why was she working as a high-class escort? Did she like the power she had over men? The power she had over him? Was this why she was leaving now, to show him that she was holding the reins? That she would decide whether to give him more of her time?

With a last look at him, Vanessa left his condo. When she was gone, and silence descended around him, he realized that he'd forgotten to pay her. Why had she not reminded him? Something about her didn't add up. But that wasn't the only thing that now bubbled to the surface of what he could only assume was a horror-addled mind.

As if he'd been drugged. How else could he explain that instead of questioning Vanessa about the vampire attack in detail, he'd made love to her? How had his body even been able to think of sex, when the horror of being attacked by a real-life vampire was still so fresh? And why had Vanessa been so calm about killing a vampire? She hadn't flinched at all, in fact, he'd seen no fear in her whatsoever. As if killing vampires was a daily occurrence for her. What was she? A prostitute slash vampire slayer?

Even he had to shake his head at that. This wasn't real. It couldn't be real. Vampires didn't exist. They only lived in literature, the movies, and on TV. Not in San Francisco. It was against all laws of science and nature. Yet he couldn't deny that the monster attacking him had been stronger than him despite his smaller size.

Cole touched the wound on his neck. It was undeniable that he was injured. He walked into his bathroom and stopped in front of the mirror. The angry red lines across his chest were clearly visible. He traced the four gashes with his fingers, and noticed that the distance between them could indeed lead to the assumption that a claw had caused them. It was also what it had felt like: razor-sharp blades cutting into his skin.

He turned his head sideways and leaned over the sink to get a better look at the injury on his neck. The lacerations were round and deep, but there were more than two. He squinted. By the looks of it there were five or six. Didn't a vampire have only two fangs? He tried to recall what had happened after the bastard had tossed him against the wall with such force that Cole had been stunned as if attacked with a taser. The moment he'd been able to catch his breath, the asshole had already gone for his neck. He'd fought him off once, forcing him back, but the second time his attacker had come at him harder, first slashing him across the chest with his hand that had looked like it belonged to Edward Scissorhands, then going for his neck again.

The second time, he hadn't been able to fight him off, and while he'd continued to try, his limbs weren't following his brain's command any longer. He'd felt paralyzed. Vanessa had come out of nowhere, and at that point he'd thought he was dreaming. In a way, he still was. But the injuries told a different story. The attack was real, not a nightmare.

And Vanessa had saved him, and then promptly left after he'd made love to her. To go to work! That gnawed on him. She was going to sleep with another man after climaxing in his arms. The thought made him furious, particularly after he'd started confiding in her why he wasn't in a relationship. She was the first woman who he'd felt comfortable to talk to about his fears. Declining his offer that he'd pay her for the entire night had stung. Was she doing this as a means to drive up her price? By showing him that he wasn't her only client? As if he didn't know how desirable she was. He was fully aware of her irresistible charms.

Next time he'd be more careful about opening up, because whenever he did, he got hurt.

His cell phone pinged with a message. He tapped on it. It was from Drake. He'd set up a meeting with the man he'd mentioned. Cole checked the time. He had one hour before the meeting. He clicked on the address and realized that it was in Pacific Heights, not too far from where he was right now. However, the address didn't seem to be a house or a restaurant, but a small park.

How will I recognize him? Cole texted back.

He'll recognize you.

Cole let out a breath. Was it wise to meet a stranger at the edge of a park in the middle of the night after everything that had just happened? It was fishy. But what were the odds that he'd get attacked twice in one right? Pretty slim though not nil.

I'll be there.

Cole placed the cell phone on the vanity and started undressing. He needed a shower to get the remainder of the blood off him and wash his hair that felt like it had been sprayed with dust. A vampire's dust. Or did they call it ash? Either way, he felt disgusted by it all. Yeah, he could accept that vampires existed, but he wasn't going to take it lying down. Next time, he'd be prepared.

Cole reached into the shower to turn on the water, and tested the temperature before he stepped inside. He closed his eyes and let the warm water wash over him. Maybe tonight he would finally get the answer he'd been looking for all his life.

12

A block away from the entrance to the Scanguards underground garage, Vanessa's car sputtered, and the engine finally cut out. She managed to steer the vehicle toward the curb, when it stopped fully. She tried to start the car again, but the engine didn't respond to her attempts. She hit both hands against the steering wheel.

"Crap!"

She pulled her cell phone from her handbag, scrolled through her contact list, and tapped on one. It rang once, before the call was answered.

"Hey, Nessie."

"Hey, Sebastian. Are you at HQ?"

"Yeah, but just for another fifteen minutes. Why?"

"My car broke down."

"So the old rust bucket finally bit it? I've never understood why you don't buy yourself a decent car. I mean, you've got the money."

"You know how long it would take before somebody broke into a new car in the Tenderloin? Like five minutes. At least nobody breaks into the Jetta or steals it."

Sebastian chuckled. "Yeah, 'cause it doesn't run anymore."

"Very funny."

Sebastian cleared his throat. "Where are you?"

"Only a block north of HQ. Can you please see if you can get it to start again? Can you meet me in the lobby, and I'll hand you the keys? I've got to see Thomas and Eddie."

"Sure, I'll see you there in a sec."

Vanessa shoved her cell phone back into her handbag and exited the car. She locked it and crossed the street. By the time she entered the lobby, Sebastian was already waiting for her.

The twenty-six-year-old half-Asian vampire hybrid was one of her favorites among the Scanguards family. Sebastian was a practical guy, who always had a way of getting impossible things done. He also loved to tinker and invent and redesign everything that could be useful to anyone of his kind. A year earlier, he'd started producing *Blood Splatter*, carbonated bottled human blood for consumption by vampires and vampire hybrids. The beverage was now served at the V Lounge, the bar within the Scanguards headquarters building where vampires and hybrids could relax after work or in between their shifts.

"Hey, Nessie."

"Hey, Sebastian, thanks for doing this." Vanessa handed him her car keys.

"I might have to tow it to the garage, so don't count on getting it back tonight," he advised. "I'm supposed to be patrolling shortly."

"No problem. Just let me know if it's salvageable." She headed toward the elevators. "Thanks, see you later."

Vanessa rode the elevator to the executive floor on the top floor of the building, where Thomas and Eddie's office was located. The blood-bonded gay couple jointly ran the IT department at Scanguards, and Vanessa couldn't really say which one of the two was more talented. As a team, they were unbeatable.

At the door to their office, Vanessa knocked before entering. It appeared the two lovebirds hadn't heard her. Eddie was standing behind Thomas, who was sitting in front of his computer, his arms around

Thomas. Eddie's face was buried in the crook of Thomas's neck, though what exactly he was doing was hidden from her.

"Sorry," she said quickly and turned her back to them. "Didn't mean to interrupt."

A chuckle came from Thomas. "Come in, Nessie."

Vanessa turned around and closed the door, before she stopped in front of Thomas. Involuntarily, her gaze drifted to his neck.

"I didn't bite him," Eddie said, grinning, "if that's what you're wondering."

Thomas smirked and winked at her, before he addressed Eddie, "But you were about to."

"As if you didn't want it..."

The loving looks the two men exchanged warmed her heart. They'd been together since before her birth, and she couldn't imagine them not being together.

"So, I heard you've got something for us," Thomas finally said, looking up at her.

Vanessa dug into her handbag. "The

wallet, cell phone, and a set of keys from the rogue I killed earlier. I already looked at the photo on the driver's license. Name's Robert Nealy. He was only twenty-four according to his ID, though I don't know if it's a fake."

"We can figure that out," Eddie assured her and reached for the wallet. He glanced at Thomas. "I'll do the background. You wanna crack the cell phone?"

Thomas nodded. "That's hardly a challenge."

Eddie rolled his eyes and looked back at Vanessa. "We'll send everything we find down to the command center so Benjamin can centralize all information we're getting on the rogues."

"Thanks, guys, appreciate it."

Vanessa entered the command center a few minutes later. Besides Benjamin who was in charge again tonight, Patrick and Ethan were present.

"Hey, guys."

"Hey."

Benjamin looked over his shoulder. "Hey, Nessie. Are Thomas and Eddie working on IDing the vampire you killed?"

She nodded. "I just gave them the guy's wallet, cell, and keys. If his ID is genuine than he was only 24 years old."

"Did you have to kill him?" Patrick asked, inserting himself into the conversation.

"Yeah, I did." Vanessa felt her jaw tightening. This had been her first kill, and while she knew it had been necessary, she still felt shaken by it. She'd ended a life.

"Couldn't you just have wounded him and brought him in? Now we can't interrogate him. How are we supposed to find out who's behind this when you kill the best lead we had?"

Vanessa turned to Patrick, making a step toward him. "You weren't there," she ground out, narrowing her eyes. "The situation required that I kill him. It was the only way to save the human he was attacking. Next time you're confronted with a rogue, maybe *you* can catch him alive. So, butt out. I'm not in the mood for your Monday-morning-quarterbacking."

"What the—"

"Patrick, you heard her!" Ethan demanded.

"Chill, all of you. We've got work to do," Benjamin said with a calm voice.

"What do you need?" Vanessa asked, turning back to Benjamin. "Do you want me to meet with Lydia to patrol? Then Quinn can do a different route."

"No, let's keep them patrolling together. I need somebody to get Scarlet. She offered to work on the suspect profile, and now that we have info on the guy you dusted, she's got something to work with."

"Why does somebody need to get her?" Ethan asked. "She's got a car."

Benjamin grimaced. "Guess you don't know your brother that well. He ordered that Scarlet can't go outside at night without protection while the rogues are roaming the city. Besides, somebody needs to babysit the twins. Both Ryder and Scarlet's father are on patrol." Benjamin grinned. "Which leaves you three. So, who wants to volunteer?"

"To babysit? You're joking, bro," Patrick protested with a shake of his head. "Count me out." Then he pointed to her and Ethan. "They are your nephews. Have fun." Patrick headed for the door.

Ethan smirked. "Hate to say it, sis, but I think it's your turn. I babysat them last weekend."

"That's just what I need. Two rambunctious boys who don't know the meaning of sleep." Vanessa let out a sigh. Just thinking of it made her feel exhausted.

"They weren't that bad last week," Ethan claimed, putting his hand on her shoulder. "Besides, they love you."

She rolled her eyes. "Fine. But I need a ride. My car crapped out a block from here."

"Hallelujah, the rust bucket is dead,"

Benjamin joked. "I hope you'll buy yourself a decent car now."

"And have it stolen the moment I park it in the Tenderloin?" Vanessa shook her head.

"Come on, sis, I'll drop you at Scarlet's and bring her back here," Ethan offered.

"Thanks, both of you. Check in with me later," Benjamin said and turned back to his desk.

In the Scanguards garage, Ethan led her to a red Lamborghini instead of his SUV. Vanessa furrowed her brows.

"You bought a Lamborghini?"

He grinned and unlocked the car. "Not yet. I'm test-driving it this week. Get in. Let's take it for a spin."

Moments later, they were shooting out of the garage, and Ethan merged into traffic, the engine roaring like a lion in the jungle.

Vanessa laughed. "You can't be serious about buying this car. It's not practical in San Francisco. You're gonna lose your transmission when you hit a dip or a bump."

Ethan chuckled. "But it's a total babe magnet. Even you must admit that. Not everything needs to be practical."

They hit a bump, and Vanessa nearly hit the ceiling. Laughing, she shook her head.

"I didn't even feel that," he claimed.

"Hopeless case."

"So how are you feeling, sis, hmm?"

She let out an exasperated breath. "Not you too. First Mom, then Dad, and now you. For the umpteenth time: yes, I went into heat out of the blue, and I took care of it. End of story."

Ethan cast her a sideways glance. "You went into heat again?"

"You didn't know?"

"Now I do."

"Oh. But if you didn't know then why did you ask me how I was feeling?"

"I asked you because you had to kill a vampire tonight. I know that's not easy for anybody. And Patrick giving you a hard time because of it wasn't cool."

She sighed, putting her hand on his forearm. "Thanks for shutting him up. I wasn't in the mood to start a big argument with him."

"I could tell. You look a little drained."

She forced a smile. Too much was going on inside her, and the inappropriate reprimand by Patrick hadn't helped. "What's wrong with him anyway? Since when is he so argumentative?"

"Since he's practically the only Woodford heir left. Since Grayson is now running New Orleans with Monique, and Isabelle is taking a leave of absence because she wants more time with the baby—and with Orlando and the club—, I think he feels that he has to step up and show some leadership qualities. Even if he doesn't like it."

"He doesn't wanna lead?"

"No, of course not. He preferred it when the limelight wasn't on him but his siblings."

"I had no idea."

"And why would you? You've got plenty of

stuff to deal with on a daily basis. Trust me, I wouldn't want your job. I'd much rather be on bodyguard assignment. Can't wait until we've caught the rogues and put a stop to what they're doing."

"Same here. None of the sex workers and the homeless are safe while they're on the loose. I'm worried for them."

And not just for them. Anybody out at night was at risk of being attacked. And Scanguards couldn't be everywhere. Even their resources weren't unlimited.

13

This time, Cole decided to take his car, even though the meeting point wasn't far. But given what had taken place less than two hours earlier, he thought it wise not to spend time outside in the middle of the night when it could be avoided. His wounds were still raw, though they were healing with astounding speed, but he wasn't ready to fight a vampire yet. However, for self-defense, he'd broken a baseball bat he'd used as a kid, and fashioned it into a rudimentary stake. He hid it in the inside pocket of his jacket.

Cole was only about three blocks away from Alta Plaza Park, where he was supposed to meet Drake's contact at the bottom of the stairs, when he had to stop at a light on Pacific Avenue. As he sat there, waiting for the light to turn green, he noticed a red Lamborghini stop outside a majestic Victorian mansion on Pacific Avenue. He was surprised to see a car like that in a city like San Francisco with its narrow streets and steep hills that weren't suitable for a race car like that. As he admired the sleek lines of the car, the light inside it came on, revealing the driver and his passenger.

Shock coursed through him. Vanessa was the passenger in the car. She smiled at the handsome young man before hugging him. A moment later, she opened the car door and got out, while the driver remained in his car, the engine running. But he didn't leave.

Vanessa scurried up to the entrance door of the Victorian house, but Cole couldn't see what she was doing there, because a tree blocked his view. He barely noticed how the light turned green. He crossed the intersection, then pulled to the curb. Now he could see the door to the Victorian. A young woman walked down the steps, but it wasn't Vanessa. She got into the Lamborghini and smiled at the driver. A moment later, the Lamborghini drove past him, and Cole turned his face away toward the sidewalk as if he was waiting for someone.

When the Lamborghini was gone, Cole stared back at the Victorian house that Vanessa had disappeared into. What was she doing there? And who the fuck was the guy in the sportscar? A client? Had she slept with him? Was he a regular?

Fuck!

Something inside him made him ball his hands into fists, ready to beat the guy to a pulp. He'd touched Vanessa. Damn it, he'd probably fucked her. The thought ate him up. He should have made it clear to her that he would pay anything to have her be with him the entire night. But he'd been too distracted by the aftereffects of the attack that he hadn't reacted fast enough.

How could she sleep with another man after she'd been in his arms, after he'd made her come with his mouth? The intimacies they'd shared had led him to hope that there could be more between them—as stupid as that sounded. And Vanessa? She'd immediately gone back to have sex with somebody else.

Cole was fuming, his stomach turning into tight little knots. He knew what was going on inside him. He wasn't stupid enough not to recognize the feeling that had burst to the surface so quickly that he hadn't been able to suppress it.

He was jealous!

How the fuck had that happened? He'd frequented prostitutes for years, and known that once his hour with them was over, they would go to their next client. It had never bothered him before. In fact, he'd liked the arrangement, because it meant he didn't have to deal with the inevitable problems of a romantic relationship. He'd gotten what he wanted—sex—, and he'd never looked for more.

Until now.

Until he'd met Vanessa.

This shouldn't have happened. He should have never developed feelings for a woman who sold her body to anyone who could afford her. And by the looks of it, the young guy—who was at least ten or fifteen years younger than Cole—had plenty of it. Owning a sportscar that wasn't even practical in a city like San Francisco was the privilege of the rich and entitled, the trust fund babies who'd never done an honest day's work.

Cole hit his fists against the steering wheel in frustration. He needed to do something, before this situation got any worse. He had to stop Vanessa from servicing any more clients. That was his first priority. Just like tech companies hired talented engineers so that their competitors couldn't hire them, he would hire Vanessa so that nobody else could hire her. Yes, take her off the market first, worry about what to do later. That was the best plan he could come up with right now—because for sure his brain wasn't functioning properly.

He was livid that Vanessa had slept with another man—even though he had no right to demand exclusivity. But he was determined to change that.

Aware that the engine was still running, he switched it off, then reached for his cell phone. He unlocked it and scrolled to Vanessa's number. His index finger hovered over it, his heart pounded like a jackhammer, and he breathed erratically. Fuck, he had it bad.

Get a grip, man!

Why was he so nervous? Was he actually worried that she wouldn't agree to see him?

Coward!

He tapped on the number and put the phone to his ear. It rang twice.

"Cole?" Vanessa's melodic voice made his heart gallop even faster.

"Vanessa, I need to see you." Way to start a conversation. An elephant in a China shop showed more finesse than him.

"Is something wrong?"

Lots of things were wrong, but none of them were suitable to be discussed over the phone. "It's important that I see you right away."

"I can't get away right now. Has something happened?"

"It's really urgent. Please, Vanessa. I need to talk to you."

She sighed. "I can't get away. I'm—"

"It can't wait. Please."

"You're making me worried now. All right. But I can't come to you. You need to come to me."

"No problem."

"The address is 2447 Pacific Avenue in Pacific Heights."

"I should be there in about five minutes."

"See you then." She disconnected the call.

He shoved the cell phone back into his pocket and leaned back, forcing himself to breathe evenly. He looked across the street at the Victorian mansion Vanessa had disappeared in. It was the number she'd given him. That she was willing to receive him there could only mean that she wasn't with a client at the moment. But before this news could calm him, another question arose. What if this mansion was just like the one Vera ran in Nob Hill? What if this was a different brothel, and Vanessa split her time between this place and Vera's? After all, a beautiful young woman had left the mansion just after Vanessa had arrived, and had gotten into the Lamborghini. What if she was a prostitute too?

Before his mind could spit out even more questions and scenarios, he got out of the car and locked it. He crossed the street and walked up the stairs to the entrance door of the stately Victorian.

He stood there, unsure of what he would encounter inside. He sucked in a loud breath, then let it out through his nostrils, while he chided himself in silence. This wasn't how one closed a deal: by showing fear. No, he had to go in there and be assertive, lay out what he wanted, and what he was willing to pay to get it. It was a simple negotiation. A business deal. Vanessa was in the business of selling sex, and he was a willing and able buyer. Nothing more, nothing less.

Cole rang the doorbell and heard it chime inside the house. It only took a few moments, until the door was opened, and light was shining into his face. He blinked. Vanessa stood in front of him.

"Hi." Her voice sounded like a faint echo as if she were an apparition, but her eyes sparkled in that intoxicating green that made her look like a fairy who would make all his wishes come true.

He had it bad. Really bad.

"Vanessa."

She stepped aside, motioning him to enter. Cole walked inside, and he heard her close the door behind him, while he assessed his surroundings. With the eye of a discerning buyer who'd viewed many properties when he'd been looking to buy a home in San Francisco, he realized that while the style was most definitely quintessential Victorian, this house was newly built, which must have cost a fortune. The other thing he noticed was that it was quiet. He heard neither footsteps nor voices.

Vanessa turned to him. "Why did you need to see me so urgently?"

Cole reached for her hand and took it into his. "With everything that's happened the last two nights... the attack... you saving me. I've been thinking..."

Fuck! Why was it so difficult for him to ask for what he wanted? He was an experienced negotiator in business. He knew how to convey to his associates what he needed. Yet with Vanessa standing so close to him, he felt like a shy sixteen-year-old kid asking the prettiest girl from high school to the spring dance. He wasn't that boy anymore.

"What is it?" She inched closer. "What's wrong? Are you in pain? Are the injuries—"

"It's not about the injuries. I'm healing. Rather quickly, actually. No, it's about you, and about what happened between us." He cleared his throat. "I want to hire you exclusively."

It was finally out.

"Exclusively?" Vanessa asked, her forehead furrowing.

"Yes, an exclusive booking. You won't be able to see any other clients. You'll only sleep with me."

Her eyes widened. "I... uhm... I need to clarify something..."

"You can name your price. I'll pay whatever you want."

She let go of his hand. "I don't understand, Cole." She shook her head. "Why would you want me exclusively? You haven't even fucked me."

He wasn't prepared for her question, or for her to state the obvious. "I want you. I like being with you."

"Without fucking me? I'm sorry, but I can't do that. If you want to have me exclusively, you'll have to actually have sex with me. And I don't mean you going down on me. Hell, I haven't even seen you naked." She went toe-to-toe with him. "I want your cock inside me. But if you can't or won't do that, then it's a no."

He shoved a shaking hand through his hair, trying to buy himself some time. But he couldn't come up with an excuse of why he couldn't sleep with her, why he couldn't undress in front of her.

Only one answer would have the desired result. "All right. We'll have sex." His cock was certainly ready for it, growing hard and heavy.

"Prove it."

"What?"

"I said prove it. Fuck me now."

"Here?"

"Here. We're alone."

He glanced around, hesitating. A look into Vanessa's eyes told him that she was dead serious. He had no choice. "Ah, fuck it!"

Cole shrugged off his jacket and tossed it over the railing of the staircase leading up to the second floor. Then he reached for

Vanessa, and pulled her into his arms, kissing her passionately.

Vanessa's lips parted, and she welcomed him, while she tugged on his shirt, her hands sliding underneath it. Feeling her touch him ignited a fire inside him, one that he could only extinguish by plunging his cock into her. There was no backing out tonight.

Cole tugged on Vanessa's top and severed the kiss to pull it over her head. Her white bra covered her firm breasts that were already topped with hard nipples. But this time, he couldn't spend time on them. He had to give her what she wanted, or he would lose her.

Again, he captured her lips, while he opened the button of her pants and slid the zipper down. He shoved her pants down over her hips as far as her knees, where her boots prevented them from sliding down any farther.

Breathing hard now, he let go of her lips.

"Turn around, brace yourself against the wall."

Excitement flashed in her eyes, and she spun around, while he already opened his own pants and shoved them down together with his boxer briefs. He hooked his thumbs into her panties.

"You want me to fuck you?"

"Yes!"

Cole pulled her panties down, then gripped her left hip and adjusted himself. Vanessa pushed her ass back at him, and he reached in between her thighs, his fingers feeling the juices that coated her pussy.

He guided his erection to her pussy, and without preamble, he thrust into her to the hilt.

"Fuck!"

Vanessa gasped. "Oh, God. You're big."

"And you're tight." While her position certainly had something to do with it, he couldn't help but notice how tightly her interior muscles squeezed him. Heaven couldn't be any better than this.

Cole began to deliver thrust after thrust, reveling in the feeling of her pussy enveloping him like a velvet glove. "Is this what you wanted?"

She turned her head to the side, and he brought his face to hers.

"Yes, Cole. This's what I want from you."

Everything inside him rejoiced. "Then tell me you love my cock." Because he needed to hear it.

"I love your cock. I love how you fuck me."

Vanessa moaned, and her body moved in synch with his, intensifying each of his thrusts. Her body glistened, and for the first time in his life, he felt happy. This felt right.

"Damn, babe, you're so hot," he murmured, his mouth at her ear.

14

Vanessa *was* hot. It was confirmed now: every time Cole was near her, she went into heat. Something about him turned her into a woman who could only think of one thing: sex with Cole. She didn't care that they were in the hallway of Ryder and Scarlet's home, while the twins were sleeping upstairs. She didn't care that he took her against the wall without even fully undressing. All she cared about was that he was finally inside her. And there was absolutely nothing wrong with his cock, even though he'd been hesitant to fuck her. All that hesitation was gone.

Cole's cock was big and hard, and every time he thrust his erection into her, she felt another flame of heat surge through her. With his large hands, he gripped her hips firmly, allowing no escape. She sought none. She loved feeling his muscular body cradling her from behind, his mouth on her neck, his breath ghosting over her heated skin, his lips pressing open-mouthed kisses to her exposed flesh.

"I love how you take me," she murmured. "As if you're my master..."

"Is that what you want?" he replied in a hoarse voice. "For me to take you, and make you do whatever I want?"

"Will that turn you on?"

A breathless chuckle rolled over his lips, and he brought his face close to hers. "Vanessa, I'm already so turned on that my cock is ready to burst any second."

"Not yet," she begged. "I love having you

inside me." She clenched her interior muscles.

Cole moaned. "Fuck!"

Yet he didn't stop fucking her. He continued thrusting, increasing his tempo.

"Just like that," she said, "that's good. So good."

"You're not just saying that?"

She turned her head sideways so she could look at him. "Are you kidding?" She let out a breath. "I've waited for you to do this since the moment I saw you at Vera's."

He lifted one hand from her hip and slid it around her front. "Ditto." He dipped his hand lower, sliding it down to her pussy. "Now be a good girl, and come for me, so I can come too."

She wasn't surprised by his request, not after their previous encounters. He wasn't the kind of lover who forgot his partner when it came to pleasure.

"If you insist," she whispered with a smile.

"I insist."

She put her hand over his, and guided his middle finger to her clitoris. "Right here. Oh, and Cole?"

"Yes?" he rasped.

"I'm about ten seconds away from coming."

Whenever she was in heat, sex was different for her, more intense, more urgent. And her orgasms came faster and lasted longer. With Cole it was even more pronounced. His scent drugged her, and the taste of the blood that she'd licked off him over two hours earlier was still in her system. And now, as he fucked her as if he couldn't get enough of her, she wished she could bite him, and heighten their pleasure even more. But that would have to wait.

Just as skillfully as Cole had made her come before, he now caressed her clit in rhythm with the thrusts of his cock, making her moan out loud. She clawed at the wall, suppressing the urge for her fangs to descend and her fingernails to turn into sharp barbs. The vampire inside her fought for the upper hand, but the satyr pushed back its rival and won the battle. A massive wave of pleasure hit her as she climaxed. Her interior muscles spasmed.

"Fuck!" Cole cursed, and a second later she felt his cock spasm inside her, shooting hot semen into her. He continued plunging into her, but his movements slowed. His breath came in shallow pants, and he pressed his forehead on the wall next to hers. His big body caged her, pressing her to him, his cock still inside her, still pulsing.

"I've never come so hard," he confessed, his voice filled with disbelief.

She knew she couldn't tell him that her blood was the reason for it. It wasn't only healing his wounds, it was also adding to his arousal and sexual prowess.

"Neither have I," she murmured and turned her face to his, offering her lips.

He captured her mouth, kissing her

tenderly. "Good. I hope that means you'll agree to my proposal of booking you exclusively."

Fuck! It was time to tell him that she wasn't a sex worker. After what they'd just done, Cole deserved the truth.

"There's something I need to tell you—"

A high-pitched scream from upstairs interrupted her.

"I thought we were alone," Cole said, pulling back, his cock slipping from her sheath.

"Except for the twins," she said apologetically, while she reached down to pull her panties up, then made her jeans follow.

"You have kids?"

She turned around to him, and noticed that he was already closing the button of his pants.

"They're not mine. I'm just babysitting," she explained, looking for her top. She saw it on the floor and picked it up.

"Babysitting?"

"Yes." She pulled her top over her head and adjusted it.

"I thought you were working tonight."

Vanessa already headed for the stairs. "Joshua, Theo, I'm coming." With her foot on the first step, she looked over her shoulder. "Change of plans. I'd better check, and see what's wrong."

She was halfway up the stairs when she heard Cole following her. Vanessa switched on the light in the second-floor hallway, then headed for the boys' bedroom. One of the boys was crying, and she quickly opened the door and walked inside. The bedside lamps illuminated the room. Three-year-old Theo was sitting in his bed, crying, while Joshua, his identical twin was standing next to his brother's bed, trying to console him.

"Nessie is here," she said in a soft voice, approaching the bed.

Theo looked up, stopped crying for a moment, then started again.

"What's wrong, Theo?" she cooed and reached for him, when she noticed that he wasn't wearing his pajama bottoms, and therefore his genitals were exposed, and with it the growth above his cock that attested to the fact that he was a satyr, and that one day it would turn into a second cock.

Hearing Cole's footsteps at the door, she quickly reached for Theo and lifted him into her arms, so his groin was covered.

"Nessie," Joshua said, looking up at her. "Theo was scared cause it was wet everywhere." He looked up at his brother, "I told you you weren't drowning."

Vanessa brushed her hand over Joshua's head then looked back at the boy in her arms. "See, it's all good. You were just dreaming. Nessie is gonna get you new pajamas, okay?"

Theo's tears dried. "Nessie." He wrapped his arms around her neck and hugged her tightly.

She heard a sound from the open door and turned slightly, still keeping Theo in the same position so Cole couldn't see the grotesque growth on the boy's groin. It would only raise questions she wasn't prepared to answer.

He smiled at her, and it looked as if he wanted to say something, but before he could, his cell phone rang. He pulled it from his pants pocket and looked at the display.

"Sorry, I'd better get that."

15

In the hallway, several feet away from the open door to the twins' bedroom, Cole hit the answer button.

He already guessed why Drake was calling him.

"Doctor?"

"Where are you? Have you forgotten about your appointment? My contact has been waiting for you. He can't wait much longer."

Drake sounded utterly pissed off.

"Apologies. I totally got turned around in

traffic with all these one-way streets. I'm only three blocks away now. Three minutes tops."

"Fine, I'll let him know. Just don't make him wait any longer. He's a busy man, and this might be your only chance to speak to him."

"I appreciate it. I'll be there in three minutes."

He shoved the cell phone into his pants pocket and walked back to the open door.

Vanessa was rocking one of the twins in her arms. The sight made a warm feeling spread in his belly, while a completely unreasonable wish rose inside him: to see this woman rocking his child in her arms. He had to shake off the image, and instead lifted his hand to get Vanessa's attention.

She cast him a quizzical look.

"Sorry, I have to leave. Can we talk tomorrow?"

"Of course. Everything okay?"

"Yes, no worries. I simply forgot

something I needed to do." He smiled. "Talk tomorrow."

He rushed down the stairs, snatched his jacket from the railing, and left the house. Seconds later, he sat in his Aston Martin, the engine roaring as he drove down the street. He took the next left turn. He could already see Anza Alta Park and was looking for the stairs that led from the sidewalk up to the highest point of the park. Another right turn, and he spotted the stairs on the south side of the square. He brought his car to a stop right in front of them, killed the engine, and hopped out, his eyes already searching the stairs.

He saw nobody. Had Drake's contact already left?

He hurried closer, walking up a few steps, while he let his gaze roam. All of a sudden, he heard footfalls. His heart pounding rapidly, Cole whirled his head in the direction of the sound.

A dark figure with a long leather coat

emerged from the shadow beneath a tree and walked toward him. When he was able to see the man's face, Cole instinctively reached into the inside pocket of his jacket, his fingers wrapping around the wooden stake.

The man was as tall as Cole, muscular, with long dark hair that reached to his shoulders. But none of these attributes sent fear into his bones. No, it was his face that made adrenaline spike in his body, demanding he make a decision between fight and flight, because one side of the man's face was marred with a large, ugly scar that reached from his ear to his chin. It made him look like an enforcer for the Mafia, or for the Chinese Triad, though he was Caucasian and not Asian.

The stranger calmly walked toward him. "You must be Cole Whitlock."

Swallowing the fear he'd felt only a moment earlier, he nodded. "Yes, Mr...? Dr. Drake didn't mention your name."

"I'm Gabriel." He offered his hand and Cole shook it.

"Apologies for being late, Gabriel. Please call me Cole."

Given the intimate nature their conversation would take inevitably, he preferred an informal address so he could at least imagine that he was talking to a friend.

"It's nice meeting you, Cole. Shall we walk?" He motioned to a path that wrapped around the park after the first set of steps.

As they walked, Cole noticed that Gabriel had chosen to walk next to him with his good side exposed to him. Cole felt foolish having stared so overtly at Gabriel's scar.

"Drake believes you may have the same problem as I do," Gabriel started. "Tell me about it so I can be sure."

Cole took a steadying breath. This wouldn't be easy. "I'm not sure how to start, so here it goes. I have a large growth on my groin, right above my penis. According to all the doctors I've seen, it's not cancerous. The biopsies came back negative."

"Hmm. Have you tried removing the growth through surgical means?"

"Yes, several times. But it always grows back. I even tried radiation therapy, but nothing will get rid of it."

"Did you know your father?" Gabriel's question was unexpected.

"My father? Yes, of course."

"Did he have the same growth?"

"Yes." Sadness crept into his voice. "He had it all his life."

"Even after he met your mother?"

"Yes, that was the whole reason she didn't want to be with him. They had a one-night stand, and nine months later, she handed me to him. She didn't want to be a mother to a freak. My father could never find love, and he spiraled down into a deep depression."

He hadn't spoken about this to anyone, and it felt like a relief to get it off his chest.

"He committed suicide when I was a junior in college."

"I'm so sorry for your loss. If only he could have held on. But I'm glad you've found me. At least you won't have to deal with the same pain."

Cole felt hope rise. "Are you saying there's a cure?" He stopped walking and turned to face Gabriel.

"Not a cure, per se," Gabriel hedged.

"But then, if there's no cure—"

Gabriel lifted his hand, interrupting. "You don't need a cure. The growth you describe, the growth you've had since your birth is the same growth that I grew up with. It's a genetic mutation, and it's hereditary. My two sons have it too. It never skips a generation."

"You have sons?"

Gabriel smiled, and for a moment, Cole didn't see the scar but only the face of the man beneath it.

"Yes, and a daughter, and a happy wife. There is love for all of us. You'll see."

"But how?" He gestured to his groin. "How can any woman love this?"

Gabriel hesitated. "What I'll tell you now might sound fantastical, but it's the truth, and I'm the living proof of it."

"What are you saying?"

"The growth I had from birth and carried with me for so many years isn't there anymore."

"It's gone?"

"Not gone, because it cannot be removed, no matter what you try. It's transformed." Gabriel looked away for a moment. "Listen, I'm not used to talking to strangers about sex organs, but here's the gist of it. After you sleep with the woman who's meant for you, the growth you have now will turn into a second penis."

Cole nearly choked on his own saliva. "A second dick?" He shook his head. "Are you fucking kidding me?"

Gabriel smirked. "I'm not. My wife would probably suggest that I show you my two cocks to make you believe, but then my wife is a doctor and not squeamish. I'm a little more reserved."

Cole let the words sink in. "How is that possible?"

Gabriel shrugged. "There's lore around this medical phenomenon. My wife will tell you that it's all science, but every piece of lore is rooted in some reality. What they call men like you and me, and the women who make us sprout our second cock—so to speak—is satyr."

"Like a minotaur?"

"Sort of, but without the hooves and all. And while my legs are hairy, they aren't more than any other man's."

"Are you saying we're descendants from some sort of mythical creature?"

"In a manner of speaking, though you are human. You just have this extra bit." Gabriel shrugged.

"And your wife? She accepts you like that?"

Gabriel chuckled unexpectedly. "She wouldn't have it any other way." There was a sparkle in his brown eyes that now looked like they had a golden rim around the irises.

"But why would you need two—" Cole stopped himself, meeting Gabriel's eyes.

Gabriel didn't speak, but held his gaze, until something in Cole's mind clicked. He suddenly realized what the second cock was for.

"I believe you just answered your own question," Gabriel said. "I knew you were a smart man."

A quiet ringing sound came from Gabriel's pocket. "Excuse me." He pulled his cell phone from his pocket and took a step away. "Yeah?"

There was a brief pause. "I'll be there in twenty minutes." He disconnected the call and turned back to Cole. "I have to get back to work."

In the middle of the night? Maybe he really was an enforcer for the Mafia. But it was best not to ask any questions. Gabriel had taken the time to explain to him what his condition really meant, and he was grateful, though he now had even more questions.

"Thank you, Gabriel," Cole said. "I wish we could talk longer."

"Let's exchange numbers," Gabriel offered. "I would love to introduce you to my family. As I said, my wife's a doctor, and my youngest son deals with the same issue as you right now. But my oldest son, he's found his mate, and he's gotten his second cock."

"You have adult sons? You don't look old enough for that." In fact, the man looked the same age as Cole.

"Good genes. And you should meet my daughter. She hasn't found her mate yet."

"Uhm..." Cole didn't know what to say. He was only interested in Vanessa, even if it was stupid to have feelings for a prostitute.

Gabriel suddenly put his hand on Cole's forearm. "I didn't mean to overwhelm you. Let me give you my number, and when you're ready to learn more about satyrs, or want to meet my sons to talk about what they're going through, just call me."

He pulled a card from his pocket, and Cole took it.

"I really appreciate it. Everything..." He nodded. "It's given me lots to think about."

A moment later, Gabriel left. His head spinning, Cole slowly walked back to his car. He got inside and locked the doors, and then just sat there, staring into the distance.

Had Gabriel spoken the truth? Might the grotesque growth really one day turn into a second cock? And if that was the case, would the woman who caused this change in him really want him and everything that it entailed? And would he want her?

But what if Gabriel had lied to him? What if all this was just one big fat April Fool's joke? Or worse, some sort of scam.

Fuck!

He didn't know what to think, how to feel, whether to be happy or angry, frustrated or hopeful, confused or relieved. Or maybe everything at the same time.

To say he was overwhelmed and a little more than just skeptical when it came to the information the scarred stranger had imparted on him was the understatement of the century.

Didn't the revelation that he was a satyr only underscore the very fact that he was a freak of nature?

He needed to think. Maybe sleep on it. Perhaps tomorrow he could figure out what this news meant for his future.

16

Cole had spent half the night scouring the internet for information on satyrs, but there was nothing that suggested that a satyr had two cocks. A permanent erection, yes, as well as an insatiable appetite for sex. Frustrated, he'd finally gone to bed around three a.m. only to dream about running around naked with two permanently erect cocks, chasing a woman with long dark hair. When he'd finally caught her, and she'd turned her face to him, he'd realized that it was Vanessa.

Light tickled his eyes and made him blink. He'd neglected to close the blinds fully before going to sleep. He glanced at the bedside clock, and shot up to sit. He rubbed the sleep out of his eyes and stretched his arms over his head. Surprised that he felt no pain from the cuts on his torso and neck, he looked at his chest wounds and saw that only a faint redness indicated that he'd ever been injured. When he touched his neck, he felt only a slight soreness as if the wound was almost completely healed.

His stomach growled, and he jumped out of bed. Naked, he walked into his ensuite bathroom and headed for the shower. A look into the mirror over the sink confirmed that new skin was already growing over the deep incisions the vampire had left. However, the horror of the attack still sat deep in his bones, but he tried to push it away, and concentrated on that part of the night that had made up for it all: having sex with Vanessa.

At the recollection of how wild she'd been, and how receptive to his cock, Cole felt himself get hard in an instant. While he reached into the shower to turn on the water, he looked down at himself. What he saw sent a shockwave through his body and made him stumble backwards and bump into the wall behind him.

"Fuck!"

Cole blinked once, twice, but the image didn't change. The grotesque growth he'd been living with for thirty-eight years was gone. In its place, an inch or so above his regular cock, was a perfectly formed second cock, which he assumed was working just like his other one. And the reason he assumed this was, because this new cock was just as hard as his old one. In fact, two erections were currently pointing upward, ready for action.

He touched the new cock, wrapping his

hand around it. It felt the same as his regular cock, though its girth was a little less, and, naturally, it wasn't circumcised like the other one.

Thoughts and questions ping-ponged around his brain, searching for answers and looking for confirmation that he wasn't hallucinating. Everything Gabriel had said to him last night came back to the forefront of his mind.

Genetic mutation.

A second cock.

Satyr.

The woman you're meant to be with.

He recalled that Gabriel had mentioned that he needed to have sex with the woman who was meant for him for the growth to transform into a second cock. But he didn't remember whether he'd stated how long it would take to grow his second cock. Surely, it wouldn't happen within a few hours. No, no, such a complicated organ couldn't just be conjured up overnight. He'd been with a prostitute a little over a week ago, just before he'd left Chicago for San Francisco. So, maybe this had taken a week. Because if it had really sprouted overnight after he'd had sex with Vanessa, then wouldn't that mean that she was the one he was meant to be with? He rubbed his scalp, trying to make his brain work faster. Or was it the prostitute in Chicago who'd caused this change in him?

Did it even matter? Wouldn't it mean in either case that the woman he was supposed to be with was a prostitute? But it did matter. It mattered to him. Why hadn't he asked Gabriel more details about how this process worked? And did this mean that only the woman who'd caused this change in him would accept him? Would he be happy with her? Or could he find happiness with someone else?

"Fuck! Fuck! Fuck!"

He pressed his hands to his temples, and exhaled a shaky breath. What now? He needed help to deal with this. But first and foremost, he needed more information. And since the internet wasn't any help, he had to speak to Gabriel again.

In the bedroom, he found the jacket he'd worn the previous night, and searched its pockets, until he found the card Gabriel had given him. He read it.

Gabriel Giles, Scanguards, Private Security.

Below it was a number. Cole snatched his cell phone from the nightstand, and punched in the number. It rang. Impatiently, he paced in front of his closet. Why the hell wasn't he picking up? It rang a fourth time, before the call was finally connected.

"Yeah?"

The voice was male and groggy.

"Gabriel? Gabriel Giles?"

"Yes? Who is this?"

"Cole, Cole Whitlock from last night. You told me about..." He dropped his voice as if somebody could overhear him. "...me being a satyr..."

"I know who you are. What's going on?" He sounded a little more alert now.

For a second, Cole felt a twinge of guilt. Had he woken the man? The previous night, he'd mentioned that he had to get back to work. Perhaps he'd worked all night.

"I'm sorry if I woke you. But this is really important. And urgent." The words fairly tumbled over his lips.

"Tell me what's going on."

"I need to speak to you in person. I can't... over the phone it's just too... Please, can we meet? I don't care where. I'm freaked out."

He heard a loud breath through the phone, then a second voice, this one female and more distant.

"What's wrong, babe?" the woman asked.

"Go back to sleep, baby," Gabriel replied. "Nothing to worry about."

Then Gabriel's voice came through a little louder. "I can't leave the house right now."

"But it's really important. I can come to you. Gabriel, please, my head is exploding, and you're the only one who can help me."

There was a short pause, then Gabriel said, "Fine, come to my house. I live in Pacific Heights. I'll text you my address."

"Thank you so much. I'll be there in a half hour," Cole promised.

"All right. I'll leave the front door unlocked. Just come into the living room. Don't ring the door bell, and please be quiet. Everybody is sleeping, because we all worked the night shift."

"I really appreciate it."

Cole disconnected the call and tossed the phone on the bed, then headed for the shower.

After a thirty-second shower, Cole had dressed in a hurry, gulped down two protein drinks straight from the refrigerator, before getting into his Aston Martin to drive to the address Gabriel had texted him. When he saw the large Edwardian mansion, he double-checked the address, but he hadn't gotten it wrong. This was indeed Gabriel's house. It appeared that private security paid well. Unless, of course, his first assumption that Gabriel was working for the Mafia was correct. Not that Cole seriously thought this was the case.

It took him five minutes to find a parking spot a block away. When he walked up the stairs to the stately old building that looked like it was very well maintained, Cole took a moment to collect his thoughts. Following Gabriel's instructions, he didn't ring the doorbell. Instead, he turned the doorknob and pushed against the door. It opened easily, and he entered a small foyer with hooks for coats and umbrellas. He shut the door quietly behind him, then took a few steps farther into the house.

The homey atmosphere of the house struck him, because for a man like Gabriel who looked rough, he'd expected a different décor. Yet the interior belonged in one of the fancy home décor magazines many American families kept on their coffee tables. The colors were warm and soothing, the rugs that swallowed the sound of his footsteps expensive.

"Come in." Gabriel's voice came from the living area ahead.

Cole walked through the open archway that led into a comfortably furnished living room. Gabriel stood near the fireplace, pivoting now to greet him. He was dressed only in a pair of faded jeans and a white T-shirt.

"Thanks for seeing me, Gabriel."

His host looked very different today. The

casual clothes made him look younger and more approachable, and even the scar on his face looked less pronounced. Looking past the scar, Cole now realized that Gabriel was actually a handsome man and not the scary mafioso type from the night before.

Gabriel motioned to the sofa, and Cole took a seat. "Thank you."

His host sat down in the armchair opposite. "I'm assuming this is regarding the things we talked about last night."

Cole nodded, his throat constricting and as dry as sand paper. In the light of day, it was even harder to speak to a stranger about something so intimate.

He swallowed, trying to lubricate his throat. "There's something that I'm not clear about. When you said that I'd get my second... uhm... cock after sleeping with the woman I'm supposed to be with... could you clarify that? I mean, when you say *to be with*, what do you mean?"

"Exactly what I said. The woman who

gets your body to change like that is meant to be your partner, your mate for life."

Fuck!

"So, you're saying she's the only one who will accept me for what I am?"

"No. There might be other women who will accept you, but she's the one you'll find most fulfillment with. Like a soulmate."

"Okay." Cole felt his hand tap nervously on his thigh, and forced himself to stop. "So, uhm, how long after you sleep with that woman will it take to get your second cock? Are we talking months, a week, a day?"

Curious, he leaned forward, eager for Gabriel's answer.

"It varies." Gabriel shrugged. "For my son Ryder, it took about twelve hours. In my case it only took a few, maybe three or four?"

Fuck!

"Is it possible that it takes longer than that, maybe a week or two?"

Gabriel gave a determined shake of his

head. "No. It always happens within twenty-four hours."

Cole tried to swallow the knot that seemed to have lodged in his throat, his mind working overtime. He knew exactly what that meant. He hadn't had sex with anybody other than Vanessa in the last ten days.

"You look a little shell-shocked," Gabriel commented.

"You could say that." He lifted his face to meet Gabriel's concerned look. "I woke up this morning. With a second cock."

His host grinned all of a sudden. "Congratulations. I'm very happy for you."

"Yeah... thanks..." Cole couldn't get his facial muscles to form a smile.

"You're not happy about it?"

"Not sure how to feel about it."

Gabriel tipped his chin up. "Is your mate not happy about it?"

"She doesn't know yet."

Gabriel leaned forward. "It sounds like

you're not happy with *her*. Don't you like the woman you slept with?"

"That's not it. I'm drawn to her as if she's put a spell on me. She's gorgeous, she's everything I ever wanted in a woman. The sex was explosive... but..."

"But what?"

Cole sucked in an audible breath. "She's a prostitute." The second the words were out, he felt guilty for judging her like that. He slapped himself on the forehead. "I'm such a fucking hypocrite! All my life I've relied on prostitutes for sex, and now that it turns out that one of them is my soulmate, I'm judging her for what she does for a living! What does that make me?"

Gabriel studied him with a kind smile. "A conflicted man. Listen, Cole. I did the same: I paid prostitutes for sex because no other woman would sleep with me." He pointed to his scar. "I had much more of an impediment than you."

Cole tilted his head toward Gabriel's scar. "How did you get that?"

"My first wife gave that to me during our wedding night. She cut me when I undressed and she saw me naked for the first time."

"You mean you didn't have sex with her before you got married?"

"She had a very strict, religious upbringing." He made a dismissive hand movement. "It's water under the bridge. What I'm trying to say is that we do what we have to do. Being a prostitute doesn't have to mean that she's not a good person. For some women it's just a way to make a living. Look at her just for how she makes you feel. If you're drawn to her, it's for a reason..." He smiled all of a sudden and looked past him. "When I met my second wife, I knew from the second I saw her that she was it. I just knew. And I also knew that I didn't have a snowball's chance in hell to win her love. She's beautiful, and could have had any man she wanted. But she chose me, despite my looks, despite the ugly growth. She slept with me in spite of it—before either of us knew what would happen with the growth."

"She sounds wonderful."

"She is. She gave me three beautiful children, a happy home, and a future to live for. The woman you slept with can do the same for you. But you'll have to accept her for who she is. Love can't grow without that."

Surprised at Gabriel's wise words, Cole let them sink in. Gabriel was right. He had to look past Vanessa's job and only look at how she made him feel.

"Do you believe in love at first sight?" Cole asked.

"I do. And I believe so do you."

"I'm beginning to," Cole admitted.

"Good. Though, of course I'm disappointed that you've already found your mate. You would have been a nice match for my daughter."

"I'm sure I'm way too old for your

daughter anyway." Because there was no way that Gabriel was older than forty, even though he claimed he had adult children.

Cole rose. "Thank you so much, Gabriel. Thanks for everything you've done."

Gabriel stood up and offered his hand. Cole shook it. "Call me to let me know how it's going. And one other thing."

Cole listened up. "Yes?"

"In most cases, the mate of a satyr male is also a satyr. That means she'll go into heat several times a year."

"Into heat?" He scrunched up his forehead.

"Yes, like a feline. When that happens, she will need sex more than anything in her life. If she doesn't get it, she will get feverish. It's very painful. It's possible that she chose to be a prostitute because of it."

That was a revelation. Maybe Vanessa didn't really have a choice. "Does this mean, she knows what she is?"

"I don't know. My wife didn't know that

she was a satyr before she met me. So this woman might not know either, and simply follows her instinct. Once you're spending more time with her, you'll be able to figure out if she's a satyr. If she is, maybe we should introduce her to my wife and my daughter so they can tell her everything she wants to know."

Hearing that Gabriel was offering this even though he knew that Vanessa was a prostitute, floored him. He felt embarrassed that he'd judged him the night before, because it turned out that Gabriel wasn't one to judge. And he now felt even worse for having judged Vanessa. She didn't deserve him to think of her as being something less, just because of where she worked. She deserved so much more.

"I don't know how to thank you."

"Thank me by finding happiness."

Cole felt a smile steal itself onto his lips. He could do that. He could find happiness. With the right woman. And with the courage to lay himself bare before her. Even if that meant that he was making himself vulnerable and risked disappointment. Love and happiness were worth the risk. He had nothing to lose and everything to gain.

17

Vanessa had awoken in the late morning bathed in sweat after sleeping only four hours. She'd heard footsteps and the closing of a door. Maybe Ethan had only just come home. But the sounds in the otherwise quiet house weren't the reason why she couldn't sleep. She was in heat again. She'd rushed into the shower and turned on the cold water, before standing under the spray for a good ten minutes. It cooled her body down somewhat, but it wouldn't last long. She knew that. She knew exactly what would help her right now.

Only wrapped in a towel, Vanessa reached for her cell phone, hesitating. Would it be desperate if she called Cole right now? Maybe not. After all, before he'd left Ryder and Scarlet's house, he'd said that they would talk today. He hadn't mentioned who would call whom. While she was still contemplating if she should make the call, her cell phone rang. It was Cole.

Her heart began to beat excitedly, and the blood in her veins raced as if she was trying to catch the last bus. She took a couple of steadying breaths, before she tapped on *answer*.

"Cole, hi."

"Hi. I hope I'm not calling too early."

His deep voice sank into every cell of her body, reminding her vividly of how he'd taken her last night.

"Not at all," she managed to say without sounding too needy.

"Good. I was thinking since we still have a lot of things to discuss, you know, about me booking you exclusively, why don't I take you out to dinner tonight?"

Fuck! She had to work tonight. With the rogues still terrorizing the city, she needed to patrol just like all her colleagues. Nobody was getting the night off.

"Oh, uhm," she said, hesitating. She had to tell him that she wasn't a sex worker, and that wasn't exactly something she wanted to discuss over the phone. "How about lunch instead?"

"Yeah, sure, that works," Cole replied.

"There's a little French bistro on Polk. I'll text you the address."

It wasn't that she loved the restaurant she suggested, but this one was only a couple of blocks from Cole's condo. And that was important, because once she was close to Cole, she was sure her symptoms would become more pronounced, and she might not have a lot of time to make it somewhere private before she would tear the clothes off his body.

"All right. Shall we say in an hour?"

"Yes."

"I'm looking forward to it," Cole replied, his voice dropping an octave lower, making him sound like pure seduction.

Vanessa felt heat rise into her cheeks, making them feel like she was ablaze. Her throat was tightening, and she was unable to speak. She disconnected the call and inhaled sharply.

Fuck!

That man could turn her into a puddle of need with only his voice.

Before she lost all her senses, she quickly texted him the address of the restaurant, then tossed the cell phone on her bed and opened her closet to pick out a suitable outfit.

By the time she was dressed, she was just as hot as before her cold shower. Maybe a bottle of blood would make her feel better.

She checked in the small fridge of her room, but it was empty. She grabbed her handbag and her jacket, and headed downstairs into the kitchen.

The fridge was mostly stocked with bottles of human blood, though there was also some human food for when Ryder's wife, Scarlet, visited. Over the last few years, Vanessa had switched to mostly bottled blood for her sustenance. It kept her strong and alert for the job she had to do every night. On occasion, mostly in social settings, she consumed human food, though she wasn't as keen on it anymore as she'd been as a teenager. Human blood simply fulfilled her needs much better than regular food.

Vanessa emptied one entire sixteen-ounce bottle and felt better. She placed the glass bottle in the recycling bin, then walked into the panty, grabbed a six-pack of bottled blood and refilled her own mini-fridge in her room. Back downstairs, she headed for the foyer, where she halted abruptly, inhaling deeply. The scent that rose into her nostrils brought back memories of being in Cole's arms.

She was clearly hallucinating. Shaking her head, she opened the front door, and left. She decided to walk to the bistro on Polk Street, since it wasn't far, and she was way too early. Besides, according to Sebastian, who'd left her a message yesterday, her car was still sitting in Scanguards' underground garage and didn't show any signs of life. She would have to get another car, but she wasn't in the mood to think about choosing one right now. Her mind was filled with too many other things.

In her mind, she rehearsed how to tell Cole that she wasn't a sex worker. Still, she was nervous, because she cared about him, and she figured that if *he*'d kept such an important fact from her, she would feel betrayed too. Not only that. This wasn't the only piece of information she'd kept from him. How she would tell him that she was a vampire was a whole other story. In hindsight, perhaps she should have wiped his memory of the attack. At least then, he wouldn't instantly associate vampires with evil.

When she turned onto Polk Street and arrived in front of the bistro, she was sweating, and this time, it wasn't only because she was in heat, but also because she was afraid that she'd kept too many things from him, and that he would never be able to trust her once he knew the whole truth.

Vanessa entered the bistro and spotted Cole sitting at a small corner table. He rose instantly and waved at her. She strode toward him, smiling, her body heating even more. Yes, he was definitely the catalyst that sent her into heat.

At the table, Cole reached for her and leaned in, pressing a tender kiss to her cheek. "I'm so glad you came."

She smiled at him. "Hi." Her throat began

tightening. Should she order food and drink first, before she sprung the truth on him?

"Take a seat." He pointed to the half-moon shaped bench.

"Thank you." Vanessa tugged on her jacket to take it off, and Cole immediately stepped in to help her like a gentleman.

"You look a little flushed," he commented. "Are you hot?"

Vanessa sat down, while he laid her jacket over one of the unused chairs. Cole took the seat next to her on the bench, close enough to touch.

"It's really warm in here." Nevertheless, she inched closer to him so her thigh touched his.

He turned his face to her, while beneath the table, he slid his hand on her thigh. "I've already had time to study the menu." He pointed to the menu in front of her. "Take your time."

"I know what I want." Both from the restaurant's kitchen and from Cole.

"Good, we'll order."

He waved at a waitress, who took their order a moment later. When she left the table again, and promised to come back shortly with drinks, Vanessa knew it was time to confess the truth.

"I'm sorry I had to leave so abruptly last night," Cole said, before she could form a sentence. He lifted his hand from her thigh and reached for her hand.

"Me too," she confessed as he held her hand in his.

"Have you thought about my proposal? About me wanting to hire you exclusively?"

She hesitated. This was as good a segue as any. "About that. Uhm, there's something I need to tell you."

Vanessa noticed a look of dread wash over his face, and saw his lips parting, getting ready for a protest, but she couldn't let him interrupt her.

"You can't hire me, because I don't work for Vera. I'm not a prostitute."

Her words coincided with the waitress placing their glasses of white wine on the table. The woman's eyes widened, but she turned away quickly and retreated.

Cole blinked, while his forehead furrowed, and he gave a light shake of his head. "But... no, no, you were at Vera's, and you slept with me. You didn't protest when I said that I wanted you."

"That's right. But you might remember that Vera tried to protest and took me aside."

"I thought that was because maybe your shift was over."

Vanessa shook her head. "Vera tried to talk me out of it, because she didn't know you. She was worried you might hurt me."

For a few seconds, Cole just sat there, saying nothing. He'd let go of her hand earlier and now shoved it through his hair, rubbing his scalp.

"But why would you agree to sleep with me when you don't work there?"

She leaned closer. "Because I wanted you the moment I saw you."

Their eyes met, and she waited for him to digest the information. Would he judge her?

"Weren't you afraid that I could hurt you?"

"No. I could see in your eyes that you're a nice man."

"Just nice, huh?" He smirked. "You know that's normally the death knell for a guy, being called nice."

Beneath the table, she placed her hand on his thigh, then slid it up to his groin.

Cole almost choked.

"Not just nice," Vanessa whispered, leaning in. "Sexy, hot, passionate. A selfless lover. What woman wouldn't want that?"

He put his hand over hers, stopping her from moving it even farther up. "Okay, so now that we've established why you slept with me, would you please tell me who the guy in the red Lamborghini was?"

Surprised, Vanessa pulled back and looked straight at him. "You followed me?"

He quickly shook his head. "No. I was on my way to a business meeting, when I noticed the car. And it's such an unusual one to find in San Francisco that I stopped for a moment to admire it, when you got out of it and went into that Victorian on Pacific Avenue. Last night, I thought he was a client of yours, but since you don't work for Vera... Is he your boyfriend?"

Relieved that Cole hadn't been stalking her, she smiled at him. "He's my brother. He dropped me off because my car broke down."

Cole let out a breath. "Thank God. But who was the woman he drove off with?"

"Scarlet, my sister-in-law. She's the mother of the twins."

"So that was her husband? Pretty young."

"Actually, she's married to my oldest brother."

"And you had to babysit for them?"

"Yes, the twins are a handful. They can't just get a regular sitter. It has to be a family member or a good friend. Nobody else will put up with them."

Because a regular babysitter would find out pretty quickly that the twins weren't human. They flashed their fangs at the most inappropriate times, and when they were naked, everybody would see the growth on their groin.

Cole nodded. "Okay, now that that's cleared, there's still one thing that I don't understand: what were you doing in a brothel?"

As he asked his question, the waitress came with their meal, and placed the plates in front of them. Vanessa caught her shocked gaze, before she pivoted and hurried away.

"I work with the City of San Francisco to look after streetwalkers, the homeless, and the drug addicts. Occasionally, I bring prostitutes to Vera's to shelter them if they get in trouble with a john or a pimp. That's what I was doing there that night."

"Fuck me," he said on a breath. "I had it all totally wrong. Will you forgive me?"

"Forgive you for what?" She shook her head. "I was the one who let you believe that I worked there. I lied to you."

Cole took her hand into his. "I don't care. Though it does bring up something else. Now that I can't hire you to sleep with me, how am I gonna get you to be with me?"

She hadn't expected him to be so easygoing. This had gone better than she'd expected. She wished telling him that she was a vampire would go just as well, but she doubted it. However, that was a matter for another day.

"In your bed?" she murmured, lifting her hand to his face to run a finger along his jaw.

"More than that. I'd like the whole girlfriend experience..."

She brushed her cheek against his, the

contact making her aware of just how hot her own skin was. "How about you get the check, and we get out of here and go to your place, before we totally traumatize the poor waitress?"

"I like the way you think." He turned his head and caught the waitress's attention. When she came to the table, he addressed her, "Can we get this food to go? And the check, please? Thank you."

As the waitress hurried away with a relieved look on her face, Cole turned his face back to Vanessa. "You know that we'll never be able to eat here again, right?"

Vanessa chuckled. "I think that's a fair assessment."

He dipped his face to hers and kissed her lips tenderly, while he slid his hand to her nape, making her entire body tingle with arousal.

18

While walking back to his condo, Cole held Vanessa's hand and realized that she felt hot despite the cool outside temperatures. Was this an indication that she was a satyr too like Gabriel had suggested? A thousand scenarios of how to reveal to her what he was whirled around his mind. What would be less traumatizing? *Show* or *tell*? Fuck, this wasn't easy. He should have asked Gabriel how his current wife had found out what he was, since clearly, she'd accepted him.

Cole recalled that Gabriel had

mentioned that his first wife had slashed his face with a knife when she'd seen him naked on their wedding night. Obviously, that hadn't been the right way to go about it. He was smart enough to learn from other people's mistakes. Telling Vanessa a few things first was probably the better way to go. *Tell* it was.

Cole unlocked the door to his condo and ushered Vanessa inside. The moment the door fell shut behind him, she wrapped her arms around him and kissed him. Her kiss felt even better than her previous ones, because he knew now that she wasn't doing this for money. Finally, he understood why she'd tasted of innocence that night in the brothel. She was an innocent, not when it came to sex, because she certainly knew how to turn a guy on, but in her heart there was something pure, he could feel it.

Vanessa's hands were already on his clothes, and as much as he wanted to continue the kiss and toss her on the nearest flat surface to bury himself in her, he had to tell her his secret. She deserved to know what she was getting into. Cole snatched her hands and pulled back, severing the kiss.

She stared at him in surprise, her lips turning into a pout.

"Hold that thought," he murmured. "I wanna make love to you just as badly, but I need to tell you something first." He let go of her hands.

"Tell me what?"

Cole filled his lungs with air. If he made a mistake now and scared her with what he planned to tell her, she could leave and refuse to see him again. So much was at risk.

He raked a shaky hand through his hair. "Maybe you should sit down."

She narrowed her eyes, suspicion coloring her face. "You're married, aren't you?"

"Married?" He shook his head

vehemently. "No. I'm single, and I'm not dating anybody apart from you." Fuck, at least he hoped they were dating, and that they would continue to date after he'd told her the truth.

"Then what is it?" She motioned to the boxes in one corner of the living room. "Are you leaving San Francisco. Is that it?"

"I'm not leaving. I'm here to stay. That is if you still want me after what I have to tell you." He knew he was stalling. What man wouldn't if he was in the same situation?

Vanessa took his hands into hers. "Of course I want you. I thought I made that perfectly clear."

Her eyes were big like saucers, and around the green of her irises, a golden hew shimmered seductively.

He exhaled. "I'm crazy about you. I want you to know that. This is not easy for me, but you have a right to know. The reason I didn't fuck you in the brothel, and then last night here in my place, was because I'm not built like other men."

Frown lines appeared on her forehead. "Of course you're not built like other men. You're a lot taller, a lot more muscular."

"That's not it. My, uhm, sex organs are not the same as a regular man's..."

She rolled her eyes. "I've felt your cock, Cole, and trust me, your cock felt perfectly normal, even though you're bigger than other men. So can we have sex now?"

He lifted his palm to stop her. "That may be the case, but that's not all of it. There's more."

"More what?"

Cole swallowed hard. "Have you ever heard of a satyr?"

Vanessa's face turned serious, but he couldn't tell what she was thinking. "Go on."

"I know most people think satyrs are just part of mythology, but there is an actual medical condition that some men have that can be explained by the myth." He studied her face for any clues that indicated that she was ready to bolt. So far, it appeared she was still listening. "Anyway, this gene mutation manifests in the male sex organs." His throat suddenly felt like sandpaper. "As in multiple sex organs."

Vanessa sucked in a barely audible breath of air, but she didn't say anything.

"Vanessa, I have two cocks."

There was a second of silence around them, and neither one of them breathed.

"Show them to me," she demanded and reached for the waistband of his pants.

Fuck! He hadn't expected that reaction. Did she think he was making a joke, and wanted to call his bluff?

"Don't you wanna know more about satyrs, and what you're getting into?"

To his surprise, a soft smile formed on her lips. "Cole, I know everything about satyrs; I grew up as one. So will you let me undress you now?"

Cole met her gaze, stunned into silence

for a moment. "That's why you feel so hot… you're in heat."

Her cheeks flushed in an even deeper red if that was possible.

"Yes, I'm in heat. You must know what I need now."

She moistened her lips, and the seductive movement sent all his blood from his brain to his groin.

"I do." He wrapped both arms around her and drew her close to him, before pressing his lips to her mouth.

This time, when her hands were on his waistband, he didn't stop her and allowed her to open his pants and shove them down. Meanwhile, he tugged at her top and lifted it, then interrupted the kiss to pull the garment over her head. He reached for the waistband of her flowery skirt, and realized that it was elastic, making it easy to pull down. It gathered around her feet.

Cole kicked off his shoes, so he could take off his pants completely, then fumbled with the buttons of his shirt, but only managed to open the top three.

"Fuck it!" he cursed and pulled his shirt over his head, then tossed it on the floor.

Vanessa was still wearing her bra and panties. Today they were black, and she looked sexier than ever. When he felt Vanessa's hands on his boxer briefs, he sucked in a breath. She lifted her eyes and met his. Without breaking eye contact she shoved his boxer briefs down and he helped her until the garment fell to the floor, and he could step out of it.

Slowly, Vanessa made a step back and lowered her gaze to his groin. He followed her gaze to where his twin erections curved toward his navel.

"They're beautiful," she whispered breathlessly.

She touched his upper cock with her fingertips, making him shudder with pleasure, before she wrapped her hand around it, cradling him gently. His eyes fell shut, and his head tipped back, and every worry he'd ever had about Vanessa not accepting him disappeared into thin air.

"I have one more question," she said.

"You can ask me anything."

"When did you get your second cock?"

He opened his eyes and met her gaze. For a second, he hesitated, because he knew that she would understand the implications of his answer. But he couldn't keep this from her. "This morning, less than twelve hours after we had sex in your brother's house."

"Oh!" A puff of air rushed from her lungs.

Cole tipped her chin up with his thumb and forefinger. "We're meant for each other, but I don't want you to feel pressured into anything you don't want. I can wait. You're so young." She couldn't be older than twenty-three or twenty-four.

"I'm not as young as I look," she protested. "And I know exactly what I want."

"What do you want?"

"Right now? I want to suck your cocks."

He gasped. He hadn't expected that. "Fuck!"

She chuckled, already lowering herself, but he snatched her and lifted her into his arms. "How about we have sex in my bedroom for a change?"

"Okay, but I get to suck your cocks first," she insisted.

As he carried her into his bedroom, he laughed out loud. "Do you seriously think that I would turn that down?" Not a chance in hell.

In the bedroom, he set Vanessa down on her feet.

"Lie down," she demanded, giving him a little push so he fell backward onto the king-size bed.

Cole watched as Vanessa kicked off her shoes, reached behind her back and opened the clasp of her bra. Like a stripper, she peeled the garment from her body, revealing her perfect breasts. When she hooked her thumbs into her panties and freed herself from them, his mouth went dry, and he felt both his cocks twitch in excitement.

"I've never been so turned on in my life," Cole confessed.

Vanessa lowered herself onto the bed and cast a knowing look at his groin. "That's pretty evident." She licked her lips.

He groaned. "Cock tease."

Vanessa pushed his thighs farther apart and kneeled in the space she'd made for herself. She lowered her head over his erections, then licked first over his upper cock, then his lower one.

His new cock was just as sensitive as his other one. "Fuck!"

In response, the vixen in his bed blew air against his cocks. He caught her smirk when he looked down. "Having fun torturing me? Wait until it's your turn."

"But it *is* my turn," she said flirtatiously. "My turn to drive you wild."

"I'd say you're doing a pretty good job already."

Vanessa pressed her lips to the tip of his new cock and parted them, sliding down on him. He watched in fascination as his cock disappeared in her mouth. Her tongue slid along the underside of his erection, caressing him, making every cell in his body tingle with excitement. When she began to suck him, he thought for a moment that he would die of a heart attack, because his heart began to thunder in his ears. And as if this wasn't enough pleasure yet, Vanessa wrapped one hand around the base of his upper cock, and one around his lower one, and tugged on them simultaneously.

He moaned out loud, and cupped her cheeks with his hands, not to force his cock deeper into her mouth, but to be able to withdraw before her caresses made him lose control.

Vanessa lifted her lids and met his gaze, while she licked and sucked his cock as if it was an Olympic discipline, and she was out for gold. There was a golden shimmer around her irises again, and he didn't know where it came from, because the sun didn't shine into the bedroom, and none of the lights were on. Maybe he was just imagining it, because she was more beautiful than ever.

Cole caressed her cheeks with his thumbs. A thin sheen of perspiration now covered her face and neck, reminding him that she was in heat and needed him. He was selfish to let her suck him—though he didn't regret it. He'd never felt anything more amazing than being cradled in her mouth.

When he pulled her head up, and withdrew from her mouth, she looked surprised.

"If you suck me any longer, I'll come," he warned.

"How about I suck your other cock?" she asked, and tried to lower her head again.

He gave a quick chuckle. "That'll have the same effect, babe."

He pulled her up to him, then rolled them, so she was on her back. When he braced himself over her, Vanessa opened her thighs, welcoming him. Even though nobody had told him what to do with his two cocks in this position, he knew. Maybe it was instinct that led him now to thrust his lower cock into her tight sheath, making his upper one slide over her clit.

Vanessa wrapped her thighs around his hips, pulling him to her. He drew back his hips, then plunged back into her to the hilt. Vanessa's long eyelashes fluttered, and her lips parted on a moan.

"You feel so good," she whispered.

"You feel even better."

Cole dipped his head and captured her lips, while his hips continued to move in a steady rhythm. He kept his tempo moderate, wanting to prolong their lovemaking, but he knew it couldn't last. Already now, he was teetering on a knife's edge, holding his climax back with sheer willpower.

Their kiss turned more passionate, and he severed it to take a much-needed breath of air, when he felt Vanessa's breathing change. She clamped her hands on his ass to force him to fuck her harder. He had no choice but to give in to her demands. She was ruling his body, his mind, and his heart now. And all he wanted was to give her the pleasure she deserved. Was that what love felt like?

He had no chance to contemplate the question, because Vanessa needed his full attention. He felt her stiffen all of a sudden, and her interior muscles spasmed around his lower cock as she came. Another thrust, another slide with his upper cock over her clit, and he climaxed. He felt semen shoot through both his cocks, one filling her pussy, the other ejaculating over her stomach. His twin orgasms sent shockwaves through his body, making him nearly delirious with pleasure. He collapsed, and with his last sane thought, he rolled off her so as not to crush her with his weight.

"Wow," he managed to say as he turned his head to the side to look at her.

Vanessa's body was a picture of love. Her skin still glistened, her hair was tangled, her lips bruised from his kisses.

"Yeah, wow."

She smiled at him and reached for his hand to squeeze it. He lifted her hand to his lips and pressed a kiss to her knuckles.

His life was finally perfect.

19

Vanessa inhaled deeply, filling her lungs with Cole's scent that permeated the bedroom. She could smell the aroma of his blood, and it made her want to sink her fangs into his neck and drink from him.

"Let me get you a washcloth," Cole offered, sitting up. "I've made quite a mess here." He pointed to the spot on her stomach where his upper cock had sprayed her with his semen.

She watched him as he walked to the bathroom, his tight butt muscles flexing with every step. She felt her fangs lengthen at the thought of biting him there.

Fuck!

She had to stop these thoughts, or she wouldn't be able to hide for long that she was a vampire.

Cole reappeared with a wet washcloth and a small dry towel and sat down next to her. With gentle movements, he wiped her clean, then used the towel to dry her, before he placed both on the nightstand.

He joined her in bed and pulled her into the curve of his body, her back to his chest, her ass pressed against his two cocks, which were still big, but currently in a resting state.

"So that's why you didn't want to sleep with me at Vera's," Vanessa said with a glance over her shoulder. "Does that mean you don't actually fuck the prostitutes and just masturbate like you did with me?"

"You noticed that, huh? But the answer to your question is no. I did fuck the prostitutes. I do need that release, and feeling a woman's body helps me imagine that there's somebody who isn't disgusted by me."

Vanessa turned halfway. "Don't say that. I'm not disgusted by you."

"I must have known that you're different, because when I saw you, I knew I couldn't undress in front of you. Sure, I would have gotten to fuck you, after all, I'd paid for it. But once wasn't... *isn't* enough. I wanted to see you again. I wanted you to like me."

"Oh Cole, if only I had known."

He brushed his fingers over her cheek. "We'll make up for it now."

Vanessa smiled. "Tell me about yourself. The boxes in the living room. You said you weren't leaving."

"And I'm not. I moved here from Chicago ten days ago. I haven't fully unpacked yet. But I'm here to stay."

He hugged her to him, and pressed a kiss to her shoulder.

"Did you move for a job?"

"I have my own company, and I can work remotely from wherever I want."

"What kind of company?"

"I developed an algorithm that's used for advertising. So, basically, I'm a computer geek."

She squeezed his biceps. "You don't get muscles like these from typing on a keyboard."

Cole laughed. "True. Hence the weight bench." He pointed to one corner of his bedroom. "Anyway, I've always moved a lot. There are only so many brothels and prostitutes a guy can visit before word gets around that I'm... you know... different."

"No more prostitutes for you."

"That goes without saying," he replied. "Can I confess something?"

She held her breath instinctively. "Yes?"

"Don't sound so scared."

"I'm not," she lied.

"Hmm. Today when you met me in the

bistro, I was fully prepared to offer you an exorbitant amount of money to be my own personal, exclusive escort. I didn't care how many men you'd slept with before me, and that you'd gotten paid for it. I would have accepted you either way."

She turned in his arms to look at him. "That's the sweetest thing anybody has ever said to me."

Cole slid his lips over hers and kissed her tenderly. "I'm so happy that you accepted me."

"You're perfect for me," she murmured. "I knew it instantly. I went into heat when you entered Vera's, even though I hadn't even seen you, and it wasn't even my time. It was spontaneous."

"Because I was nearby?"

She nodded. "Yes. I go into heat four times a year on a pretty regular schedule."

"How old were you when it started?"

"Fifteen."

"And did you have to... I'm sorry, it's none

of my business to ask that." He dropped his lids.

She stroked her hand over his cheek. "If your question was whether I had to have sex then, the answer is yes."

"You were so young."

"That's why I asked a friend of my family. He's only two years older than I am, so he agreed to help me."

"Did you date him?"

"No. We never dated. He's still a very good friend, even though it's been fourteen years since I had sex with him."

"Excuse me? How long? You can't be older than twenty-four."

She laughed. Of course, he'd noticed that she looked young. A vampire hybrid's appearance didn't change anymore after the age of twenty-one. "I'm actually thirty-two."

"Impossible."

She rolled her eyes. "Guess I have good genes. Anyway, my friend helped me all those years until I was old enough to pick up other guys to have sex with when I went into heat. I hope that doesn't shock you."

Cole chuckled. "You're talking to a guy who paid for sex all his life. You did what you needed to do. Just, please, if I ever meet this friend of yours, don't tell me it was him. I'd rather not know who he is."

She understood that. "I promise." She kissed him. "So, what made you move to San Francisco, when you could choose any place in the world?"

"I found a note and a phone number in my dad's old diary that made me wonder if somebody here in San Francisco knew of a cure to my condition. Turns out, I didn't need a cure, just the right woman."

"And your dad?"

"He committed suicide 17 years ago. I never knew my mother. She dumped me at his doorstep after I was born with that ugly growth."

"I'm sorry." She kissed him softly on the

cheek, and trailed more kisses down his neck and along his shoulder.

"He never found the woman who was meant for him." There was sadness in his eyes, and her heart broke for him. "He spiraled into a depression that he couldn't climb out of." He sniffled. "I'm sorry, Vanessa, I didn't mean to spoil the mood."

She gave him a peck on the lips. "It's part of you, the happy and the sad. It's what makes you, you."

Cole pressed his forehead to hers. "You saved me, not only from being killed by a vampire, but from giving up hope of finding happiness."

His stomach suddenly growled loudly.

He smirked. "And apparently you also kept me from eating my lunch." He gave her a playful slap on her ass. "How about we eat the takeout?"

"Yes, we should definitely do that. You need to keep up your strength, because I can feel another wave of heat coming on."

"Guess that means that my services will be required again shortly."

There was a sparkle in his eyes that made her heart beat excitedly. But would that sparkle still be there once she told him that she was a vampire, and that instead of French food for lunch she'd rather drink his blood?

When exactly was the right moment to bring this up?

She wasn't quite ready for it. Their relationship was still too new, and if she sprung this on him right now, she might destroy the happiness she saw in his eyes.

20

They'd eaten their takeout, and Cole had noticed that Vanessa only picked at her food, barely eating any of her salad, while he'd finished his steak and French fries in no time.

Vanessa was wearing his oversized bathrobe and looked adorable in it. He could get used to this sight. He was wearing a pair of shorts, his body still too heated from the incredible sex they'd had. It almost felt as if she wasn't the only one who was in heat. At the thought, he suddenly realized something he hadn't even considered before. He hadn't worn a condom, neither the night before—which could be excused because he'd acted without thought—nor today where he'd had no excuse.

"Vanessa, there's something…" he started.

"About?"

He pulled her closer, lifting her onto his lap. "Since you go into heat, doesn't that mean this is pretty much your most fertile time? I mean, I could have already gotten you pregnant." Even as he said the word, he knew that he would be ecstatic if that happened.

She hesitated and cast her gaze downward. "It is, but don't worry, I'm taking a contraceptive."

He tipped her chin up with his index finger, forcing her to look into his eyes. "I'm not worried, babe," he assured her, wondering if she was telling him the truth. Was it possible that she was lying to him, because she thought he would be angry if she didn't take anything, when it was just as much his fault for not thinking of it? "Vanessa, if you weren't taking anything, I'd be okay with that too."

Her eyes seemed to sparkle all of a sudden, and she shifted on his lap.

Feeling himself get hard, he undid the belt of her robe and slid his hands underneath it to touch her naked skin. "In fact, that thought makes me positively horny."

"I can feel that," she said seductively, and pushed the robe over her shoulders. "Please fuck me, Cole."

He touched her cheek and her forehead. "You're burning up. Let's get you into the shower, and then I'm all yours to do with as you please," he suggested, and stood up with Vanessa in his arms, not waiting for her reply.

He carried her into the bathroom, while she kissed his neck, and rubbed her luscious breasts against his chest. In front of the shower, he set her down on her feet, and dropped his shorts. Cole reached into the shower, and turned on the water to a cool temperature.

Taking Vanessa's hand, he led her into the shower, then drew her into his arms, and let the cool water rain on them. He knew she needed sex, and his satyr body was more than ready to give her what she needed. His twin cocks were rock hard, pressing against her stomach.

"I've got you," he murmured and captured her lips for a passionate kiss.

Her mouth was hungry when she kissed him back, her tongue relentless in its demands, eagerly stroking against his, demanding he explore her. Fuck, Vanessa was on fire. He could feel her urgent need as if it was his own. Her arms were around him, her hands exploring him.

Knowing what she demanded, he pressed her against the shower wall, his hands already hooking under her thighs to lift her. Automatically, she spread her legs as he lifted her and positioned himself at her center, before he ripped his lips from hers.

"Guide my cock into your pussy."

Without hesitation, Vanessa took hold of his lower cock and brought it to her sex, placing it at the entrance to her pussy. When the tip of his shaft touched her nether lips, he moaned, and Vanessa leaned her head back, panting.

"Don't make me wait," she rasped.

Cole moved his hips and plunged deep inside her, while his upper cock slid over her center of pleasure, before being imprisoned between their bodies.

"Oh, God, yes." Vanessa moaned, her chest rising and falling, air rushing out of her lungs.

He pulled back, so only the tip of his cock was still submerged in her, then thrust back to the hilt, his balls slapping against her, his second cock sliding over her clit again.

"Cole!"

"I know, baby, I'll take care of you."

He could feel her channel stretch to accommodate him and her hips undulate to beg him for more. She gripped his shoulders, her fingernails digging into his flesh to force him to fuck her harder.

He wouldn't deny her, or himself. His thrusts turned more ferocious, his chest heaving from the effort to hold her suspended against the wall, his breath coming in rapid pants. His jaw was clenched tightly as he tried to hold on to his self-control. Vanessa needed to climax more than he did, so he pushed away his own needs, and concentrated on hers.

Vanessa tilted her head to the side as if her neck was an offering. Instinctively, he knew what she wanted. He kissed her there, pulling her skin into his mouth, running his tongue over it, before he scraped his teeth against her neck without biting her.

Vanessa shuddered, and her entire body spasmed, her interior muscles squeezing his cock and sending him over the edge.

He filled her pussy with his seed, lubricated her channel even further, while his upper cock sprayed semen against her stomach. He didn't stop thrusting, instead he continued fucking her, until her spasms subsided. Breathing hard, he leaned his forehead against hers.

"Fuck! I can't believe it's getting better each time."

Vanessa panted. "I love the way you fuck me."

"It's not just fucking." Cole kissed her lips gently. "It's making love." Because what he was feeling when he was with her was more than just physical. It went deeper, despite the short time they'd known each other.

She lifted her head and met his gaze.

"Yes." Her eyelashes fluttered. "Next time you make love to me, I want both your cocks inside me."

"You mean…?"

He didn't have to finish his sentence, because he knew exactly what she meant. Because it was what he'd fantasized about from the moment he'd seen his second cock. He hadn't expected her to be ready for it so soon.

"Yes," she murmured and brushed her fingers along his jaw. "I want to know what it feels like."

"Are you saying you've never had anal sex?"

"Never."

That revelation made something akin to an electrical charge shoot through his body, igniting every single cell inside him.

"I'll make sure you'll enjoy it. I promise. I won't hurt you."

Vanessa cupped his cheek. "I know you won't."

The trust he saw in her eyes and heard in her voice made him feel as if his heart was expanding in his chest.

"Oh, baby," he whispered, and kissed her tenderly, while sliding out of her sheath and setting her feet back on the ground.

As if he'd done this many times before, he reached for the soap and began to wash Vanessa's body. She turned in his arms and leaned back against his chest. He lathered her breasts and massaged them, loving the feel of her firm flesh in his palms.

"I could do this all day and night," he confessed.

"I wish we could," she said, turning her head. "But I have to get going."

His forehead furrowed. "Going where?"

"To work."

"But it's almost evening," he protested.

Vanessa turned in his arms. "Yes, and that's when I work. I have to go on patrol to make sure the sex workers are okay."

"That's too dangerous. Have you already

forgotten that I was attacked by a vampire last night?"

She tilted her head to the side. "You seem to have forgotten that I saved you. I'll be all right."

"Vanessa, you can't just go out there on your own. It's too risky."

She sighed. "Cole, please, I've been doing this job for years. I know how to handle myself."

"That might be the case, but do you really think I'd let you go out there alone, knowing that those vile creatures are out there?"

She blinked and remained silent for a moment, as if she was contemplating something. "There's nothing you can do about that."

"Yes, there is."

"And what is that?"

"I'm coming with you."

Because he wasn't going to risk losing her, now that he'd finally found the one woman who he was meant to be with. The only woman he'd ever fallen in love with. Because, yes, he was falling hard and fast. And if he were honest with himself, he would admit that he'd fallen in love with her the moment he'd seen her at Vera's. And if he had to learn how to kill vampires to protect her, then he would do just that.

21

"Turn left up here," Vanessa instructed, pointing to the next intersection.

Tonight, Cole had decided to take the Land Rover, since the Aston Martin would attract too much unwanted attention in the neighborhood where Vanessa wanted to patrol. He was still ticked off that she insisted on working tonight despite what had happened the night before. But he could be insistent too, and there was no way in hell he'd let her go out there alone.

He made the left turn. "Where to?"

"Middle of the block, on the right. You can partially block that driveway with the black SUV. I won't need long to change my clothes."

Cole pulled to the curb, blocking part of the driveway that had space enough for two cars side-by-side, leaving enough space so the SUV could leave without him having to move his car. He switched off the engine. Vanessa already jumped out of the car, and by the time he reached the sidewalk, she was waiting for him at the bottom of the stairs leading up to a large Edwardian mansion. His gaze was drawn to the house. Fuck, he'd been here before. In fact, he'd been here earlier today. How had he not put two and two together as to who Vanessa really was?

Vanessa already put a foot on the first step, pulling her keys from her handbag, when Cole touched her arm to get her attention. She looked at him, but continued walking up to the entrance door.

"This is your parents' house?"

She inserted the key in the lock. "Yes. Nice, huh?"

"You're Gabriel's daughter?" The assumption wasn't too farfetched. How many satyrs could there be in a city the size of San Francisco? Not too many, that was certain.

She cast him a quizzical look. "You know my father?"

"Long dark hair, big scar?"

She nodded. "Small world." She pushed the door open and waved him in.

Cole followed her inside the foyer and let the entrance door snap closed behind him. The house was quiet, though he could hear footsteps from one of the upper floors. It appeared that somebody was home.

In his mind, everything he'd told Gabriel earlier in the day came back in a flash. How would he make sure that Gabriel didn't find out that his daughter had been in a brothel and slept with him pretending to be a prostitute?

"Let's go to my room, so I can get changed," Vanessa said, and took his hand. "And then you can tell me how you know my dad. He's never told me about you."

As he walked to the second floor with her, he wondered how to explain to Vanessa that once her dad found out that she was the woman he'd been talking about, the woman who'd made his second cock appear, Gabriel would know the circumstances under which they'd met. He didn't want Vanessa to be judged for it. Fuck! He should have never told Gabriel that his intended mate was a prostitute. Why hadn't he kept his mouth shut? Maybe because Gabriel had been so helpful and understanding.

Vanessa opened a door on the second floor and ushered him inside. He was surprised to find himself in an enormous self-contained suite with a living area, a sleeping area, and an ensuite bathroom.

Vanessa opened the door to a large walk-in closet and grabbed a pair of pants, a T-shirt, and a sweater from it.

"So, how do you know my dad?" she asked, while she started to undress.

It was hard to think straight looking at her like this. The self-confidence with which she took off her clothes, knowing that she had an absolute perfect body that he couldn't get enough of, made him want to toss her on her bed and make love to her again. But this wasn't the place for such thoughts—or deeds—not with her parents at home—which they probably were, since Gabriel had said that everybody worked the night shift.

"Cole?"

"Sorry, yes, your dad... I only met him yesterday for the first time. He's the one who told me that I'm a satyr."

She gave him a quizzical look. "Unless he saw you naked, how would he know about you?"

"This doctor referred me to him. Drake. He's got a clinic in—"

"Drake, the psychiatrist?"

"You know him?"

"Yeah, he's the go-to guy that everybody from the office consults when they have issues." She smirked. "He's a pretty odd duck."

"Have you ever been to his practice? The furniture is more than just odd."

Vanessa slipped into the T-shirt and smoothed it down. "I've never been to his office, but I've heard his décor is a bit goth." She pulled the sweater over her head and fed her arms through the sleeves. "Done," she declared. "Let's go."

Cole stood closest to the door and opened it for her, letting her step into the hallway ahead of him. When he followed, he was forced to stop right behind her. The reason was the couple that had just descended from the third floor and now stood only a few feet away from him and Vanessa.

The man was Gabriel. The woman was as stunningly beautiful as Vanessa, and looked barely a few years older than her. She had the same long, dark hair as Vanessa. There was no doubt that this was Vanessa's mother. They were carbon copies of each other.

"Cole?" Gabriel stared at him in utter surprise, his head ping-ponging between him and Vanessa.

"Gabriel," Cole said, searching for what to say.

Gabriel turned to his wife. "Maya, this is Cole, the man I told you would make the perfect mate for Vanessa." He looked back at Cole. "So, uhm, wanna explain to me why you're coming out of my daughter's bedroom, when your intended mate is a prostitute?"

"Gabriel, I'm really sorry," Cole started. "I think I wasn't very clear earlier this morning when we talked. I might have given you the wrong impression—"

"You were here this morning?" Vanessa interrupted, touching his arm.

"He was," Gabriel answered in his stead. "He had some important news."

Was Gabriel trying to suppress a smirk, or was his scar twitching?

"No wonder I went into heat," Vanessa added.

"I think you two are making our visitor uncomfortable," Maya said and extended her hand. "I'm Maya, Vanessa's mother. It's nice to meet you, Cole."

"It's nice to meet you too, Maya." Cole shook her hand, then addressed both her and Gabriel, sweat building on his forehead and nape. He wasn't prepared for this *meet-the-parents* thing. "I uhm, I don't want you to think badly of your daughter, because of how we met..." Fuck, this wasn't easy.

"Vera's?" Maya asked, addressing Vanessa.

Vanessa nodded, smiling. "Must have been fate." She slipped her hand into Cole's.

Maya gave them both a warm smile, and Gabriel put his arm around his wife, then offered his hand to Cole. "Welcome to the family."

Surprised that neither Gabriel nor his wife seemed to judge Vanessa for having slept with him pretending that she was a prostitute, and him for believing that she was, he felt his worries dissipate into nothing.

He shook Gabriel's hand. "Thank you, Gabriel, Maya. I'm so grateful for everything you've done for me."

Gabriel chuckled. "See, I told you I had a beautiful daughter." He exchanged a loving look with Maya. "I should have been a matchmaker."

"A matchmaker, you, Dad? No way!"

The young man who'd spoken, came out of a room on the same floor. Cole recognized him as the driver of the Lamborghini, Vanessa's brother.

"That's Ethan," Vanessa said.

"Hi, Ethan, I'm Cole."

"Hey. What's up?"

Gabriel looked over his shoulder. "You on patrol duty?"

Ethan nodded. "Chinatown's mine tonight. Better get going."

"Want us to drop you on the way?" Gabriel asked. "We're leaving in a minute."

"No, I have to drop the Lamborghini at the dealership on Van Ness first."

"I'm glad you're not keeping it," Maya said. "It's so impractical in the city."

He winked at his mother and pressed a kiss to her cheek as he squeezed past her. "Yeah, but it would be a total chick magnet. See you guys." Ethan hurried down the stairs.

"Well, we'd best be on our way too," Maya said.

"I'm leaving too," Vanessa said.

"Where are you patrolling?" Gabriel asked.

"Tenderloin."

"Yeah, about that," Cole interrupted, addressing Gabriel. "Could you please talk Vanessa out of going out there at night, putting herself at risk?"

Gabriel looked at his daughter, then back at him. "That's Vanessa's job. I'm sure she's told you that."

"She has. But now I know who she's up against: vampires, vile bloodsuckers. I can't let her go out there. Please talk some sense into her, because she sure isn't listening to me."

Gabriel and Maya exchanged a quick glance. "Vampires? You know about vampires?"

"I do. Don't you?"

Gabriel stared at Vanessa. "You told him?"

"Vanessa didn't have to tell me," Cole

said quickly. "I was attacked by one last night."

"Oh." Gabriel motioned to Vanessa. "A quick word in private." He gave a curt nod. "Excuse us."

Vanessa and Gabriel disappeared in Vanessa's room, and Cole was left with Maya. Given the surprised, almost shocked look on Gabriel's face, there was a good chance that Vanessa's father would make her see reason.

"Cole, why don't we wait downstairs for them?" Maya asked with a pleasant smile.

"Of course."

22

Gabriel turned to her as soon as the door fell shut behind him. "He was attacked?"

Vanessa nodded. "Last night. It was pure luck that I heard him scream. I was on my way to work."

"So, Cole's the victim you protected? Whose attacker you killed."

She braced her hands at her hips. "What should I have done otherwise? The bastard would have killed him! With Ginger I reacted too slowly, and thought I could capture him, and Ginger nearly died because of it. And if you think—"

"Hey, sweetheart," Gabriel interrupted, putting a hand on her shoulder. "I'm not reprimanding you. You did good. I would have done exactly the same as you, if the victim had been somebody I love. 'Cause you love him, right?"

"He's an amazing man. When I'm with him, everything is perfect." She felt as if she was overflowing with emotions. "But I have no idea how to tell him what I am, what we are. Not after he got attacked last night. Now all he'll be able to see is that vampires are brutal, evil, vile..." She lifted her lashes to meet her father's gaze. "What am I gonna do, Dad?"

Gabriel embraced her, and she felt tears well up in her eyes. He stroked over her long hair, soothing her like he'd done when she was a little child. Sometimes, she still felt like that child.

"You'll find a way. He adores you. Even when he thought you were a prostitute, he wanted you."

"What if he's disgusted when he finds out what I really am?" She peeled herself out of his arms.

"He'll get over it. Look at all our friends. They all managed somehow for the human they love to accept them for what they are."

"But I'm physically stronger than him. What will that do to his male ego? A man like him won't like a woman like me."

"Says who?" Gabriel shook his head. "Look at Yvette and Haven. When they met, he was human. And she was way stronger than him; I mean she was a formidable fighter. That didn't stop Haven from falling in love with her. So trust me, Cole's ego will survive it. Besides, once he experiences what the bite does to him, he'll count himself lucky."

"What if we don't even get that far?" She pressed her hands to her temples. "I should have followed procedure and wiped his memory of the attack."

"It's too late for that now. Besides, you must have had a reason for why you didn't."

Her father wasn't wrong. "I wanted him to be prepared. To know that there are dangers out there. Because I can't protect him every minute of every day." A thought pierced her mind. "We need to train him. He should go through the bodyguard training at Scanguards. At least then he can defend himself."

Gabriel put a hand on her forearm. "That's for later, and only if that's what he wants too. For now, you need to help him understand that not all vampires are bad. And you need to do it fast. With these rogues terrorizing the city, it's only a matter of time until you expose yourself in front of him. That's not how he should find out."

She knew that. "What if I'm not brave enough?"

Gabriel smiled. "We've all had to

overcome the same obstacle, and we all muddled through it."

Vanessa tilted her head to the side. "It was a little different with you and Mom."

"Yes, but not less traumatic. She had to deal with being a newly turned vampire. That's no walk in the park. At least Cole now knows that he's a satyr, that's a step in the right direction. He's a preternatural creature even if it's not that obvious to anybody— other than to you, of course."

She decided not to comment on the physical sign that identified Cole as a satyr. She bit her lip.

"You can do this, Nessie."

She forced a smile. "And what are we gonna tell him about going patrolling tonight?"

"It's your choice, but as your boss, I don't think I need to tell you that we need everybody we can spare to be on the lookout for those rogues."

"He'll insist on going with me."

Gabriel shrugged. "Let him. Who were you supposed to patrol with tonight?"

"Adam."

"I'll call Quinn to use him somewhere else. You stick with Cole, it'll be good for him to see what you do. But you have to protect him. When did you last feed?"

"This morning." And she was craving blood after her marathon sex session with Cole. "Thanks for the reminder." She walked to the small fridge in her living area, opened it and took a bottle of human blood out of it.

"Good. You need your strength."

Vanessa gulped down the cold liquid and disposed of the empty bottle in a closed recycle bin.

"I'm ready."

Together they left her room. Vanessa heard voices from downstairs. Her mother was making small talk with Cole in the living room. When Vanessa and Gabriel came down the stairs, Cole looked in their direction, falling silent.

"I'm afraid, Cole," Gabriel said with a shrug, "my daughter is a stubborn one. She'll do her job tonight, no matter what. But I can assure you that she's trained for it. She underwent the bodyguard training at Scanguards, just like my sons and I have. She's an excellent bodyguard. She can handle herself."

Cole's head whipped to her. "You work for the same company as your father? I thought you're a social worker for the city."

"I am," Vanessa said quickly. "The city hires Scanguards for certain things, including taking care of the sex workers and the homeless. That's my job, and since I'm out and about at night, we thought it would be best if I'm trained in self-defense, personal security, and a few other things."

Cole already opened his mouth to respond, when Maya interrupted, looking at Gabriel. "Babe, it's time to go. I've got patients to see." She smiled at Cole. "We'll see you again soon, Cole. It's been a pleasure."

"Thank you, Maya, you too."

When her parents left, and silence descended on the house, Vanessa crossed the distance between her and Cole and put her hands on his chest.

"We should get going too," she said.

"So you're a bodyguard, huh?" He shook his head in disbelief. "Is there anything else I should know?"

She pursed her lips and tilted her head to the side. "My dad is also my boss? And my brothers are my colleagues?"

"And you all work for this company, Scanguards?"

"That's about it." Except for one other thing, but she wasn't ready to reveal her last secret yet.

Cole pressed a kiss to her lips, and pulled her into an embrace. "All right, then let's go patrolling, or whatever you call it."

He released her.

"Just one rule: if we encounter a vampire, please let me handle him," she demanded.

Cole simply grunted, and it wasn't hard to guess that he wasn't going to stick to that rule.

23

Cole parked the Land Rover in a parking garage near Union Square. As he and Vanessa left the building, he took her hand into his, and they walked in the opposite direction away from Union Square. Some shops were open late, and there was also a good number of theaters in the area, as well as restaurants, accounting for the busy traffic on the streets and lots of pedestrians on the sidewalks. He figured while they were walking along these streets, it was unlikely that a vampire would attack in front of so many witnesses, making this the ideal time to talk.

After meeting Vanessa's parents and brother, and finding out that she was a trained bodyguard, it made a little more sense why she had been able to kill his attacker with such ease. But it had also thrown up a lot of other questions.

"Your parents seem very easygoing," Cole started.

"They are the best."

"You look a lot like your mother. And she looks barely a few years older than you." It had been downright puzzling when he'd conversed with her while waiting for Gabriel and Vanessa to finish their private talk.

Vanessa gave a one-shouldered shrug. "She takes care of herself. And I guess she has good genes."

"Apparently Gabriel does too."

"You think he looks young? I guess I can't really tell. To me he's just Dad. Maybe it's because he dresses young," she suggested.

"Hmm. Maybe. I was quite surprised to hear that you're a trained bodyguard. That's an unusual choice for a woman like you."

She cast him a sideways look. "What do you mean like me?"

Cole smiled at her. "Beautiful with a body for sin."

Her eyes sparkled at the compliment. "Perhaps I use my physical attributes to distract my opponents, and they don't know what hit them."

He let out a laugh. Vanessa had a way of avoiding answers to his questions, but he wouldn't let her get away so easily. "I agree. You can be very distracting. But in earnest, why bodyguard training? Is that a prerequisite for working at that company? Scanguards?"

"Not a prerequisite per se. But every new employee is required to do the training with them so they can be used anywhere in the field. There are a few exceptions though."

"Like?"

"My mother. She's a physician, and she runs a clinic for Scanguards."

That sounded odd. A clinic for a private security company? "Are you saying that every Scanguards employee goes to her clinic if they get sick?"

Vanessa hesitated. "Uhm, it's more like when anybody gets injured on the job. Sometimes we bring victims of violent crimes to her."

"But that's what the emergency room of a hospital is for."

"Victims of crimes like you who were attacked by..." She lowered her voice to a whisper. "...a vampire."

Cole stopped and pulled Vanessa toward a building and out of the path of a group of pedestrians. "Are you saying that what happened to me last night, happens frequently here?"

He noticed the hesitance with which Vanessa nodded, and leaned closer. "How many freaking vampires are running around here trying to suck people dry? And how do you even know about them?"

He'd wanted to ask this earlier, but with everything that happened between them, there hadn't been the right time, because he hadn't wanted to spoil the romantic mood between them. But now, they were patrolling the city on the lookout for vampires, and it seemed the appropriate time to ask these questions.

Vanessa took a visible breath, her chest lifting.

"What is it?" he added. "Something wrong?"

She shook her head quickly. Maybe a little too quickly, before she answered, "It's complicated."

"I've got time."

"Just promise me not to tell anybody what I tell you now."

The suspense sent his heartbeat into the stratosphere. "I wouldn't know whom to tell."

"Let's walk," she suggested and hooked her arm into his.

He agreed by walking arm in arm with her.

"The company my entire family works for is a private security company, which you probably already know. The City of San Francisco hired them to deal with crimes by or against vampires, so that the public doesn't find out that there are vampires living among them. It would only cause a panic, and a lot more bloodshed."

Cole lifted his hand halfway in confusion. "Did you say crimes *against* vampires?"

"Yes, there is vampire-on-vampire crime and human-on-vampire crime. So we deal with that too."

"But why? You should be glad when they kill each other off. And if a human manages to kill one, good for them."

"There are many good people among the

vampires. They live their lives, and don't bother anybody. They need to be protected—"

"You can't be serious," he interrupted. "How can those creatures be good? I mean, the guy who attacked me, he was brutal, violent... it was disgusting..."

"The vampire who attacked you was a rogue."

What the hell did she mean by that? "A rogue?"

"Yes, a vampire who isn't playing by the rules. We think he was recently turned by somebody, and then let loose on the population to cause trouble for everybody else."

Vanessa stopped and motioned for them to step into the covered entrance of a closed shop to continue their conversation.

"The night before you were attacked, one of the prostitutes that I look out for was attacked by a different vampire. He got away, and luckily Ginger survived, but we know now that there are more of those rogues. My colleagues found another victim two nights ago, a tourist. There will be more attacks, that's why we've ramped up patrols."

"Fuck!" The more he heard, the wilder this whole situation became. "Then who's turning these rogues as you call them? It's another vampire, right?"

"Yes, but in order to figure out who is turning them, we have to figure out *why* he's turning them. And so far, we only have the identity of the one I killed last night."

"How?"

"When a vampire turns to dust, certain things on his person don't turn to dust: coins, cell phones, keys, wallets. That kind of stuff. Our IT guys have identified him, but we have no idea yet what connects him to the other rogues. There must be a pattern."

"You mean like a profile?"

"Exactly. My sister-in-law, Scarlet, has been working on a profile of the rogues so we can predict who might have already been turned and who is at risk of being turned. That's why I had to watch the twins last night —Scarlet is a psychologist for Scanguards."

Cole understood. "Like an analyst in the Behavioral Analysis Unit of the FBI."

"Yep."

"What has she got so far?"

"Not much, since we only have one confirmed rogue. If we capture or kill a second one, we might be able to find something that connects them. A common denominator that could lead us to more of them, and eventually to the vampire behind this, so we can eliminate them."

"So, you're saying you basically need at least two datapoints to figure out why these guys are chosen and turned by a vampire, right?" Cole asked, an idea forming in his mind.

"Yes, otherwise how would we be able to find out what they have in common?"

"Normally, I'd say you're right. But there's another way."

"What do you mean?"

"I told you that I have my own company."

"Yeah, something about an algorithm for online advertising." Vanessa looked at him quizzically.

"That's what it's sold for, yes, but it has another application." He felt excited now, because he could help Vanessa and her family eliminate the danger vampires presented. "The algorithm can create models using only one set of data, in this case, the vampire you killed."

"I'm afraid you lost me there," she said. "I'm not an IT genius."

"Scanguards has an IT department, I assume?"

"Yep."

"If I can show them what the algorithm can do, they'll understand it. All I need is to get my computer and my data drives from my condo."

For a moment, Vanessa said nothing, but judging by the way she bit her lip, he could see that her mind was digesting his words.

"Let's do it. I'll call Thomas and Eddie; they head up the IT department."

Cole took Vanessa's hand, turning toward the direction they'd come from. His idea would kill two birds with one stone: removing Vanessa from patrolling tonight so she wouldn't be in danger of getting attacked by a vampire, and helping Scanguards find and eliminate the bloodsuckers.

24

While Cole had gone into his home office to fetch his computer and data discs, Vanessa had remained in the living room and made a phone call to Thomas to apprise him of their arrival. Since they couldn't let Cole come to the executive floor, which was accessible only to vampires and their mates—though this rule had been broken more than once—, Thomas and Eddie would meet them in the computer lab in the basement. Even though Cole knew of the existence of vampires, it was imperative that he not find out that

Vanessa and most of Scanguards were vampires too. Thomas promised to inform the staff accordingly.

At the gate to the Scanguards underground garage, Vanessa swiped her access card at the card reader and pressed her thumb on the scanner, and the gate lifted to let Cole drive into the garage. She directed him to a vacant parking spot designated for visitors.

"Looks like a pretty big building," Cole commented when they got out of the Land Rover and walked to the elevators.

"It's half a city block long and half a block wide." Vanessa pressed the call button next to the elevator.

"I didn't realize a security company needed that much office space."

The elevator doors opened, and Vanessa ushered him inside, swiping her access card again, before selecting the level for the computer lab.

"It's not just offices. We also train

bodyguards here, so there are several rooms for hand-to-hand combat, an underground shooting range, a medical facility, rooms for research and supplies, and of course the servers and the computer lab. Some of our work deals with cyber security, so we're pretty well-equipped in that respect too."

That there was also a lab where two witches, Charles and Wesley, concocted magic potions and worked on spells, she left out, just like she left out the fact that there was also a bottling facility. There, Scanguards bottled human blood it purchased from blood banks around the country, posing as a medical supply company. There was also a weapons vault with all kinds of weapons that worked on vampires and other preternatural creatures. Not to forget the V lounge, where vampires rested in between shifts and where human blood on tap—arranged by blood type—was served at no cost to the employees. It was meant as an encouragement not to feed off unsuspecting humans.

"Whom are we meeting?"

"Thomas and Eddie. They run the IT department. They are geniuses."

Cole took her hand and lifted it to his lips, kissing her knuckles. "And they all know about vampires? The entire company?"

She nodded, feeling guilt rise up from her gut, turning her stomach into knots. How long could she keep from him that he was walking right into a vampire nest?

"How did you and your family find out about them? I meant to ask you earlier—"

"Uhm—" The elevator door opening interrupted him. To Vanessa's relief, Thomas, dressed in a casual white shirt and black leather pants stood waiting in front of the elevator, saving her from answering Cole's question.

"Hey, Nessie." Thomas nodded and extended his hand. "I'm Thomas. You must be Cole."

Stepping out of the elevator, Cole shook Thomas's proffered hand. "Nice to meet you, Thomas."

"Let's go to the computer lab, and we'll see what you've got for us."

"Thanks for making time for me," Cole replied.

Thomas flashed him a smile. "We welcome any help finding those rogues." He pushed a door open and entered ahead of them.

The large room had at least two dozen work stations with multiple computers. Along one wall was a glass-enclosed office.

Thomas pointed to it and looked over his shoulder to address Cole, "Eddie is already waiting for us. He's got a brilliant mind."

Vanessa had to chuckle. "And so do you."

Thomas winked at her and entered the office where Eddie, dressed in leather pants and a white T-shirt, sat in front of a bank of computers. He jumped up when they entered, and approached them.

"So, you're Cole, hmm?" Eddie said, running his eyes over Cole.

She caught sight of Thomas shaking his head and rolling his eyes at his mate checking out Cole. "Hands off, babe," Thomas said, even though they all knew that Eddie would never touch a man other than Thomas.

Eddie locked eyes with Thomas for a fraction of a second, exchanging a loving glance with him, before extending his hand to Cole. "Nice to meet you, Cole. I'm Eddie."

Cole shook his hand. "Hi, Eddie. Am I making you guys work late?"

Eddie shook his head. "Security is a twenty-four-hour business. So, what have you got for us?"

Thomas gestured to a large table with several chairs around it. He cleared it off, moving the files to the top of a filing cabinet.

Cole placed his computer and data discs

on the table, and sat down, while the others joined him.

"Hit us with it," Thomas demanded.

"You probably know that online advertising platforms use algorithms to figure out which customers to advertise which product to. Let's say you're selling golf clubs, the algorithm will try to find the ideal customer for you who's not only willing but also able to buy your product at the price you're advertising."

Eddie shrugged. "That's nothing new."

"You're right. But as we know, these algorithms take time to learn, until they find the ideal customer, which can cost you quite a bit in advertising dollars until you're hitting the right targets." Cole made eye contact with all of them, clearly to test that everybody was still following.

Everybody nodded.

"Good," Cole continued. "I've developed an algorithm that works differently. It takes the customer—let's say the entire adult population of the US, about 258 million—and finds out everything about every person: what they want, need, can afford, dream of, hate, and so on, so it can pair them with the perfect product. So, before you spent even a penny on advertising, you already know who your ideal customer is. There's no learning phase, no wasting money on customers who'll never buy from you."

"But how is that gonna help us?" Vanessa felt compelled to ask.

Eddie and Thomas exchanged a look, and it appeared that they were silently communicating via their telepathic bond as blood-bonded mates.

"I think I know how," Thomas said, nodding at Cole. "The customers are the rogue vampires."

"And the product is the vampire who turns them," Eddie finished his mate's sentence.

"Exactly," Cole said excitedly. "And the algorithm works from either side, if you know the product or the customer. And we already have that information, right? Vanessa said you were able to identify the rogue that attacked me."

Thomas nodded. "Yes. We've got all his info in the system."

"Good. All we need to do is to enter this guy's information into my program, and it will find other people who would act the same way, want the same thing, hate the same thing. Was the guy local?"

"Yes," Eddie said, "he lived in San Francisco, went to school here too."

Cole opened the lid of his laptop. "Okay. So, let's assume all the other rogues are also local. We can find them by taking the guy we know as well as the product, and the algo will create a model of the ideal customer: what makes this guy vulnerable or likely to being turned. With that model, we can identify who else is at risk of being turned, or was already turned."

"It's brilliant," Thomas praised. "What do you need to get started?"

"I need to know a little more about the process of turning a human. I'm assuming the vampire attacks them, and then turns them somehow."

Thomas shook his head. "Not necessarily. It's more likely that they agree to being turned."

Deep lines appeared on Cole's forehead as disbelief spread on his face. "What would they gain by becoming vampires?"

"Immortality," Vanessa started, "physical power, enhanced senses."

"But they kill people because they drink their blood," Cole protested.

Vanessa put her hand on his forearm. "Yes, the rogues do that. But in general, the vampire population in San Francisco doesn't hurt humans. A vampire feeding on a human doesn't kill the human, nor does it hurt, not when it's done right."

"Vanessa is right," Thomas interjected.

"Most vampires keep to themselves. And as long as they don't hurt anyone, we leave them alone. But somebody is turning humans without teaching them the rules. Whoever it is, is most likely offering them something they don't have now."

"My money is on power," Eddie said with a nod.

"I feel like I've landed in *Men in Black*." Cole pressed his lips together in a grim gesture. "Oddly enough, if they are really doing this voluntarily because they are promised something valuable in return—power, immortality—it makes it easier for the algorithm to find who's susceptible to such an offer."

Cole logged into his computer and looked at Eddie. "Can you give me the dead rogue's info? Name, date of birth, address. You probably don't have his social."

"We do," Eddie said and walked over to his computer, and tapped on a few keys. "I'm ready when you are."

"Great! That makes it easier. I'll set it all up in my cloud, and then I'll send you the access code so you can watch from your computer."

"How long until we get results?" Thomas asked.

"A few hours, since we're only covering San Francisco. If we don't get enough data from that, I'll expand it to the East Bay and the Peninsula."

"That works," Thomas said.

As Eddie dictated the rogue's information, and Cole entered the data into his computer, Vanessa ran her eyes over him. She would have never pegged Cole for a computer genius, but it was clear that he was in his element. The way he carried himself, the way his entire body was all muscle, no fat, he didn't strike her as the kind of guy who spent hours sitting hunched over his computer, writing code. But there was no doubt that what he'd told them had impressed Thomas and Eddie, and was clearly giving them hope that he could deliver on his promise to find other humans vulnerable to be turned into a vampire.

A sense of pride filled her. Her intended mate wasn't just a pretty face and a hot body. He had a brilliant mind on top of it. The more time she spent with him, the more layers she unpeeled, the more facets of his character he revealed.

Vanessa slid her hand onto his thigh, wanting to feel physically connected to him. Cole cast her a loving smile, their eyes locking for a brief moment, before he turned his gaze back to the computer screen.

To make her happiness complete, there was only one more thing for which she needed to find the courage: to confess that she was a vampire hybrid lusting for his blood.

25

While Cole knew that his algorithm would eventually produce the desired results, he hadn't expected it to work so quickly. Only a little over an hour after he'd fed the data into his computer, it spit out promising leads.

"Samson and Gabriel are ready to meet with us in the conference room," Thomas announced, and put down the receiver.

"We'll need my computer, so I can show them the data." Cole closed the lid of his laptop, ready to take it with him, when Eddie stopped him.

"It's all networked. I'm feeding your data from the cloud to the monitor in the conference room."

Cole nodded, but wasn't surprised. From what he'd been able to glean, Scanguards was extremely well-equipped when it came to IT, and both Eddie and Thomas were a step up from every IT professional he'd ever worked with.

He met Vanessa's smile. "I knew you could do it." Was that pride shining from her eyes?

"Your mate is a pretty smart guy," Eddie added.

Cole blinked. Mate? Did everybody already know that he and Vanessa were made for each other? It certainly hadn't been Vanessa who could have told Eddie and Thomas about it, since he'd been with her ever since he'd found out himself. Which only left her family.

"You guys know about that?"

"Good news travels fast," Thomas said with a smirk.

"Guess it does." Cole took Vanessa's hand. "Lead the way."

The four of them traveled several floors up in the elevator, before alighting on the first floor, where Thomas swiped his keycard and opened the door to a mid-size conference room without windows.

Inside it, Gabriel was already waiting for them. Next to him stood a tall man with black hair and hazel eyes.

The man extended his hand. "I'm Samson Woodford, owner of Scanguards. Nice to meet you."

"Cole Whitlock, nice to meet you too." Cole shook Samson's hand, while he perused the guy in more detail.

Samson carried himself with the authority of a man who knew he wouldn't be challenged in any of his decisions, even though he looked no older than thirty-five.

So far, everybody he'd met from Scanguards looked extremely young, something he was used to from tech startups, but certainly not from a company that provided bodyguards. How could they have sufficient experience at their young age?

"Take a seat, Cole," Gabriel said, pointing to the conference table. "We're eager to hear what you've figured out." Then he pointed to a large video screen. "Scarlet, my daughter-in-law, is joining us from home. Since we're talking about the victim profile, I figured it best if she joined us. Scarlet, this is Cole."

Cole looked at the screen and recognized the woman he'd seen exit the Victorian mansion. "Hi, Scarlet, nice to meet you."

"Likewise," Scarlet replied. "Sorry I can't be there in person, but there's nobody who can look after the twins." She pointed over her shoulder, and now Cole could hear the sounds of two kids running around, laughing.

Meanwhile, Eddie had retrieved a computer from a drawer sunken into the table, tapped on a few keys, and a large monitor next to the one on which Scarlet could be seen illuminated, mirroring what could be seen on the laptop.

"Here you go, Cole," Eddie said and moved the laptop in front of Cole.

"Thanks." Cole cleared his throat. "I'm not gonna bore you with the technical aspects of what we did. If it's all right with you, I'll dive right into the results."

When there were no objections, Cole continued, "Let's start with the vampire Vanessa killed: Robert Nealy was 24 years old, unemployed, and still living in his parents' basement. He dropped out of college, has no real friends, nor has he had any girlfriends. His IQ was average, and he spent his days and nights playing computer games with online friends. By all accounts he was a loser." He let his gaze roam to see that everybody in the room was listening attentively, before looking at the livestream from Scarlet, who nodded in agreement.

"He was active in an online forum, and that's where we see what was going on inside him. He had a deep-seated hatred for women, rooted in his inability to have a romantic relationship with any woman. The rejections he's received appear to have turned him into a very bitter young man. The other men on this online forum show the same traits." Cole paused for a moment to let the information sink in. "He's what is referred to as an incel."

He looked at Scarlet.

"An involuntary celibate man," Scarlet added. "That's a pretty typical profile. And unfortunately, nowadays with social media and the pressures that young people are under, there are more and more of these men that feel insecure and isolated, which then turns to bitterness. And eventually hatred for women."

"Exactly," Cole agreed. "My algorithm identified that because of this feeling of being a loser, unable to attract a woman, an incel is out for revenge. He craves power to show these women that they were wrong to reject him. He wants them to pay for his unhappiness."

"So you're saying this man will only attack women?" Samson asked.

Cole shook his head. "No. While women are his preferred target, he'll also take out his frustration on men who he believes get any woman they want. In his eyes, they are his enemies too."

Gabriel and Samson looked at each other, then at Scarlet.

Scarlet chimed in, "Cole is right. Any man whom an incel believes to be more successful or desirable becomes a target, though in general, the incel will take his frustration out on women first."

Cole lifted his hand toward Scarlet, in a sign of agreement. "An incel would be extremely susceptible to what a vampire can offer him: power, because power can finally give him the means to exact his revenge."

Samson leaned forward in his chair. "It all makes sense. The other three victims apart from you were women. But it doesn't explain why this vampire would offer these incels to be turned. What's in it for him?"

"I'm afraid we won't know that until we catch him," Cole replied. "But what we do have is a list of incels in San Francisco who fit the profile. We found 13 men that are extremely likely to be turned."

"Maybe they've already been turned," Vanessa interjected.

"That sounds like a low number," Scarlet interrupted. "I would have expected the number to be much higher."

Cole looked at her. "We've run a very narrow search and at this stage only focused our attention on those men who tick all the boxes. If we don't have any luck with them, we'll widen our search."

"Sounds good," Scarlet said.

"So, we know where the incels live. If they've been turned already, it's very likely that they keep coming back to their parents' basements, since that's where they feel safe." Then he remembered something that he hadn't asked before. "I'm assuming vampires can't be out in daylight?"

Gabriel nodded. "Correct. Pureblooded vampires would burn in the sun."

"Pureblooded? What does that mean?"

There was a second's pause, before Gabriel explained, "Uhm, that's just what we call them. So, if any of these incels got turned, they would have to stay out of daylight." He exchanged a look with Samson.

Samson nodded. "Let's put together teams to go to the addresses of these incels. It's nighttime right now, which means if they've already been turned, they'll probably not be home, but we can have our people wait for them there, and have all available patrol units use their photos to look for them in the city.”

“What will you do with the incels who’re still human? I mean, they have to be watched too, right?”

“Of course,” Samson said. “We’ll put surveillance on them to see who they’re meeting with. But our priority right now is to find the ones who’ve already been turned. And to bring them back alive. Only they can lead us to the vampire behind this.”

The plan sounded solid. Even Cole had to admit that. But he still had concerns. “These bloodsuckers are strong. I’m a big guy, and even I couldn’t fight a skinny hundred-and-seventy-pound vampire off. How are you gonna catch one alive? No offense but that sounds dangerous and pretty damn near impossible.”

“Don’t worry,” Gabriel said. “We have the right weapons.”

"Stakes?"

"No, that would defeat the purpose," Gabriel replied. "We can restrain them with silver chains. It's the only metal they can't break. It burns their skin like acid."

That knowledge calmed him a little. At least the people from Scanguards knew enough about vampires to fight them.

"When we have a little more time, you must tell me how you all found out about vampires," Cole said, looking at Gabriel and Samson.

For a second there was only silence in the room, and all he could hear was the sound of the twins coming from the livestream. He noticed Gabriel casting a look at his daughter.

"Yeah, sure, when it's a bit quieter," Vanessa finally said. "But I think tonight we've got too much going on."

"Gabriel," Samson ordered, "get everybody up to speed, and have Quinn put together teams, so we can check on all thirteen addresses simultaneously, just in case they are communicating with each other. We don't want them to tip each other off."

"Got it," Gabriel said and rose. He turned to the monitor, "Thanks, Scarlet. We'll let you know when we need you."

"Bye, guys." The screen went blank.

Everybody got up.

"Nessie, why don't you take Cole to the lounge? Maybe he wants to eat something while we get this mission set up. And then we need you upstairs for the briefing."

"All right, Dad."

"Gabriel, are you saying that Vanessa is gonna be one of the teams to hit the incels' addresses? You know how I feel about—"

Gabriel put a hand on his forearm. "We need her at the briefing, that's all. I won't assign her to any of the search teams tonight."

Relieved, Cole tamped down his pounding heart and took Vanessa's hand in his. When he met her gaze, she looked less than pleased.

"You're not gonna be able to stop me from doing my job," Vanessa said. "This is what I do."

"But not tonight." And he would make sure to come up with plenty of reasons to stop her from putting herself in danger.

"Uhm, Cole," Gabriel said, "you're not gonna win that fight with her."

"Yeah, might as well give in now," Thomas added with a smirk.

"I don't give in easily," he replied without breaking eye contact with Vanessa. "Particularly when it concerns someone dear to my heart."

And there was nothing and nobody dearer to his heart than Vanessa.

26

Patrick kicked the gas pedal of the Scanguards blackout SUV down, while Ethan sat in the passenger seat, directing him to the address of the incel they'd been assigned to check out.

"You think Cole is right about these incels? That they would agree to be turned?"

"You heard the others. Thomas and Eddie were impressed by the data, and your dad as well as mine are confident that his data will lead us to the rogues," Ethan replied.

"So, about this Cole... Have you met him?"

"I ran into him before I left the house this evening. Didn't get a chance to talk to him, but Dad told me he tried to dissuade Nessie from going patrolling, because he didn't want her to put herself in danger. Of course, he doesn't know that she's more than capable of looking after herself."

Patrick cast a sideways glance at his friend and colleague. "Ahh, the famous protector instinct of a man who's found his mate."

"Yep. Looks that way." Ethan pointed to the next intersection. "Turn right here."

Patrick followed the instruction. "So, is he a satyr like you? Or just a regular human?"

"According to Dad, he's a satyr. Envious?"

"Of two cocks? What guy wouldn't be envious?" Ever since he'd found out that satyrs existed and what their physical attributes were, he'd been just a little bit envious of Ryder, Ethan, and Gabriel.

Ethan laughed. "Sure, once you actually have the two cocks, but until then it's not exactly ideal when you wanna get a girl to sleep with you. That growth isn't particularly attractive."

Patrick had seen Ethan's growth before—they'd both been young boys, and just like all young boys they'd been curious about their bodies. "You don't seem to have any problems getting laid."

"I get a fair amount of rejections." Ethan shrugged. "But I don't let that bother me. It's a numbers game. Besides, I've learned how to hide what I don't want the women to see."

"Mind control?"

"On occasion. Though I prefer not to use that skill if it's not absolutely necessary. I often don't undress fully. A dark room works wonders, and if I fuck them from behind, they'll never know."

Patrick shook his head, laughing. "Lucky you!"

"As if you don't get your share of pretty women. I've seen how the girls check you out when we go clubbing."

"Don't you get tired of going clubbing and picking up girls for mindless sex?"

"Uh, oh." Ethan gave him a sideways look. "Don't tell me you're ready to settle down."

"No, of course not!" Patrick protested quickly. Perhaps a little too quickly, because in his own mind, he didn't believe his own words. "Just saying, I need a little more than just mindless one-night stands. I wanna meet a woman who doesn't throw herself at me the minute she sees me. You know, a little challenge."

"It's a curse to be handsome and rich," Ethan said, his words dripping with sarcasm.

Patrick slapped him playfully over the back of his head. "Idiot!" He concentrated on the traffic again. "Besides, I'm not rich. My father is."

"Same thing. And with Grayson running the show in New Orleans, and Isabelle more interested in her mate and baby than in the company, you're next in line at Scanguards."

"You know as well as I do that I'm not interested in running the company. I told Dad the other night."

"And what did he say?"

"That I might change my mind one day."

"Will you?"

"Doubt it. I don't wanna be stuck in an office." He made a gesture toward the street. "This is what I live for: taking down bad guys, getting in on the action, protecting people."

"Well, you'll have your chance tonight." Ethan pointed out the window. "Last house on the right. Park right in front of it."

Patrick looked at the clock on his dashboard, noting that they had almost five minutes to spare until the prearranged time to strike the rogues simultaneously. He tapped on the SUV's communication system that was connected directly with the control center at Scanguards.

"Unit 12, Patrick and Ethan. We're in place."

"Understood, unit 12," Benjamin replied. "Mission is a go. Repeat: all units are in place. Execute mission in 4 minutes."

"Roger that," Patrick replied and muted the communication system.

"Let's do this," Ethan said.

Patrick killed the engine and got out of the car. Ethan was already standing on the sidewalk, looking at the house.

"It's dark. Little early for everybody to be in bed," Patrick said, his forehead furrowing.

Ethan let out a hum. "Unless nobody's home."

Patrick reached into his inside pocket and retrieved his lockpicks. "Watch my back."

He walked up to the front door, Ethan on

his heels, and listened for sounds from inside the house, but it was quiet. As quickly and as quietly as he could, he picked the lock with his tools. Everybody at Scanguards had to learn that skill during their bodyguard training. While vampires certainly had enough strength to kick in regular doors to gain access to a room or a building, it was a noisy act that would take away the element of surprise.

"It's open," Patrick whispered.

He put his lockpicks back into his jacket pocket and pulled out his leather gloves. He slipped them on, then pulled a silver knife from the sheath at his belt, before looking over his shoulder. Ethan was now also wearing leather gloves. But instead of a knife he was holding a silver chain in his hands. The thick leather gloves were necessary to protect their hands from the silver, because just like pureblooded vampires, vampire hybrids could also be injured or killed with silver. In this case, they would only injure the rogue if necessary, and capture him alive.

They'd left their stakes in the car, so they couldn't be used against them by the rogue, although it was entirely possible that the rogue was armed with a stake too. However, given that this incel had no training in any fighting style, and according to his records was a five-foot-nine weakling, Patrick didn't doubt they could subdue him quickly.

Ethan gave a quick nod. "Ready."

Patrick opened the door slowly, then spied through the gap between door and frame to look into the dark corridor. Even with his superior night vision, he couldn't see anybody in the hallway. He opened the door wide enough to slip inside, when a pungent smell greeted him. His heart sank into his gut, and his body recoiled.

"Fuck," he hissed under his breath, glancing over his shoulder at Ethan, who wrinkled his nose in disgust.

"That bastard," Ethan murmured.

Patrick indicated where he was heading, and Ethan nodded in agreement. Like they'd been taught at Scanguards, they went from room to room, covering each other, until they reached the kitchen in the back of the house. There, the stench was worst, and his suspicion was confirmed. The aroma of decaying human flesh filled the room, its origin the older woman on the linoleum floor, her clothes torn, her eyes wide in complete terror, her throat ripped out, and blood splatter everywhere he looked. She'd been savagely attacked.

"His mother?" Ethan asked in a low voice as he bent down to her.

Patrick looked around the kitchen and saw a handbag on a counter. "Most likely." He reached into the handbag and found the woman's wallet. Her driver's license confirmed his guess. "Yes, she's his mother."

"He must have really hated her to kill her so brutally."

Patrick tightened his jaw, and tried not to

breathe too deeply. Nevertheless, the scent of decomposition was impossible to block out. "Looks like she's been dead for a few days."

"Yeah, my guess is three to four days," Ethan agreed. "We'd better call it in. We need a clean-up crew."

"Let's check the rest of the house first." He tipped his head up toward the ceiling.

"I can't hear anything from upstairs," Ethan whispered.

"Do you remember from the info we got if she has a husband?" Patrick asked, wishing he'd had more time to go over the information that had been sent to his and Ethan's cell phones. He'd barely glanced at it before jumping into the car to drive here.

"She's divorced," Ethan replied. "But there was no info whether she had a boyfriend."

Walking swiftly, but without making any noise, they headed for the stairs to the second floor. Upstairs, the corridor was dark too, but from underneath the door to one room in the back of the house, a faint light shone through. Patrick pointed to it, and they crept toward it. Patrick put his ear to the door, but there was no sound. With a quick glance at Ethan, he pushed the door open, his silver knife ready for attack.

But the room was empty. Only a lamp on the bedside table was switched on. The bed had been slept in. While Ethan checked the closet and the bathroom, Patrick approached the bed. He dipped his head to the sheets and inhaled. The scent was human, and though he couldn't tell whether it was the mother's scent because the scent of her decaying body smelled entirely different, his best guess was that she was the one who'd slept here.

"Nothing," Ethan confirmed. "The other rooms?"

They checked the other two rooms too, and they were empty as well. One was used as a sewing and craft room, which smelled similar to the aroma Patrick had smelled in the bedroom. The other room was a kid's room with posters of Spiderman and other superheroes. But the bed hadn't been slept in, and the air smelled musty. Nobody had been in this room for a while.

"This house doesn't have a basement," Patrick said, feeling discouraged. The bird had flown the coop.

"No, but it has a garage," Ethan said. "And the car is parked in the driveway."

Their eyes met, and Patrick realized that they were thinking the same thing. All wasn't lost yet. Without another word, and walking on tiptoes now, they went downstairs. Patrick tested the door to the garage, turning its knob gently. It wasn't locked. With a nod, he ripped the door open. Within a fraction of a second, he assessed the interior of the garage. It looked like a man cave complete with an old sofa and easy chair, a large TV mounted on the wall, a computer in one corner, and heaps of dirty clothes on the washing machine and dryer. The makeshift room was messy, which fit with the profile of the rogue. So, where the hell was he?

"I can smell him," Ethan said from next to him.

"Me too."

The sound of a key scraping against a lock drifted to Patrick's ears. He whirled around and drew the door to the garage closed, then he pressed himself against the wall next to the door, several brooms and cleaning mops hanging from hooks on the wall hiding him partially. Ethan pressed himself to the wall on the other side of the door, where he would be hidden from view once the door was opened.

The entrance door opened, then slammed shut. The man entering grumbled something unintelligible. Footsteps came closer, then retreated toward the back of the house. Patrick exchanged a look with Ethan, when the sound of footfalls became louder again. A moment later, the door was opened loudly, and the man flipped a light switch in the garage. Patrick remained hidden until he could see the aura of the person. There was no doubt: he was a vampire.

Patrick pushed himself away from the wall, his silver knife at the ready. The rogue whipped his head in his direction, his eyes flaring red, his fangs instantly descending to full length, ready to attack.

"Don't even try it," Patrick said calmly. "You'll lose."

The rogue growled. "Fuck you!"

The vampire lunged, but was instantly jerked back by the silver chain Ethan had slung over his head and around his neck in less than a second. A painful cry issued from the captive, who—stupid as he was—reached for the chain with both hands, trying to pull it off him. Instead of achieving his intended goal, his fingers and palms burned from the acidic metal, and he cried out like a wounded animal.

"Gotcha," Ethan said from behind the rogue. Forcefully, he tugged on the chain, and his captive fell on his ass.

"Well done," Patrick praised his colleague. "Though I would have liked to use my knife on him." He stepped over the vampire and looked down on him. "But unlike you, I don't hurt people who can't defend themselves." He spit in the guy's face. "Killing your own mother. That's low, man. You're gonna pay for that."

Patrick met Ethan's gaze. "Let's put him in the trunk. They'll be happy to see him at HQ." He tapped on his iWatch to connect to the communications system and brought his wrist closer to his mouth. "This is unit 12. We've got our guy. Alive."

Benjamin's voice came from the watch a second later. "That makes you officially number one. See you back at HQ. The interrogation room is ready for you."

Patrick grinned at his colleague. "I love my job."

27

With Cole by her side, Vanessa watched as the elevator doors opened, and Ethan and Patrick stepped out with their captive in tow. They weren't the only ones who'd been waiting for them ever since their unit had reported that they'd captured one of the rogues alive. Her father, as well as Samson, Amaury, and Zane were waiting too. The other teams hadn't come back yet.

The rogue vampire, who'd been identified as Mike Harris, groaned in pain.

Vanessa knew instantly why. Ethan was holding on to a silver chain wrapped around the captive's neck. In addition, his hands were shackled with silver handcuffs behind his back. His eyes were glaring red, and his fangs extended.

"Well done," Samson praised, nodding at the two hybrids. "Bring him straight into the interrogation room."

As Harris, flanked by Ethan and Patrick, walked past her, the bastard's nostrils suddenly quivered, and he lunged toward Cole, the only human in the corridor.

Vanessa instantly jumped in front of Cole to protect him.

"Vanessa!" Cole snatched her and pulled her into his chest, turning sideways in the same moment to shield her from the vampire.

It turned out it wasn't necessary, because Ethan jerked Harris back by the silver chain around his neck, eliciting painful screams from his captive.

"You touch anybody here," Ethan hissed, "and I'll kill you slowly and painfully."

"Easy, son," Gabriel cautioned.

Ethan met Gabriel's gaze. "He butchered his own mother and left her body rotting in the kitchen. He deserves no mercy."

Horrified, Vanessa sucked in a breath, while the others let out suppressed curses. She felt Cole pull her closer to him. When she'd jumped in front of him, he'd instantly tried to protect her, and that thought made guilt churn up inside her. She still hadn't told him that she was a vampire and wasn't the one who needed protection from the rogue, because she could defend herself.

"Agreed," Samson said.

Behind him, Zane, the bald vampire who was their go-to guy when torture was warranted, grunted his approval.

"But first, we need to find out what he knows," Gabriel said, pointing to a door at the end of the corridor, where the interrogation room was located.

As Patrick and Ethan pulled the resisting rogue along the corridor, Cole took her hand and made a step in the same direction, but Vanessa didn't move. She knew she couldn't take him there, because during the interrogation it would quickly become evident that the rogue's captors were also vampires. This wasn't how she wanted him to find out.

"Sorry, Cole," Gabriel said, putting a hand on his shoulder. "You and Vanessa can't go in there."

"But—"

"It's not your job," Gabriel insisted. "It's mine."

"Without me," Cole protested, "you wouldn't have found this guy. I'm involved in this. I only want to watch the interrogation. I won't get in the way."

Gabriel hesitated, then looked at Samson, who shook his head. "You know the rules." Samson trained his gaze at Vanessa.

She knew what he was trying to tell her. He would let Cole watch the interrogation from a room with viewing windows only if Cole was made aware that she and her family and friends were vampires too. And only once he'd accepted that fact, was it safe for all of them to let him see what was really going on here.

Silence stretched over them for several seconds, and Vanessa was painfully aware that it was up to her to make a decision.

"What's going on?" Cole asked, his eyes ping-ponging from one person to the next, only to land on her and become more insistent. "Vanessa? What are you not telling me?"

Vanessa inhaled a deep breath. Cole deserved the truth, and it wasn't fair to keep this last secret from him any longer. She was scared of how he'd react, but maybe she was worrying over nothing. He'd accepted that he was a satyr, and she his mate. Maybe he would accept the fact that she was a vampire hybrid just as easily. After all, all she and her family and colleagues had shown him was love and respect, and he had to see that they were nothing like the rogue he'd encountered. Every species had good people and bad people, and it wasn't any different in the vampire population.

"Cole, there's something I need to explain," Vanessa started. "Let's go somewhere private."

Cole's eyes narrowed, and she could practically see the worry and suspicion that rose to the surface. "It's bad, isn't it?"

She took his hand into hers and ushered him down the corridor. Nervous energy prickled off him, and she could hear his heartbeat accelerate. By the time they'd reached her little office a floor higher, and closed the door behind them, her own heart was beating against the lump in her throat.

Alone with Cole now, Vanessa let go of his hand. "Maybe you should sit down."

"I'd rather stand." He broadened his stance as if bracing himself for bad news. "Out with it. What is it you want to explain to me?"

Vanessa swallowed twice, but the lump in her throat didn't budge. This was harder than she'd imagined. Her brother Ryder hadn't had any trouble making Scarlet accept him as a vampire, even though she'd found out the hard way: seeing Ryder's vampire side without warning.

"I want you do know that what I'm telling you now might come as a shock to you." Fuck, she was stalling. "But please remember that I love you, and I would never hurt you."

Vanessa's declaration of love was both welcome and strange. Welcome, because she was actually telling him what he'd hoped to hear from her since the moment he'd laid eyes on her, and strange, because of where and how she was declaring her love to him. At any other time, he would have swept her into his arms and told her that he loved her more than anything in the world, and that he couldn't imagine life without her. But he knew instinctively that something wasn't right.

"Why do I get the feeling that there's a *but* coming?"

He scrutinized Vanessa's face, and saw that she was battling with herself, and he was tempted to put his arms around her and tell her she could tell him anything. But something held him back: an odd sense of foreboding. As if he'd suddenly developed a sixth sense.

"Cole, my family and I, we're not just satyrs like you. We're different. You've met them, and I want you to remember how kind and helpful my father was to you, and that my parents are over the moon that you're my mate, and—"

"Damn it, Vanessa, out with it! What are you trying to say? Just say it, because the suspense is worse than whatever you are trying to tell me." He let out a shuddering breath. At least he hoped the suspense was worse than the news she was trying to impart.

Her green eyes bored into him, and their gazes locked.

"My family and I, we're vampires."

For a second, his brain couldn't process the words coming out of Vanessa's mouth. It felt as if fog was clouding his brain, making him unable to understand anything. He felt as if he was standing outside his own body, watching a bizarre scene he wasn't part of. It was too surreal, like a waking dream, a nightmare of sorts, a nightmare during which he was awake.

His body did what it had to. He shook his head as if he could shake off the words his brain was now processing and giving meaning to. "No." He kept shaking his head. "You're lying."

"I'm not."

Vanessa remained still while she spoke, and he ran his eyes over her. Shreds of memories came and went. Memories of the vampire attack, and of Vanessa killing the rogue. Memories of Vanessa dragging him to his condo, even though a woman of her size shouldn't have the strength to move his heavy body.

He could still feel the fangs of the rogue in his neck, still felt the pain and horror. It all came back to him in vivid color. A cold shudder crept up his spine and settled in his nape. Disgust rose from his gut and wrapped around his heart.

"Cole..." she murmured, and stretched out her hand.

When she touched his arm, he recoiled from her, stepping back in horror.

"You're a bloodsucker like that rogue who attacked me." He couldn't keep the bitterness out of his voice, nor expel the disappointment from his heart. "How could you keep that from me? How could you lie to me about what you are?"

Inside him, disappointment, pain, and disgust collided, and he wasn't sure which emotion was stronger. It didn't matter. The woman he'd fallen in love with was a violent creature living off the blood of humans, hurting them, killing them.

"Cole, I'm still the same person. I'm not like that rogue. I love you."

He shook his head and tightened his jaw. "You can't love anybody! You kill people! You attack them and feed off them!" A creature like that didn't have a heart.

He ran a hand through his hair, and realized it was trembling.

"I don't hurt people. We don't attack them... we don't kill them. Please, Cole, just let me explain everything," she begged.

"Don't! I don't know how I could have ever felt anything for you! You deceived me from the moment I met you. What was your plan, huh? Gain my confidence? And then what? Keep me locked up somewhere so you could feed from me whenever you wanted blood? How could I have been so stupid?" He glared at her. "I wish I'd never touched you!"

"Don't say that, Cole. I would never hurt you."

He made a step to the side and glanced at the door behind her. "Then let me leave."

"Please, stay, and let me show you that my family and I aren't the bad guys."

"So you're not gonna let me leave, is that it? Well, I guess that proves my point. You're just as bad as that rogue."

He steeled himself for the inevitable. When would she attack him? Would it be as painful as when the rogue had sunk his fangs into his neck? Would he feel a second time how his life was slipping through his hands? Would he feel that same helplessness again? Or would it be worse, because he would die at the hands of the woman he'd loved and trusted?

Vanessa suddenly stepped away from the door and trained her gaze to the floor. "You're free to leave. I won't force you to stay with me if you don't want to."

Her voice sounded different now, resigned. But was it a trick? He hesitated, but Vanessa didn't move. He walked to the door and opened it. She didn't stop him when he left the office and walked to the elevators to get out of the building. He reached his car in the garage without anybody running after him or stopping him. Still, his nape prickled, and he felt like prey.

When he drove out of the garage and merged into traffic, he kept looking into the rearview mirror, but from what he could tell, nobody was following him.

On the drive home, he felt as if he were in a trance. He got lost twice, before he found the right street that led him toward his neighborhood. Every word of his conversation with Vanessa replayed in his mind.

So many things made sense all of a sudden. Yet, so many other things didn't. He'd seen Vanessa walking outside during daylight. Did that mean that vampires didn't burn in the sun? He'd also watched her eat regular food—though not a large amount. When she'd saved his life that night, she'd killed the rogue with such precision and nonchalance that he had to assume that this was nothing new to her.

How could he have been so wrong about her? He'd seen her as an innocent, a vulnerable, caring woman, yet she was a bloodsucking monster, a killer without a heart. Just like the rest of her family. Now that he thought back to his interactions with Gabriel, he understood so much more.

The good genes Gabriel had claimed were keeping him looking young were nothing but a lie. He was a vampire, and therefore didn't age, just like his wife and

Vanessa herself. No wonder Gabriel hadn't been worried about Vanessa going out patrolling at night. More like prowling! After all, she was a predator. They'd dished up so many lies, and he'd eaten them up. Why? Because he didn't want to see the truth. He wanted to live in the fantasy that he'd finally found a woman he could be happy with—only to be proven wrong. He couldn't be happy with a vampire. What kind of life would that be?

By the time he reached his condo building, and was back inside his place, his mind was spinning. The tangled sheets of his bed reminded him of making love to Vanessa. He'd made love to a vampire. And he'd loved it, and still craved it, craved her. What did that make him? An idiot? A hypocrite?

Even now, as he sat down on the bed, his head in his hands, he wanted nothing more than feeling Vanessa pressing her body to his, their lips locked in a passionate kiss. At the thought of it, he felt both his cocks rising. Fuck! How could he get hard at the thought of fucking a vampire? It only proved how perverted he was, how desperate to fulfill his sexual need. Was he condemned to long for Vanessa because she was his mate? What if he had no choice because they were meant to be together? Or was he using this argument as an excuse, because deep down in the recesses of his mind he still wanted her, no matter who or what she was? Just like he'd wanted her when he'd thought she was a prostitute. Had his heart really made its choice? Or would the love he felt for Vanessa dim now that he knew the truth about her?

"Goddamn it!" he cursed and looked up toward the ceiling. "What other trials do I have to pass before I can be happy? Isn't it enough already? What have I done to deserve this?"

There was no answer.

"Dad?" he murmured, tears welling up in

his eyes. "If you can hear me, Dad, please help me make the right decision."

To leave San Francisco now and never come back, or to stay and accept his fate: to let Vanessa turn him into a vampire so they could have a life together.

28

Patrick shackled Mike Harris, the rogue vampire, to the metal chair that was affixed to the floor in the large underground interrogation room. The room was high, and from a two-way mirror just beneath the ceiling, observers could watch and listen to the interrogation without being seen. Ethan was in the room with him, and since they were the ones who'd brought in the suspect, they got the first crack at questioning him.

Samson and Gabriel were watching from the observation room, and Patrick wanted to show his father that he was more suited to this kind of work than running the company.

Patrick still wore his leather gloves, which he'd needed to handle the silver chains. He now took them off and tossed them on the metal table on which several instruments were displayed. They were the standard clamps, blades, and pliers used for light torture, as well as a few other items, though it was rare that any of the tools were used to elicit information from a captive. They served mostly as a veiled threat of what would happen if answers weren't forthcoming.

"See this, Harris?" Patrick asked, pointing to the torture instruments. "Do I need to use them, or are you gonna answer me truthfully?"

Harris cast a look at the table, then spat in defiance. "Fuck you, asshole!"

"Big mistake." Patrick exchanged a look with Ethan. They were a well-oiled team, and knew their roles in this game.

Ethan twisted his mouth into a scowl. "Just as well that I haven't taken my gloves off yet." He calmly walked over to the table and lifted a pair of pliers. "Hey, bro, how about these?"

Patrick shook his head. "That will barely hurt him." From the corner of his eyes, he noticed Harris crane his neck to get a better look at the items on the table. "I'd go with the syringe. Very effective."

Ethan smirked. "Bro, you're one sick son of a bitch." He took the prefilled syringe from the table and stepped closer.

Patrick watched how Harris shrank back in his chair.

"What is that?"

Patrick took a few steps closer to him and jerked his thumb over his shoulder. "You mean that? A syringe."

"You think I'm afraid of a needle?" Harris growled, his eyes shining red.

Patrick looked at Ethan. "Not the brightest bulb in the shed."

"You want me to explain to him what silver nitrate injected into his veins will do to him?" Ethan asked, his voice sounding calm and friendly.

Patrick made a dismissive hand movement. "Nah, I doubt he understands chemistry. Just inject him, and he'll get it pretty quickly. I really don't wanna be here all night."

"All right then," Ethan agreed and made a step toward the rogue.

Harris yanked at the handcuffs at his back, the rattling sound echoing in the nearly empty room. "Stay away from me!"

"I can't," Ethan said with a nod in Patrick's direction. "I do what the boss tells me to do."

Harris's eyes shot to Patrick. "Don't let him inject me."

"But don't you wanna know what silver nitrate in your blood will do to you?" Patrick asked innocently.

"No! I can guess."

"Oh, so you're aren't that stupid after all," Patrick said and leaned over him. "I guess that means you'd rather answer my questions."

"Yes, yes, I'll answer." He tipped his chin in Ethan's direction. "Just keep that guy away from me."

Patrick suppressed his smirk. This was way too easy. "Let's get down to business. When were you turned into a vampire?"

"About two weeks ago."

"Voluntarily?

"Yeah, so?" Defiance colored the rogue's voice.

Patrick ignored the last word. "About the body you left in the kitchen of your house... When did you kill her?"

"I didn't!"

Patrick laid his hand around the jerk's neck. The silver chain, which had been around Harris's neck earlier had left the skin raw and the flesh below exposed, eliciting a wince of pain from his captive.

"Don't lie to me, or my friend will inject you with what's in the needle. Now, again: when did you kill your mother?"

Harris's throat worked, and Patrick loosened his grip a fraction so he could speak. "Three nights ago."

"Why?"

"The bitch deserved it. Always nagging me. Always complaining."

Patrick let go of his neck and took a step back. The guy disgusted him. Had he admitted to losing control due to his insatiable hunger for blood that as a newly-turned vampire he had trouble controlling, he would have had a pinch of compassion for Harris, but this guy was a psychopath.

"Yeah, like you're the model son," Patrick hissed. "Who's the vampire who turned you?"

Harris made an attempt at shrugging his shoulders, but the movement caused him visible pain.

Patrick looked over his shoulder to

Ethan. "Bro, just give him the needle already."

As Ethan approached with determined strides, Harris yelled, "No, no! Not the needle. I'll tell you his name. Thomas. He said his name was Thomas."

Patrick felt adrenaline shoot through him. They all knew a vampire named Thomas: Scanguards' own IT genius. The name had to be a coincidence. "What's his last name?"

"He didn't say. I swear! And I only saw him twice. Please, believe me!" Red tears were welling up in his eyes now.

Patrick glanced over his shoulder up to the observation window, before turning back and demanding, "Describe him!"

"I don't know. Taller than me. Short light brown or dark blond hair."

"Facial hair?"

Harris shook his head.

"That's not a very good description. That

could be anybody." But hopefully not Thomas.

"I only met him briefly. And it was kind of dark, and frankly the guy creeped me out."

Patrick shook his head. "Yet you agreed to be turned by him."

"Yeah, I mean... he was offering everything I wanted..."

"Back to the vampire who turned you. Where did you meet him?"

"Online at first."

"Via the incel forum you're on?"

Surprise flashed in Harris's eyes. "How do you—"

"We know what you've been up to," Patrick interrupted. "Where did you meet this guy in real life?"

"Somewhere behind a bar in the Castro."

Patrick sucked in a breath. Many of the bars in the Castro were known as gay hangouts, and he was certain that Thomas and his partner, Eddie, had been to many of them. Did that mean that Thomas could indeed be involved in this?

Patrick pulled his cell phone from his pocket and navigated to an app, typed in Thomas's name in the database, and it spit out his photo. He turned the display so that Harris could see it.

"Is that him?"

Harris shook his head instantly. "No. I've never seen that guy."

Patrick turned back to the observation window. "It's not Thomas." But with the vague description that they had, they needed to bring in the big guns to find who this vampire was. "I think we need Gabriel down here."

"He's already on his way down," Samson said via the speaker system.

The door opened in the same instant, and Gabriel strode in. He walked up to the captive, who shrank back, clearly scared of him, because with his imposing figure and the large scar on one side of his face, he looked like a violent criminal. Only those people who knew him, knew that he was a considerate man who abhorred needless violence, and only employed it when his friends or family were in danger.

"Are you gonna use your skill?" Ethan asked from behind Patrick.

Gabriel nodded. "It's the only way to know for sure."

He stopped right in front of Harris and stretched his hand over the vampire's head without touching him. Patrick knew about Gabriel's skill of being able to look into other people's memories, but he'd never witnessed it firsthand.

"What the fuck are you doing?" Harris asked, his eyes darting nervously from Gabriel to Ethan and Patrick. "What is this?"

"Shut up, and let me concentrate," Gabriel demanded.

"I would do what he says," Ethan advised. "He's not as gentle as my colleague and I." He pointed to Patrick.

Scared into silence, the rogue clamped his jaw shut.

It took less than a minute before Gabriel pivoted away from Harris. "I saw who turned him. It's definitely not our Thomas, but I've never seen the guy."

Harris's eyes widened. "What the fuck?"

Everybody ignored him.

"What now?" Patrick asked.

"I'll go through our database of known vampires and see if I can find him in there. It'll take a few hours, but with some luck he's in there," Gabriel said and already headed toward the door. "And put the guy in the lockup. Don't kill him yet, just in case we still need him."

"Kill me? What the fuck! I answered your questions. I told you everything I know," Harris whined.

Gabriel looked over his shoulder. "You savagely killed your mother. And not because you couldn't control your thirst for blood. Vampires like you need to be put down."

Harris screamed and fought against his restraints, but he couldn't break them.

Patrick wasn't surprised that Gabriel had decided that Harris deserved death. Had it been his decision, he would have come to the same conclusion. A man who killed his mother deserved no better than death.

Patrick grabbed the rogue by his shirt collar, and bared his fangs. "I'm looking forward to killing you."

"Who said you get to kill him?" Ethan asked, stepping closer.

"I called dibs."

29

Vanessa sat on the two-seater sofa in the office where she'd told Cole the truth about her and her family. She was curled up, her arms hugging her knees, tears streaming down her face in little rivulets. The red color of her tears stained her top, but she didn't care. Cole didn't love her enough to accept her the way she was. Nothing mattered now. She'd lost. She was the first and only hybrid among her friends who'd been rejected by her mate.

Everything had been perfect between

them. He'd accepted that they were both satyrs, and that fact had given her hope that he would also accept that she was a vampire. But she'd been wrong. He hated vampires. And why wouldn't he? A vampire had nearly killed him. He was traumatized. She should have waited longer, until his love for her was stronger. Maybe then, he would have accepted that she was a vampire. She'd rushed it. It was her own fault.

A shudder wracked her frame, and with it came another wave of tears. She almost didn't hear the door opening.

"Nessie." It was Ethan.

He rushed to her, and put his arms around her, hugging her to him. "I was told that Cole was seen leaving the garage without you."

She briefly lifted her head, looking into her brother's eyes. "He didn't want me. He hates vampires. He hates me."

"He doesn't hate you," Ethan protested, his voice soft and beseeching. "I saw how he reacted, when you tried to shield him from the rogue. He wanted to protect you. It's his instinct. You're his mate."

Vanessa shook her head. "He's rejected me. He sees vampires only as evil and violent. I didn't even get the chance to tell him what it is like between mates." She sniffled. "I love him, Ethan. I've never felt like this for anybody."

"I know, Nessie, I know." Ethan pressed a kiss into her hair, and stroked his hand over her back, comforting her. "Just give him some time. I know he'll come back. I saw how he looked at you. He loves you."

"He doesn't love the vampire in me."

Ethan put his fingers under her chin and forced her to look at him. "Sis, I promise you he will come back to you."

She doubted it. Cole had made his choice.

"In the meantime, how about I drive you home, and you'll rest a little?" he suggested.

Wordlessly, she nodded and rose. Her

vision was tinted and blurry from the tears. Ethan took her by the hand, and ushered her out of the office. A couple of minutes later, they sat in a Scanguards-owned SUV, and Ethan drove out of the garage.

In the interior of the car it was stifling hot. She reached for the temperature dial on the dashboard and turned it all the way down, then hit the air conditioning button. Cool air blasted toward her, but it wasn't enough to cool down the car.

Ethan glanced at her, and pressed the back of his fingers to her left cheek. "Fuck, you're burning up. Are you going into heat?"

Vanessa didn't answer. Instead, she lowered the window, hoping the cool night air would help. It didn't. She had to admit it. She was going into heat, and there was nothing she could do to alleviate her condition.

"I'm gonna drive you straight to Cole's."

"No!" Vanessa protested, clamping her hand over his wrist to prevent him from turning the steering wheel to make a turn. "I don't want his pity."

"Damn it, Nessie, you need sex now. So if you don't want me to bring you to Cole, then I'm bringing you to Vera's. She can give you one of her clients."

"I'm not gonna have sex with anybody else." She wanted only Cole's hands on her, his cocks inside her. She didn't want mindless sex with a stranger just because she was in heat. She would get through this.

"Nessie, be reasonable. You have to have sex."

"No, I can get through this. Just take me home. Please. It'll pass," she lied, even though she knew that it was only going to get worse over the next few hours, until she would reach the peak of this cycle, and her feverish state would break. She would survive the pain.

Ethan looked at her, but he continued driving toward home. "Maybe call him, and try to explain things to him over the phone. He'll have to listen."

"He's made his choice. I'm not gonna turn into some crazy stalker and hound him about changing his mind about me. It would only prove his point."

"What point?"

"That he has reason to be afraid of vampires."

"Are you saying you think he's afraid of you?"

"You didn't see how he looked at me." She turned her head away and looked out at the houses they were passing. "As if I was an apex-predator. And he was the prey. And he hasn't even seen me in my vampire form." She whipped her head back to her brother. "What then? What happens when he sees me with glowing red eyes, my fingers turning into claws, my fangs extended? He'll run. Or worse, he'll grab a stake and kill me."

"It's never gonna come to that," Ethan insisted. "Just look at it this way. It's not easy for a man to accept that the woman he loves is stronger and more powerful than him. He's not used to that. I mean he's a big guy, and probably never had to be afraid of anybody. And suddenly you tell him that you're stronger than him, when *he* thought he had to protect *you*. That could confuse anyone."

"He didn't look confused. He looked betrayed." And hurt.

Ethan pulled up in front of their parents' house and turned to look at her. "You need to talk to him."

"I can't. It won't change anything. I can't force somebody to love me. That's not how it works."

"But he needs to see your side, and he can only see that if you talk to him."

More tears rose to the surface, and ran down her cheeks in a steady stream. Through her blurry vision, she looked at her brother and shook her head. "No. It's over."

She reached for the door handle and opened the car door.

Vanessa hurried up the stairs to the entrance door, wanting nothing more than to crawl into a corner and stay there until she couldn't feel anything anymore. Her hand shook when she unlocked the front door and opened it. Inside, it was quiet. Upstairs, in her room, she switched on the lights and headed straight for the shower, undressing on the way and leaving her clothes where they fell on the floor. She turned on the water in the shower, and stepped into the spray of the cold water, hoping it would cool down her body and distract her from the pain in her heart and her body. The pain of losing Cole.

30

Cole slammed his fist against the wall in his bedroom, anger and betrayal surging through him, the pain so severe, as if somebody was ramming a burning poker through his heart. He'd never thought that he was capable of such deep emotions, not after all the years of schooling himself not to hope for something that was unattainable. He'd never allowed himself to hope for real love, even less for finding his soulmate. But his heart had betrayed him. It should have warned him that Vanessa was too good to be true. It should have stopped him from falling so completely and hopelessly in love with a dangerous and violent creature: Vanessa. A vampire.

But every time she appeared in his mind, he didn't see the vampire, he didn't see the evil and violent creature. He only saw the woman. The lover. The temptress. He tried to force himself to imagine her with glowing red eyes and extended fangs like the creature her brother and his colleagues had brought to Scanguards. But whenever he tried, all he could see was the warm glow in her eyes, her soft lips, her tender kisses. How could a vampire do that? How could a vampire kiss so tenderly?

Fuck! He recalled how she'd taken his hard-on into her mouth, sucking him with such skill and such tenderness and passion, when she could have sliced his cock off in a second. She'd never hurt him physically, even though she could have. On the contrary, she'd saved his life, she'd killed for him.

Even when he'd demanded to leave Scanguards, she'd stepped aside and let him pass, when she could have lashed out at him because he'd rejected her.

Cole plopped down on the edge of his bed, running a hand through his hair. What had he done? He'd seen red the moment she'd told him that she was a vampire. His only thought had been the vampire who'd nearly killed him, the trauma of it still haunting him. He hadn't been able to process anything else. His instinct had kicked in. Fight or flight? Knowing how strong his attacker had been, and therefore how strong Vanessa had to be, he'd opted for flight.

But now, safe in his four walls, the adrenaline shooting through his veins had simmered down, and the analytical side of his brain was working again. Like a film, every interaction he'd ever had with Vanessa played back in front of his inner eye, and he was able to assess everything that had happened between them. He had to admit that there hadn't been any moment when he'd felt any danger emanating from Vanessa. Even when she'd let him leave Scanguards earlier, he hadn't seen a single flicker of violence or danger directed toward him. She'd simply moved aside and let him go. Any other woman would have yelled at him for leaving her. But Vanessa had accepted it without lashing out at him. Of a vampire, he would have never expected such self-control. Such poise. Such grace.

Didn't that prove that she wasn't a violent creature? That there was humanity in her? Maybe more humanity than in some humans. Or why else would she patrol night after night, looking out for the less fortunate, the hookers, the druggies, the homeless? Or had that all been a lie?

Fuck! How would he ever know the truth? Certainly not by sitting here in his condo making himself crazy. The only person who could really tell him the truth about Vanessa, was Vanessa herself. But did he have the courage to confront her?

A loud banging on his door made him jump up. His heart beat in a loud staccato, and his breathing changed. Who was at his door at this time of night? Was it Vanessa?

He hurried to the door, then looked through the peephole. He sucked in a breath and reared back.

"Cole, I can hear you breathing," Vanessa's brother Ethan said insistently from the other side of the door. "Open the fucking door before I kick it in."

Knowing that Ethan wasn't making an empty threat, and certainly had the strength to kick the door in, he decided to follow his command and opened the door wide.

Ethan didn't lose a second and pounced, grabbing him by the front of his shirt and slamming him against the nearest wall, while kicking the door shut with his foot. Cole had never seen anybody move so fast.

"What the fuck do you want?" Cole managed to press out.

He wouldn't let Ethan know that he was just a slight bit intimidated by the vampire's strength and speed. He didn't even want to admit it to himself, but that ship had sailed. He knew he had no chance fighting him off, but that didn't mean he would cower.

"What I want is you going back to Vanessa and making up with her."

The words made one thing clear instantly: Ethan wasn't here to kill him.

"You broke her heart, you jerk!"

Cole tipped his chin up. "How could I break her heart when she doesn't have one?"

Ethan let go of his shirt and took a step back, shaking his head. "You know nothing about vampires. You think we're so different from you? We have hearts just like you humans. We feel more deeply than a human ever could. So, congratulations, you managed to break my sister's heart."

Cole felt his mouth open, but no words came out. He exhaled, then took in another breath. "Are you saying she really loves me?"

Ethan let out an exasperated breath and tapped on Cole's forehead. "Hello? Anybody in there?" He shook his head again. "Don't you get it at all? Vanessa loves you more than anything or anybody. She would give her life for you if she had to."

"Did she send you to tell me that?"

"Send me? Fuck, no! If she knew I was here, talking to you, she'd kick the living daylights out of me. I'm here because she's in heat, and she refuses to have sex with anybody but you. And I'm not gonna stand by, and let her suffer."

Ethan's jaw tightened visibly, and he stabbed his index finger into Cole's chest.

"So, you, pretty boy, are gonna go to her, and fuck her for as long as she needs it. And

I don't care what you have to tell her. Lie for all I care. But she needs sex now. And you're the only one she'll sleep with, because she loves you, and nothing is gonna change that. Because when a vampire falls in love, it's forever."

Ethan's words triggered something in Cole. He blinked and stared at him, a memory surfacing. "How can she even be a vampire? How could I have missed that? She was out during the day. I was with her. But your father said that vampires turn to dust in the sun... Was that a lie?"

"No. Pureblooded vampires do indeed turn to dust in the sun. But Vanessa isn't a pureblooded vampire. She's a hybrid, like all children born to a vampire. Like myself and my brother. We have all of the pureblooded vampires' traits, but can't be killed by the rays of the sun."

Cole felt as if his head was exploding with all the information he tried to process. He nodded to himself. "I guess that's not important right now." The words were meant more for himself than for Ethan. "Fuck. What have I done?" He sought Ethan's gaze. "I love her. I didn't want to hurt her, but when she told me that she's a vampire, I panicked."

Ethan appeared to relax. "Well, that happens. Guess it didn't help that you were attacked by one of the rogues."

Seeing understanding in Ethan's eyes, Cole nodded. "What if Vanessa doesn't take me back? What if she can't forgive me?"

For the first time, Ethan smiled and slapped his hand on Cole's shoulder. "I think some groveling will come in handy for that. Oh, yeah, and sex. Start with that. That's what she needs most right now."

"I can do that."

"I bet." Ethan chuckled. "Oh, and one other thing: if she wants to bite you and drink your blood, let her."

"But..." How could he let her do the same as that rogue?

"Trust me on this. When a vampire bites his or her lover, it's sensual. There's no pain, no horror, only pleasure."

Cole furrowed his forehead. "But how is that possible? I felt that vampire's bite, and I can still remember the pain."

"Like I said: when it's done right, there won't be any pain. I've been bitten plenty of times, and I've bitten my lovers too, and there's nothing better than to share that pleasure with the one you love."

Ethan's eyes suddenly began to shimmer golden. It reminded him of how Vanessa's eyes had shimmered when they'd made love.

He stretched out his hand. "Your eyes... they're golden... just like Vanessa's when..."

Ethan smirked. "I'll let Nessie explain that to you. Now, let's move. She needs you."

Cole reached for his car keys.

"We'll take my car," Ethan said "I'll have to let you into the house, because she's not gonna open the door in the state that she's in."

"If I just show up there, isn't she gonna know that you let me in?"

"If she asks, and I doubt that she will, tell her you picked the lock. Under no circumstances can you let her know that I made you go see her. Understood?"

"Ethan…"

"What?"

"You're not making me do anything. I was already pretty close to going to talk to her before you came."

"I'm happy to hear that, bro."

Ethan opened the door, and Cole snatched his house keys, and followed him out.

31

After Ethan unlocked the front door to the Giles's Edwardian home, Cole entered the house. He looked over his shoulder, waving back at Ethan who was returning to his car, and pulled the door shut behind him. The lights in the foyer and the hallway that led to the stairs were on, but the rest of the house was wrapped in darkness. Cole listened for sounds. It was quiet except for the sound of water running through the old pipes in the house.

Cole ascended the stairs to the second

floor and stopped in front of Vanessa's room. He lifted his hand to knock, but then decided otherwise and simply opened the door and entered. Inside the bedroom, only a small lamp on the bedside table was illuminated, but the room was empty. From the open bathroom door, more light shone into the room. He could clearly hear the shower running. As he walked toward it, he noticed Vanessa's clothes strewn all over the floor.

At the entrance to the bathroom, he stopped. Vanessa was cowering in one corner of the shower, curled up into a ball, her arms hugging her knees, her head on her thighs, while water rained down on her. She hadn't heard him yet. When he noticed how her torso trembled, he recognized that she was crying, and his heart contracted in pain. He had done this to her. He'd hurt her, and now it was up to him to fix what he'd destroyed—because he never wanted to see Vanessa in pain again. He loved her too much for that, he acknowledged that now.

Cole kicked his shoes off, pulled his shirt over his head, and dropped his pants, tossing them behind him, before he approached the shower only wearing his boxer briefs. With a start, Vanessa lifted her head. Their eyes met, and shock charged through him. Blood was streaming from her eyes down her cheeks.

Concerned, he rushed toward her. "You're injured."

"What are you doing here?" Her words were clipped. She turned her head away.

Cole stepped into the shower and crouched down to her. "Vanessa, your face is bloody. Let me help you."

When he reached for her, she pushed his hands away. "I don't need your help. I'm not injured."

"But there's blood on your face."

Defiantly she tipped her chin up. "It's tears. Happy now?"

The revelation that a vampire's tears were blood-red made him see her in a vulnerable light. "No, I'm not happy about you crying. I'm sorry."

"I don't want your pity," she spat.

Cole grabbed her shoulders. "You think I pity you?" He shook his head. "I'm here to apologize for what I've done. For hurting you."

She met his gaze then, the expression in her eyes changing, but she didn't speak. It appeared that he'd have to work harder to be forgiven.

"Vanessa, baby, I didn't mean the things I said to you. I should have never said them. And I'm willing to do anything to earn your forgiveness. But right now, we have more important things to do. You're in heat. You need sex."

He rose, pulling her up with him, but she drew back and shook off his hold. "I don't want pity sex."

She was a stubborn one, his mate. But

he could be stubborn too. He took her hands and led them to his groin, pressing them to his cocks that had turned hard the moment he'd seen her naked in the shower.

"Does that feel like I'm doing this out of pity?" he challenged. "'Cause I'm fucking horny whenever I'm near you." He pulled her closer so their bodies touched. "Feeling you in my arms. Damn it, baby, don't you understand? I love you, and I don't care what you are. As long as we can be together."

Even if that meant that one day she'd have to turn him into a vampire so he would stop aging and could spend eternity with her. But that was a discussion for another day.

Vanessa lifted her head. "Cole..."

With his thumb he wiped away the streaks of bloody tears on her cheeks. How had he ever doubted that vampires had a heart? He could see Vanessa's spilling out from her eyes, showing him that she had feelings that were just as deep as a human's if not deeper.

"You don't have to say anything, baby. And you don't have to forgive me right away. I'll prove myself to you. But I beg you: let me make love to you now. We both need this. I can feel how hot you are. I can ease that fever for you."

Vanessa inched her face closer. "It's so bad this time. Worse than all the other times before. I think I need... I need..."

He framed her face with his hands. "I know what you need: both my cocks inside you. Just like it's meant between satyr mates." Nothing less would do tonight.

"Yes." Her answer was but a tender breath.

Cole slanted his lips over hers, capturing them for a searing kiss. He felt Vanessa's hands on him, sliding them into his boxer briefs as she kissed him back. Cold water rained down on them, but he didn't bother switching it off, knowing that Vanessa needed it so her body wouldn't burn up. He pressed her against the tile wall, while he caressed her naked body and dueled with her tongue.

Vanessa yielded to his touch, her body responding to him just as passionately as when they'd made love earlier today. To know that she was a powerful creature, and that he, a mere mortal, could turn this woman into putty in his arms, was a powerful turn-on. Her sighs and moans bounced off the tiles, and her body's heat seeped into him, making every cell in his body vibrate with pleasure.

Still pressing Vanessa against the tiles, he severed the kiss and dipped his head to her breasts. Her nipples were hard little buds, pointing up at him, asking for his touch. He sucked one into his mouth, while he pinched the other one between thumb and index finger. A gasp burst over her lips, and she thrust her breast toward him, demanding more.

"Your teeth," she begged. "Use your teeth."

He understood now why she'd enjoyed it when he'd bitten her lightly when they'd had sex before: it was something a vampire did with a lover, and he wouldn't deny her anything now. Gently, Cole brushed his teeth over her skin, then pressed harder until his teeth sank into her flesh without breaking the skin. He felt a visible shudder run through Vanessa's body, confirming that she enjoyed his rough caresses. He switched to her other breast and did the same there, while he dipped one hand to the apex of her thighs.

Vanessa lifted one leg and wrapped it around his hip, giving him better access. His fingers found her female folds moist with her juices, and rubbed over her warm cleft, before drawing them to her clit. The tiny organ was engorged, begging for his touch, and he painted circles around it with his finger, his tempo and pressure increasing with every second. Vanessa panted heavily, and her hips moved in synch with his touch.

"Oh God," she let out, and the sound was like music to his ears.

He realized just how much he loved giving her what she needed, making her body hum with pleasure. She was all woman now, and she was all his. He'd never before felt this kind of possessiveness toward anyone but the woman in his arms.

While he continued caressing her clit, easing up when he felt she was getting too close, then speeding up to get her close to the edge again, he alternated between licking her nipples with his tongue and biting her breasts.

"Baby, baby, please, let me come," she begged, her voice sounding like she was miles away.

He lifted his head from her breasts. "Anything you want, baby." He captured her lips with his and delved into her mouth, reacquainting himself with the delicious cavern of her mouth, while farther below, he rubbed his finger over her center of pleasure in a faster tempo.

Suddenly he felt Vanessa's body spasm, and she moaned into his mouth. He let go of her clit and drove his finger into her pussy, just in time to feel how her interior muscles clenched around his digit as she climaxed.

Cole let go of her mouth and looked at her face. Her eyelashes fluttered, and her eyes shone golden, eliminating the green in her irises completely. Her lips looked bruised from his kisses, and heavy pants rolled over them. She looked thoroughly loved. Any sign that she'd cried only minutes earlier was gone.

"Now you're ready for me," he murmured at her lips. "For both my cocks."

She opened her eyes fully and gazed at him, excitement sparkling in them. "Yes."

Cole pulled her with him and stepped onto the bath mat. "Do you have lubricant?"

"Top left drawer next to the sink."

Vanessa pointed toward it. Cole rid himself of his wet boxer briefs and opened the drawer. He found the tube of lubricant immediately, and squeezed a generous dollop onto his palm. When he turned around, Vanessa stood right in front of him, looking sexier than she ever had. Quickly, he lathered his upper cock with the lubricant. His cocks were super sensitive now, the anticipation ratcheting up his arousal even more.

Without a word, Vanessa turned to the sink, gripped it, and stepped back, while she placed her legs hip-width apart, her ass pointing up at him.

"Fuck!" He wouldn't last long. Not with Vanessa giving herself to him like this; submitting to him by offering her body to him.

"Don't make me wait," she murmured, looking over her shoulder. "You know you want it too."

He let out a nervous chuckle. "I think I want this more than you."

She smirked. "How about we compare notes afterwards?"

"Good idea."

There was no more stalling. Cole stepped closer, positioning himself. With one hand, he guided his lower cock to the entrance of her pussy, with the other he held on to his upper cock and pressed it against her anus. For a moment, he hesitated. He didn't want to hurt her.

"Please take me," Vanessa murmured.

Slowly, he pressed forward. His lower cock easily dipped into her pussy, while his upper cock sank into her anus. The tightness of the puckered hole made him gasp, before he pushed farther in. Another push, and he was inside her to the hilt, his upper cock in her ass, his lower one deep in her pussy. Her twin channels held him tightly as if he'd slipped into gloves that were a size too small. The sensation of

Vanessa's interior muscles squeezing him sent a sensual shockwave into his balls. He gripped her hips, stopping her and himself from moving.

Their eyes met in the mirror. He saw his own desire mirrored in Vanessa's eyes, and knew that as long as he did what his body dictated, they would both experience pleasure. It was like a new instinct he'd developed. Was it the satyr in him that instinctively knew what his mate needed?

Without breaking eye contact, he withdrew his cocks until only their bulbous heads were still inside Vanessa's body, before he plunged back faster than the first time.

Vanessa gasped in surprise, but she didn't voice any protest. "Yes, take me hard. Let me feel that I'm yours and yours alone."

Her words did something to him. They cut the leash with which he'd previously held himself back so as not to scare her away. But now he knew there was no chance that he could ever scare her away, no matter how rough he was with her, and how hard he fucked her.

A never before heard growl dislodged from his chest, and he withdrew and thrust hard into her ass and her pussy.

"Yes, you're mine," he grunted, his breath quickening. "And I'm gonna fuck you until you beg me to stop."

"I won't beg," she promised, the golden hue in her eyes intensifying.

As he thrust in and out of her, plunged deep and hard without a second's reprieve, he admired her body in the mirror. Her breasts were bouncing up and down, left and right with every thrust, her wet hair clinging to her skin, moans and sighs tumbling over her luscious lips. Lips that were parted, showing her perfectly white teeth.

But it wasn't regular teeth he wanted to see. "Show them to me," he demanded.

Her eyelashes fluttered and her gaze connected with his. "You mean…"

"Yes, your fangs. Show them to me now, or I'll stop fucking you." He paused his thrusts, but kept his cocks lodged deep inside her tight channels. He didn't know why he suddenly wanted to see her vampire side, but he did.

"Oh, Cole…"

She opened her mouth wider, and slowly, her canines extended and became perfectly shaped, razor-sharp fangs.

His heart made a somersault. He could hardly believe what he saw, and what he felt at that sight. He'd never felt so turned on in his life.

Without tearing his eyes from the sight of her beautiful and deadly fangs, he resumed fucking her with both cocks, slamming harder and faster into her with every second.

"Fuck, you're even more beautiful with your fangs."

"Oh Cole..."

Her response was spoken on a surprised breath, while a jolt seemed to go through her body. Both her channels suddenly spasmed as she climaxed, squeezing his cocks so tightly that there was no chance stopping his coming orgasm. He felt semen shoot through both his cocks as pleasure washed over him, making his entire body feel weightless.

Still inside Vanessa, he wrapped his arms around her, and pulled her against his chest. He nuzzled his face in the crook of her neck. He was spent, but he'd never experienced anything even close to what he'd felt with Vanessa: a deep satisfaction, not just physical, but also emotional.

Cole lifted his face, and Vanessa turned her face to him.

"I love feeling both your cocks inside me." She brushed her lips over his. She reached behind her, placing her hand on his backside to drive his cocks deeper into her again.

He chuckled softly, pleased that she enjoyed the experience as much as he had. "I love it even more."

Her breath blew over his lips. "Then I hope you don't mind if we do this at least daily."

In response to her words, he moved his still hard cocks back and forth a few times, thrusting slowly this time. "You're insatiable... Just as well that I was going to suggest the same thing."

Vanessa laughed softly, before he kissed her and drowned out her laughter.

32

Samson opened the door to Gabriel's office. "You wanted to speak to me?"

Gabriel nodded. "Come in, close the door."

Samson pointed over his shoulder. "Mind if Patrick joins us?"

Gabriel motioned them to enter. Patrick closed the door behind them.

"What's wrong?" Samson asked.

Gabriel turned the computer screen so that Samson and Patrick could see it. It showed the photo of a man he hadn't laid eyes on in over three decades. He'd practically forgotten all about him.

He looked away from it and met Gabriel's eyes. "What are you saying?"

"That's the vampire who turned those incels."

"Are you sure?"

"Absolutely. I saw him in Mike Harris's memories. It's him. I never met him back then, but when I read the notes in his file, I realized who he was. Now I understand why he told the incels that his name was Thomas. That's sick."

Samson dropped into the chair in front of Gabriel's desk. "Fuck!" He rubbed his nape. "I never expected him to come back."

Gabriel's scar seemed to pulse. "Nobody did, I'm sure. But he's back. And I can guess what his motives are."

Samson nodded. "Revenge."

"He waited a bloody long time for it."

"Dad, Gabriel, you know this guy?"

Patrick asked, his gaze bouncing between them. "Who is he?"

Samson turned his face to his son. "That's Milo. He was Thomas's lover a long time ago."

"Okay? So, why would he want revenge?" His forehead furrowed. "Because Thomas dumped him, I'm assuming?"

Samson exchanged a look with Gabriel. While Gabriel knew the full story, Samson had never told his children about Milo. There'd never been a need to. But it appeared, it was time to talk about the past.

Samson took a deep breath. "Milo tried to have your mother killed."

"Fuck!" Patrick cursed. "When? How?"

"A long time ago. I'd only just met her. She was auditing Scanguards at the time, and Milo and my ex, Ilona, who turned out to be his sister, tried to get access to my money to steal it. They knew that Delilah would figure it out during her audit, and would be able to stop them, so they tried to get rid of her."

"Oh, fuck!" Patrick let himself fall into a chair, all air rushing from his lungs. "Why didn't you tell me earlier? Do Grayson and Isabelle know about it?"

Samson shook his head. "None of them knows. Why burden you kids with that knowledge? After all, we'd prevented the theft, and your mother was safe."

"Safe? But if Milo and his sister are back, nobody's safe."

"Ilona isn't back. Amaury killed her when she made a last-ditch effort to kill Delilah, and injured me." How gravely he was injured back then, impaled on spikes of a wrought-iron fence, he decided not to reveal to his son. Delilah had saved him with her blood.

"And Milo got away?"

Samson shook his head. "It was up to Thomas to punish Milo. He decided not to kill him." He locked eyes with his youngest son. "You see, Thomas still loved him. He couldn't kill him."

"But—"

"I respected his choice. Thomas exiled him. We made sure he left the country the same night. And we notified the council and every vampire clan we knew, that if they harbored him, we would destroy them, and then hunt him down."

Gabriel grunted.

Samson nodded. "We never got any alerts that Milo was trying to seek help from any of the clans in the US. He probably knew that nobody would dare to give him shelter. I guess he figured, if he couldn't join another clan, he would create his own."

"After such a long time?" Patrick asked. "How many years ago was that? Forty?"

"Thirty-seven years ago," Samson confirmed. "And now he's back to take his revenge."

"With a bunch of incels he turned into vampires?" Patrick asked, shaking his head.

"The one Ethan and I captured was so easy to overwhelm, I can't imagine them to be a real threat to us."

"That may be the case when it comes to a fight between us and the incels, but there are more ways than one to destroy what we've built for ourselves here in San Francisco. Unleashing the incels on an unsuspecting human population will wreak havoc, and has the potential to expose our secrets."

"But—"

Gabriel interrupted Patrick's protest. "Your father is right. Milo doesn't have to attack us directly to harm us."

"I need to tell Thomas," Samson said. He dreaded the conversation.

"It'll be a blow for him," Gabriel guessed.

Samson rose slowly. "He'll blame himself.

"As he should," Patrick added.

Samson turned his head to his son. "No, he shouldn't. I don't blame him, and neither should anybody else. He'll be his own harshest critic."

For a long moment, Patrick didn't say anything. "So, what are you gonna do now?"

"You and Gabriel get everybody to HQ for a crisis meeting. And I mean everybody, particularly the hybrids, even Isabelle. Have Virginia fetch Grayson and Monique and her brothers from New Orleans. We'll need every hybrid we can get."

"Why every hybrid?" Patrick asked.

"I'll tell you at the meeting," Samson said, an idea already forming in his head. "In the meantime, I'll talk to Thomas. Alone."

And that wasn't a conversation he was looking forward to. But Thomas had a right to find out the identity of their enemy, before he announced it to everybody at the meeting.

33

Vanessa snuggled up to Cole, her cheek resting on his chest, her hand caressing his muscled torso, one leg across his thigh. She'd never felt so satisfied and happy than when in Cole's arms, knowing that he accepted every part of her. After the most amazing sexual experience with him, they'd taken a quick shower together.

Now, they were in bed together, but they weren't sleeping. There were so many things she wanted to talk to him about.

"You surprised me," she began.

"Surprised you how? By coming to see you?"

She lifted her head to look into his face. "No. By asking me to show you my fangs."

A soft rumble rolled over Cole's lips. "I honestly don't know what came over me, but when you showed them to me, fuck, it was such a turn-on..." He stroked over her ass, simultaneously moving her closer so her thigh rubbed over his cocks. "Just thinking of it now..."

She followed his gaze to his lower body, and noticed that his cocks were slowly but surely hardening again, even though he'd come only a few minutes earlier. Now was probably the best time to confess one last thing.

"Cole," she said, hesitating.

"Yeah, babe?"

"There's something you should know."

He met her gaze. "You can tell me anything. I promise whatever it is, you won't get rid of me anymore. I'm here to stay."

She felt a smile curve her lips upwards. She knew he was telling the truth. She could feel it.

"The night you got attacked..."

He nodded. "Go on."

"You were badly injured. The rogue had already taken so much blood from you, and you would have bled out within minutes, if I hadn't done what I did." Just the thought of that moment sent an icy shudder down her spine.

"That night you said the injuries weren't that bad, and honestly, when I looked in the mirror, I noticed that they were only superficial."

"I know that's what I said. But that was a lie. Because had I told you what I did to heal you as quickly as possible, you would have pushed me away."

His forehead furrowed. "What did you do?"

"When you passed out on the street, I licked over your wounds to close them. A vampire's saliva heals skin, but it wasn't enough. The injuries on your neck were too deep. I carried you back—"

"I knew it. That's why you said before that I was in and out of consciousness, because I wouldn't have believed that you'd be capable of carrying me while I was fully unconscious. I don't doubt that anymore." He pressed a kiss to her nose.

"Trust me, you were heavy nevertheless. But I had to get you off the street. I couldn't risk that anybody could see what I had to do." She paused for a moment. "I had to give you some of my blood to drink, so you could heal from the inside. It was the only way."

A short gasp escaped Cole's throat. "Your blood? But wouldn't that mean that I'm a vampire now too?"

She shook her head. "No, that's not how humans are turned. You'd have to be on the brink of death for a vampire's blood to turn you. But there's a side effect other than healing that comes with ingesting vampire blood."

"Side effect?" He moved a little, raising his head higher. "What side effect?"

"Sexual arousal."

She watched him take in the news, and could see exactly when he realized what that meant.

"Does that mean that when I made love to you on the couch, when I went down on you, it was because of your blood?"

She nodded. "I'm sorry."

"I'm not."

He smirked, and pulled her on top of him. Her legs opened and rested at either side of his hips so she was straddling him.

"I don't suppose you'd be willing to give me more of your blood to prove what you just told me?"

"Don't you believe me?"

He winked at her, a soft smile on his lips. "Oh, I believe you, babe. I just want to experience that side effect again."

"You're a rascal," she chided, while her heart warmed. "But I believe it's my turn now."

"You mean…"

He lifted his hand to her lips. Without a word, she parted them and allowed her fangs to descend to their full length.

"Fuck, baby."

With his index finger he stroked over one fang. Vanessa jolted and reared back.

"I'm sorry," he apologized, an expression of true worry on his face. "Did I hurt you? I didn't mean to."

She snatched his hand and brought it closer to her face again. "No, you didn't hurt me. But a vampire's fangs are erogenous zones."

He blinked and stared at her in rapt fascination. "Are you telling me that it turns you on when I touch your fangs?"

"Yes, if you touch them… or if I sink them into your flesh. It has the same effect."

"Oh, babe." He pulled her face down to

him. "What are you waiting for then? Don't you want to drink my blood?"

An excited breath tumbled over her lips. "Only if you want it."

He brushed his lips over hers, then licked his tongue over one fang, while he cupped her face so that she couldn't pull back. His sensual touch turned her interior to molten lava, sending a spear of heat into her center of pleasure.

"Bite me, Vanessa, please. I want to give you everything you need."

"I love you," she whispered. Then she added, "Oh, and before I forget, when it's done right, the host experiences the same pleasure and arousal as the vampire. I hope that's okay with you..."

A surprised gasp issued from Cole's throat. "Fuck yeah!" He gripped her hips and made her rise to her knees. "Oh, and before *I* forget, I have one condition for you drinking my blood."

Though she could guess what he was

trying to say, she asked, "And what's that condition?"

"I get to make love to you every time you bite me."

Vanessa shifted above him and reached for his lower cock. She positioned it at the entrance to her pussy. "I can live with that." She impaled herself on his shaft, and reveled in the sight of bliss spreading on Cole's face.

When Cole tilted his head to the side to offer his neck, Vanessa lowered her face to the spot. She licked over the spot where his neck and shoulder met, and felt the pulsing vein beneath her tongue. She could already smell his rich blood. When she set the sharp tips of her fangs to his skin, opening her mouth wide, her own heart was beating out of control. Savoring the moment, she slowly sank her fangs into him, breaking the skin, and lodging them deep in his flesh. An instant later, deliciously rich blood rushed into her mouth and overwhelmed her taste buds.

If there was a paradise on earth, then she'd just found it.

***

Cole had expected to feel some initial pain, and was surprised that there was none at all. Vanessa licking his skin had sent a tingling sensation through his body, and a moment later, her fangs drove deep into him, and he could feel her sucking on his vein. He wasn't prepared for the sensations that followed, despite Vanessa's claim that the bite would heighten his arousal.

It was much more than that. More than mere arousal, more than sexual pleasure. Her bite seemed to heighten his senses, making him feel everything more intensely. His heart was beating out of control, his breath raced through his lungs, and the places where he and Vanessa were connected felt as if they were on fire.

Vanessa rode him, her hips moving in an even pace, up and down on his cock, while his second cock was rubbing over her center of pleasure, the contact doubling the pleasure his lower cock in her wet pussy gave him. As she drank from him, moans bounced against his skin. Cole gripped her hips, aiding her movements so she wouldn't grow tired too quickly. He wanted to make this last for as long as he humanly could. But already now, he was dancing precariously close to an orgasm.

"Babe," he murmured. "You're gonna make me come too quickly."

His voice sounded as if he were drugged. And maybe he was. Drugged by her bite. Delirious from the pleasure she bestowed on him. This was where Vanessa's true power as a vampire lay: in the bite that made him want to do everything she demanded of him, because the sensations she unleashed in him were addictive. He understood now how people could get hooked on drugs or alcohol or gambling, because he was surely getting addicted to her bite—on the first hit.

"I love you," he whispered on a short breath.

And even though she didn't answer him, because her fangs were lodged in his neck, he could feel that she loved him too. With her fingers she stroked over his cheek and touched his lips, lingering there for a brief moment.

The need for release rising with every movement, Cole eased up on the grip on her hips, giving Vanessa leave to move faster. Instantly, her tempo increased. He kept up with her, thrusting his cock upwards, whenever she made a downward movement, doubling the impact. Perspiration covered their bodies, making them slide more smoothly against one another.

When he sensed Vanessa trying to draw

her head back to stop drinking from him, he put his hand on the back of her head and pressed her down.

"Don't stop, I beg you."

He'd never begged a woman for anything. But Vanessa was giving him pure and total bliss, and if he had to beg for her so she wouldn't stop, he would do that. He'd do anything to feel like this. To feel arousal run through his veins instead of blood. To inhale bliss into his lungs instead of air. To feel connected to her as if they were one.

As Vanessa continued to suck on his vein and drink his blood, he suddenly felt her interior muscles spasm around him, squeezing his cock so tightly that he lost the reins with which he'd tried to hold onto his self-control. There was no holding back now. He surrendered to his orgasm and to the woman who showered him with pleasure. Both his cocks exploded at the same time, one shooting his semen deep into her pussy, the other spilling on their bellies. He let out a moan that came deep from within his heart, almost like a battle cry, raw and primal.

Vanessa withdrew her fangs from his neck, and again, he felt her tongue as she licked over the incisions, before she lifted her head.

Their eyes met. Vanessa's were a deep golden color. Her fangs were still extended, blood dripping from them. He pulled her face to him, then swept his tongue over one fang to lick it clean.

"Cole, oh." She let out a moan, and her pussy clenched around his cock once more.

Pleased that his action had the intended effect, he did the same to her other fang. Again, her tight channel squeezed his cock like a vise, and he welcomed the sensation. He knew then that he too had a power. The power to give her pleasure and make her surrender to him.

When her pussy relaxed again after a few moments, Cole framed Vanessa's face with both hands. "You were amazing." She inhaled a deep breath. "I can't believe I was ever scared of what you are."

A wet sheen appeared in her eyes.

"Baby, did I say something wrong?" he asked, instantly worried.

She shook her head and sniffled. "No. I'm just... I'm so happy that you liked it."

"Liked it?" He chuckled. "I didn't just like it. I loved it. Please tell me you need to drink blood every day, 'cause I don't think I can go without this for too long."

Vanessa smiled. "Yes, every day. I've never tasted anything as delicious as your blood."

"It's all yours, baby," he murmured and pressed his lips to hers, kissing her, when a ringing sound interrupted him.

Vanessa severed the kiss and looked toward the origin of the sound, her handbag. "That ringtone is for important Scanguards messages only. Sorry."

She lifted herself off him and retrieved

her handbag, reached inside and pulled out her cell phone. She tapped on the screen, then read the message. A moment later, she looked up. "We need to get dressed, and go to HQ."

Her serious expression made him sit up instantly. "What's going on?"

"I'll tell you on the way."

34

After taking an Uber to stop by Cole's condo building to get his car, Vanessa and Cole arrived at Scanguards' headquarters at the same time as many of her colleagues. Everybody headed for the large conference room, piling into it until there was only standing room left. Several of her colleagues eyed Cole, and she put her hand into his to indicate that he was with her. Vanessa caught her father's look, and she could see his question in his facial expression. She nodded in his direction, letting him know that she'd told Cole the truth that they were all vampires. A quick smile played around Gabriel's mouth, before he turned back to exchange a few quiet words with Samson.

While they waited for the meeting to begin, Vanessa pointed out to Cole who some of the assembled staff members were. She would introduce him later to some of her friends and colleagues who hadn't met him personally yet, though she was sure that the news that she'd found her mate had already spread among them like wildfire. Nothing remained a secret in their society for very long.

Slowly, the conversations in the room quieted, and Thomas stepped forward to the lectern. He cleared his throat.

"Thank you all for coming," he started.

Vanessa couldn't help but notice that he looked a lot more earnest, if not downright upset, when he cast his gaze at the assembled staff members.

"The reason I'm speaking to you first, is because I'm the reason for the mess we're in."

Surprised gasps and murmurs bounced around the room.

"Had I made a different decision, a better decision, 37 years ago, none of this would have happened."

"Thomas," Samson interrupted.

"No, Samson, it has to be said. It's my fault. And I take full responsibility for it."

He tapped on a mouse, and turned sideways so that everybody could look at the picture on the large screen behind him. "This is Milo. He was my boyfriend back then. Thirty-seven years ago, he and his sister Ilona tried to rob Samson and Scanguards of all their funds. We foiled their plan, and killed Ilona, but I made the mistake of letting Milo live."

More whispers traveled through the crowd, and Vanessa listened attentively. She'd never heard anybody talk of Milo.

"Milo is back. He's the vampire who's been turning incels into vampires and letting them loose on the city to wreak havoc among the human population. We can only assume that he's back to take his revenge, not just for us killing his sister, but also for thwarting his plan to rob Scanguards."

Thomas nodded at Samson, and stepped away from the lectern. Vanessa watched him as he walked to Eddie, his blood-bonded mate, who put his hand on Thomas's arm, squeezing it, while he gave him an encouraging look.

Samson took his place at the lectern, continuing where Thomas had left off.

"I want you all to memorize this photo. It's also being sent to your cell phones, so you can refresh your memory when you're out in the field canvassing the neighborhoods. It has taken Milo 37 years to return. That means he's had plenty of time to come up with a plan. Gabriel and I talked about this earlier, and we don't think that turning incels is the only part of his plan. We have to assume, that he's also turning other people, but in the absence of any other leads, we'll need to start with what we know."

Samson gave a nod in Gabriel's direction, who now approached.

"Our first order of business is to find Milo," Gabriel announced. "This will be mostly in the hands of our IT staff, who will comb through CCTV footage and traffic cams, trying to find Milo. We'll run facial recognition, and have asked every IT staff member to report for duty. We believe that he's holed up somewhere in the city to watch his plan unfold, and see the city descend into chaos, when more and more humans are being attacked. There'll be a panic when this happens."

"While the IT staff is busy with this," Samson said, taking over from Gabriel, "our second priority is to pick up all the incels.

Unfortunately, tonight our teams didn't have much luck, since most of them were out, most likely hunting for blood. That's why we'll do it differently this time."

Samson let his gaze sweep over the assembled vampires and hybrids. "The hybrids will be teamed up, and they will go to the incels' homes during the daytime. They won't expect you to come, thinking they are safe in their homes during daylight. We think that most of them don't even know about hybrids, and aren't aware that they can brave the sunlight. This will give us the advantage. You'll take the blackout vans and all equipment necessary to get the newly-turned vampires into the vans and transport them back to HQ. We'll be locking them up here for now."

"How about the incels that haven't been turned yet?" Benjamin asked.

"They will also need to be brought in, since they are at risk of being turned. We don't want to give Milo any more easy targets."

"But won't that show our hand?" Cole asked, lifting his hand. "I mean, won't that give away that we know what he's up to?"

Samson pointed to Cole. "Everybody, this is Cole. He's Vanessa's mate."

Some of the vampires turned to Cole to look at him, before Samson continued, "That's a good point, Cole. The fact is that by showing Milo that we're onto him, we're forcing his hand. He'll have to do something that he might not be ready for, so he might make a mistake. In any case, it will give us a better chance of finding him. And by locking up the incels, we're not only making the streets safer, we're also in a better position to get information out of the incels. One or more of them will have seen Milo's car, or where he came from. If we're lucky, we'll get a good lead as to where he's hiding. And then we'll come down on him with everything we've got."

Vanessa understood what Samson was saying. Milo wouldn't get out of this alive. She glanced at Thomas, and noticed that his jaw looked tight and his body rigid. Guilt and regret rolled off him in waves.

Her attention snapped back to the lectern, where Gabriel now cleared his voice.

"There are still ten incels we haven't captured or killed," he started. "Quinn and I put a list together of who's assigned to which incel. Each team will consist of two hybrids. Grayson, Monique, and her two brothers are on their way here from New Orleans. Virginia is bringing them through the portal shortly."

Vanessa felt Cole tug at her arm.

"Portal?" he asked, his brow furrowing.

"I'll explain later," she whispered.

"Unfortunately, since we only have sixteen hybrids available, it means that the teams that bring in their incels first, will be sent out again to bring in remaining ones."

"Can't we just go in alone?" Ethan asked.

"It really wasn't hard to snatch Mike Harris. He was totally hapless."

Gabriel instantly shook his head. "Out of the question. Nobody goes in alone. We can't take the risk."

Vanessa noticed how her brother let out a breath, but he didn't protest, even though she could tell that he wanted to.

Gabriel lifted several sheets of paper for everybody to see. "You can find your partner on these sheets together with the corresponding incel with his photo and home address. Sunrise is at six forty-seven. Get yourselves ready to go in at seven a.m. sharp. Make sure you're armed. Quinn will assign you your vans, and Amaury, Haven, and Yvette will help you equip them with everything you need."

Vanessa looked at the clock on the wall. They had a little over an hour until they needed to leave HQ.

"Once you're outside the incels' homes, send a message to the command center so we know you're in place," Gabriel added. "Be safe out there."

Everybody began talking at the same time, while some of the hybrids already headed for Gabriel to pick up their assignments.

Cole put his hand on her arm. "I'm coming with you."

Vanessa automatically shook her head. "You can't. This is a mission for the hybrids only. It's too dangerous for you."

"But I can't let you go out there unprotected. What if you get hurt?"

Patrick interrupted them, "Don't worry, bro, I'll make sure she doesn't get hurt." Then he looked at Vanessa. "You're on my team."

Vanessa rolled her eyes at Patrick. "Yeah, and I'll make sure *you* won't get hurt."

She reached for the piece of paper and looked at the information and the incel's photo. "This is our incel: Jeff Cramer. Five foot six and a hundred and twenty pounds soaking wet?" She made a dismissive hand movement. "Easy-peasy."

Cole looked over her shoulder at the paper. "Yeah, but he's a vampire. The one that attacked me wasn't much bigger."

She could hear the worry in Cole's voice, and took his arm. "Give us a moment, Patrick." She brought her face closer to Cole's, and lowered her voice, though she was sure that some of the people in the room would still be able to hear their conversation.

"Please, Cole, trust me on this. I can handle myself. You know it. You've seen it. And Patrick is a strong guy. And we both are as well trained as anyone at Scanguards. We've got this. I don't want you anywhere near this mission. I would only have to worry about you, and that would take my focus off the task at hand. And when I lose focus, things go wrong."

She noticed Cole take a deep breath. At first, it looked like he wanted to protest again, but then he nodded. "All right. Be careful out there."

Before she knew what he wanted to do, his lips were on hers, and he kissed her with the same passion as he'd showered her with when they'd made love earlier.

35

Vanessa sat behind the steering wheel of a Scanguards blackout van, while Patrick perused the information of their target again. She was glad that Cole hadn't fought her about wanting to ride along with them. In fact, it had even surprised her a little that he had given in rather quickly. Maybe the knowledge of how strong she was as a vampire hybrid had finally sunk in.

"We're almost there," Patrick confirmed.

They were in the Haight-Ashbury neighborhood of San Francisco, the center of Flower Power in the 1960s, a neighborhood with lots of Victorian single and multi-family homes as well as large apartment buildings built in the same style. The buildings butted up to each other, leaving very little to no space between them, other than perhaps a slim corridor that served as a space where the garbage bins were kept. The house where their suspect lived together with his parents was a single-family home and boasted a two-car garage, which was practically unheard of in this area where parking was a contact sport. In front of the house was a fire hydrant, which now provided a convenient parking spot since nobody else dared park in the red zone.

Vanessa parked in front of the fire hydrant and switched off the engine. "Let's get this bastard."

Patrick nodded in agreement, and they both exited the car. Vanessa walked around the car and caught up with him on the sidewalk. She glanced up and down the street. People were on their way to work, carrying coffee cups as they hurried to the bus stop or the MUNI stop. Nobody took any notice of them. Very few cars passed them, since most San Franciscans used public transport to get to work.

They walked up the few stairs to the entrance door. The plan was simple. They would ring the doorbell. The file had indicated that the incel's mother worked from home, and should therefore be home. The father worked at a bakery and would be at work already. They would claim that they were friends of Jeff, and ask to speak to him. If the human gave them any trouble, they would use mind control to gain access to the house. The rest would be easy. They'd grab the incel and cuff him with silver handcuffs, then Vanessa would go out to the van to get a heavy black tarp with which to cover the incel so they could get him into the van without turning him into dust. To finish their assignment, they would wipe his mother's memory, and leave with their suspect in the back of the van.

"Ready?" Patrick asked.

Vanessa nodded and pressed the doorbell. She heard the sound echoing from inside the house. She listened closely, but for a few seconds she heard nothing. No footsteps, no doors opening or closing, nothing at all. Had this incel also killed his parents like the one Patrick and Ethan had found the night before? Was that why nobody was coming to the door?

She exchanged a look with Patrick, who was already reaching into his jacket pocket to pull out his lockpicks, when there was a sound coming from inside the house. The shuffling of feet. Somebody was coming to the door.

A moment later, the door lock disengaged, and the door opened inwards by only a few inches, just enough for somebody to stick their head out. A human woman in her fifties held the door and gave them an indifferent look.

"Yes?"

"Mrs. Cramer. We're friends of Jeff's. Is he home?"

Her expression didn't change. "Yes, he's home." She made no effort to open the door wider to let them enter.

"Could we come in to talk to him, please?" Vanessa added, pasting a smile on her face.

Mrs. Cramer opened the door wider. "Yes, you can come in." Her voice was expressionless just like her face.

"Thank you," Vanessa said and entered the dark hallway.

Patrick entered the house behind her, and a moment later, Vanessa heard the door shut behind her.

"He's expecting you," Mrs. Cramer said from her spot at the door.

Vanessa looked over her shoulder, alerted by her odd words, when she caught a glimpse of the woman's wrists. They had abrasions that she recognized instantly: ligature marks. The woman had recently been tied up.

"It's a trap!" Vanessa yelled, alerting Patrick.

But it was too late. From the three open doors in the hallway, vampires emerged, two black men, and one Caucasian, charging at them with guns. Vanessa realized instantly that resistance was futile. It would take her longer to pull her own gun than it would take any of the three vampires to shoot her or Patrick. Her colleague had obviously come to the same conclusion, and lifted his hands just like Vanessa.

"Fuck," Patrick hissed, his gaze snapping to the white man. Vanessa recognized him too: Milo. Dressed in all black with garish dark-purple cowboy boots, he looked like the villain he was.

As two of the vampires approached, Milo remained standing with his gun pointed at them, it was clear what had happened. Mrs. Cramer had been tied up somewhere in the house, and the vampires had to untie her so she could open the door. In order to make her comply, they used mind control on her, which explained why she'd been so expressionless.

Vanessa cursed. She should have noticed this earlier.

The two black men disarmed her and Patrick, taking their guns, stakes, knives, and cell phones, before shoving them into a dark room.

"You're not gonna get away with this," Patrick threatened, glaring at Milo. "We know who you are." He made a dramatic pause. "Milo."

Milo laughed, and the cold sound slithered down her spine like a deadly snake. If only she'd acted faster, and recognized more quickly that something about Mrs. Cramer wasn't right, they could have realized that this was a trap and acted accordingly.

"Of course, you know who I am. That's all part of the plan," Milo claimed.

One of the black men put silver handcuffs around her wrists. Vanessa gritted her teeth, not wanting to show that the silver burned painfully into her flesh. Patrick was cuffed in the same way, with his hands behind him. He too clenched his jaw, not showing the pain the cuffs caused him.

Milo tipped his head into the direction of one of his henchmen. "Tie up the human bitch again. Or suck her dry. I don't care. We don't need her anymore."

The callous words echoed in the room where heavy curtains hung in front of the windows facing the street. The small window along the side that faced the wall of the house next to it, was covered with a thinner curtain which moved back and forth, indicating that the window wasn't fully closed.

Seeing no immediate way to get out of this situation, Vanessa addressed Milo, "What do you want?"

"Isn't that evident?" Milo chuckled. "I want everything."

Not sure what he meant, she decided to get him talking. Maybe HQ would figure out that they were staying far too long at their target location and come looking.

"We know about you turning those incels. The game is over," Vanessa said.

"The incels? You think that's my plan, turning some idiots who're totally worthless?" He motioned to the black guy who was still in the room, while the other had gone to tie up Mrs. Cramer. "Didn't I tell you that Scanguards are totally predictable?"

"You said it, boss."

Milo shook his head, turning his gaze back to her and Patrick. "The incels were only a diversion. I knew Thomas would figure out the pattern, and think himself a genius by sending his troops to pick up the incels."

Fuck! Milo had planned this? He'd wanted them to find the incels and capture them? She exchanged a look with Patrick.

"You'll never get away with this. Scanguards will get you," Patrick promised.

"I doubt that very much. After all, I've built an army in the last thirty-seven years. Men like this one here. Strong, loyal. Not useless like the incels." He shrugged. "You should be grateful. I saved you some work. The incels are all dead. Didn't want them to get in the way when the real plan starts."

Vanessa glanced at the door, where the other black vampire appeared, blood around his lips. He'd taken Milo's suggestion and fed from Mrs. Cramer. Whether she was still alive was anybody's guess.

Milo nodded at his henchman, then stepped closer to Patrick. "So, you're one of Samson's sons." He huffed. "Do you know what your father did?"

"Nothing as evil as you, I'm certain of that," Patrick replied.

A snarl issued from Milo's throat. "He killed my sister."

Patrick didn't flinch. "She deserved it."

Vanessa had to admit that Patrick was braver than she'd expected. He had a lot of his father in him, more than she'd previously seen.

Milo growled. "If I didn't already have a plan for you, I would stake you right here, boy. But I still need you. You'll be a nice bargaining chip."

"What do you want from my father?" Patrick asked.

"Didn't I already say that?" He huffed. "Maybe you should learn to listen, boy."

"I don't listen to scum like you."

Milo slapped Patrick so hard across his face that Patrick lost his balance and fell to the floor, hitting his shoulder on the tile around the fireplace.

"Not another word from you!" Milo

bellowed, before he waved to his henchmen. "Let's get them in the van. We're done here."

Vanessa looked at Patrick and knew he was hurting, but there was nothing she could do right now. She had to trust in her friends and colleagues at Scanguards that they would find them wherever Milo was taking them. One thing was clear: If Milo wanted to use them as bargaining chips, he needed them alive. At least for now.

36

Fuck!

The worst-case scenario had happened, just like Cole had feared. He hadn't been pleased about the fact that Vanessa and Patrick had gone to pick up the incel without him. Luckily, he'd gotten a quick glance at the sheet of paper with the incel's home address. After Vanessa and Patrick had left, he'd hurried back to his own car and made his way to the incel's house in Haight Ashbury. As expected, the

Scanguards blackout van was already parked outside the house.

He'd parked his car, illegally blocking a neighbor's driveway so he would be close enough, and exited his car. He didn't want to be seen by Vanessa and Patrick when they were leaving the house, so he'd slunk down the three-foot wide path next to the house that acted as a lightwell for the few windows on the side of the incel's house and that of his neighbor. When he'd noticed that one of the old sash windows wasn't fully closed, he'd seen his chance to find out what was going on inside the house.

The four-inch gap between the window frame and the window made it possible for him to hear what was going on inside the house, even though the curtain in front of it only offered a blurred view into the dark room. When he'd heard the menacing voice of the rogue vampire, and Vanessa's and Patrick's voices confirming that they recognized the man as Milo, he'd realized that they'd stepped into a trap.

Holding on to the window ledge with both hands, Cole lowered himself down to the ground. He jumped the last foot, and ran toward his car as fast as he could. He had to get in before Milo came out with his hostages. His pulse raced as he jumped into the driver's seat and turned on the engine. His heart pounded, and his palms were damp with perspiration, the fear of what was happening to the woman he loved, cutting off his oxygen.

He looked into the rearview mirror to watch the driveway and the garage. Nobody was parked in the driveway, which meant that the kidnappers had parked their getaway vehicle in the garage, most likely because as full-blooded vampires they couldn't get into their van while the sun was up. It seemed to take forever until the garage door finally opened. An instant later, a dark van similar to the one Vanessa and

Patrick had driven, shot out of it, and turned right.

Cole blessed his luck that the street was a one-way street, which meant that the kidnappers' van had to pass the spot where he was parked. After they passed him, he merged into traffic and followed them.

He reached into his pocket, and pulled out his cell phone. He had to call Scanguards, but he didn't have their main number. All he had was Gabriel's cell phone number. But it would have to do. Keeping one eye on the van, he scrolled to his recent call list, when in front of him, a motorcycle swerved and nearly collided with him, had he not stepped on the brake. His cell phone fell into the crack between his seat and the console in the middle.

"Fuck!"

He couldn't waste time reaching for the phone now. The traffic light ahead of him had already turned yellow, and the kidnappers' van had crossed the intersection. In order not to lose them Cole stepped on the gas to cross just as the light turned red.

Not being very familiar with San Francisco, he didn't know which way they were heading. All he was concerned with was not losing sight of the van that held Vanessa and Patrick. He could only hope that the van's driver and passengers didn't notice him following them. He was glad that he was driving the Land Rover and not the Aston Martin, which would have been much more conspicuous. At least the Land Rover wasn't much to look at. The paint was a dark greyish green and had dulled over the years. Nobody would give the car a second look. He hoped the kidnappers didn't either.

Traffic got heavier, and Cole read some of the street names. He recognized Van Ness Avenue, which they stayed on for only a few blocks, before veering off again onto a smaller street. Cole didn't catch the street name. Another car was between him and the van now, and while this probably helped should the kidnappers look in their rearview mirror, Cole knew that at every traffic light, he was running the risk of being separated from the van, unable to catch up with it.

Perspiration was running down his nape, disappearing beneath the collar of his shirt. He had no experience in tailing somebody, and surprised himself that he was still able to follow the van. He promised himself that when this was over, he'd take a master class in vehicular pursuit, if there was such a thing. And another class in how to defeat and kill a vampire. And whatever else was necessary so he would be able to accompany Vanessa next time she was sent on a dangerous mission. Because he knew enough about her already to know that she would never give up her job. He'd never be able to make her quit. So he might as well join her. But that was a conversation for later. Right now, he had to figure out where the kidnappers were taking their hostages.

After going underneath an overpass of one of the freeways, the van took a sharp left turn, then right again, before it turned into an alley. Cole was about to turn into the same alley, when he realized that it was a dead end. If he did that, they'd realize pretty quickly that he was tailing them. Cole stopped the car and looked down the alley. Milo's van turned to a garage on the left. It opened quickly, and the van pulled into the building, before the garage door closed with a loud rattling sound made by metal chains.

Cole took a breath. He'd made it this far. He put the car in park, but left the engine running. He reached between the front seats and fished his cell phone out. Quickly, he scrolled through his recent call list and found Gabriel's number. He punched it and put the cell phone to his ear.

"Cole?"

"Gabriel, listen carefully. Vanessa and Patrick stepped into a trap. Milo was waiting for them at the incel's house."

"Fuck!" Gabriel cursed. "How do you know—"

"I followed them. But that doesn't matter now."

"Are they alive?" Gabriel's voice trembled.

Cole glanced down the alley again, making sure the van didn't come back out. "Yes. Milo and his goons took them. They wanna use them as bargaining chips."

Cole could hear several voices in the background. It appeared that Gabriel had put him on speaker. "Oh, God."

"I know where they are," Cole said quickly, knowing that Gabriel was just as worried about Vanessa as he was. Maybe he should have led with that.

A sigh of relief came through the line.

"But I don't know the area," Cole added.

"Drop me a pin from your cell phone," Gabriel demanded.

"Right." Cole switched to his map app

and did as Gabriel had asked. "Here it is. Do you know where this is?"

"Yes. Are they in a building?"

"Yes, just off the alley that ends in a cul-de-sac."

"Got it."

Cole took a breath. "What are we gonna do now? We have to rescue them."

Suddenly, loud voices could be heard from Gabriel's phone, and several phones seemed to ring.

"What's going on, Gabriel?"

"Oh, fuck!" Gabriel cursed.

"Damn it, Gabriel. I asked you what we're gonna do now. We can't leave Vanessa and Patrick in the hands of that vampire! You need to get the other hybrids to where I am, so we can rescue them."

"Cole, listen carefully." Gabriel's voice was shaking. "The other hybrids were taken too. We just got word from Scarlet, Naomi, and Anita, the blood-bonded mates of three of them. Ryder, Damian, and Cooper contacted them via their telepathic bond that they were captured too."

"What?" He shook his head. "What telepathic bond?"

"I'll explain later. Just know that all of our sixteen hybrids have been kidnapped. Some are reporting that they're still in vans being transported."

"Fuck!" Cole cursed and looked into his rear window.

"Listen, you need to move your car, and park where you can see the entrance to the alley, but where they won't notice you," Gabriel said.

"But shouldn't I block them from bringing more hostages there?"

"No!" Gabriel's protest almost burst his eardrum. "We can't let them know that we already know where they brought the hostages. It'll put Vanessa and Patrick in danger. So, go and move the car. Do it quickly. I'll stay on the line."

Cole put the car in gear and crossed to

the far-left lane, then made an illegal U-turn and pulled into an available spot on the other side of the street. From there, he still had a perfect view into the alley.

"Okay, I'm in place. What now?"

"Do you have one of those phone holders in your car that has a suction cup?"

Cole felt his forehead furrow at the odd question. "Yeah, why?"

"Listen, and do exactly as I say..."

37

The silver handcuffs around Vanessa's wrists chafed, and she cursed quietly. She and Patrick weren't only handcuffed, a long silver chain was looped through the cuffs, chaining them to massive iron rings that were anchored in the concrete floor. And they weren't the only team that had gotten captured. Within a half hour after their arrival in the large industrial looking building, more of her colleagues arrived, similarly bound before they were chained up in the same manner.

The building looked like it had once been a large auto repair shop, though it also had a second floor. Two sets of stairs led to the upper story, and her sensitive hearing picked up footfalls from above. How many men were on the second floor, she couldn't tell.

In the van, Milo's men had put hoods over their heads so that they couldn't see where they were being held, though she was certain that they were still in the city. They hadn't driven for long.

When she saw both her brothers being brought in, Vanessa was both worried but also relieved. She managed to get close enough to Ryder to whisper to him.

"Have you contacted Scarlet?"

Because Ryder was blood-bonded, he had the unique ability to communicate telepathically with his mate, Scarlet. Just like the other two blood-bonded hybrids could: Damian and Cooper, both of whom had just arrived.

Ryder nodded, and whispered back, "She's already called HQ and alerted them that we were taken."

"Could you see where they brought us?" Vanessa asked.

Below his breath, he said, "No."

"Fuck," she cursed. It appeared the ability to communicate to HQ wouldn't help much if they didn't know where they were.

"Don't worry," Ryder added, keeping his eyes peeled on the vampires guarding them, and waiting for a moment when they weren't looking at them. "Cole followed you and Patrick. He's given Dad our location."

Relief washed over her. Cole was a stubborn man, and any other time she would have torn him a new one for not trusting that she could handle herself, but now he would actually be their salvation.

Ryder smiled at her. "I'm looking forward to meeting him properly."

Then Ryder fell silent and leaned back against the wall. Vanessa caught a glimpse of Damian too, and noticed that he was letting his eyes roam in the dimly-lit building, most likely telepathically sending information to his mate, Naomi.

Vanessa glanced around too. Milo was huddled in the far corner of the first floor, talking to several of his henchmen. She wasn't sure how many vampires were in his camp, but if he'd sent three to each incel's house to lay in wait, he had to have over forty men working for him.

By now, all hybrid teams had arrived in the building. Even Isabelle, Samson's daughter, was among them. She'd taken part in the mission, and while she showed no fear, as a mother of a toddler, she was most likely scared of what would happen if she didn't make it back. Vanessa could admit it to herself: she was scared too, because it was still morning, still daylight for another ten hours or so, which meant the cavalry wouldn't be arriving anytime soon.

Scanguards had sent all their hybrids out

into the field. There were none left who could mount a rescue operation during daylight hours. They could certainly use some of their human staff, perhaps aided by Wesley and Charles, the two witches in Scanguards' employ, but knowing Samson and her own father, she was almost certain that they wouldn't risk their children's lives by sending anybody but the A team. Which meant that they had to wait for nightfall.

Not all of Milo's vampires were in the same area as Vanessa and her colleagues. Some of them could easily be on the upper floor, or in some other corner, hidden from her. It was of course also possible that they were hiding in a neighboring building, maybe to attack from the flanks and the back once Scanguards tried to rescue the hostages.

After a while, Ryder leaned closer and whispered, "Were any of the men that took you and Patrick hybrids?"

She found the question odd. "No, why?"

"HQ wants to know."

She glanced down to the area where Damian was chained up. He too was whispering something to the hybrids next to him, and she could only assume that he'd been posed the same question by their superiors.

It could only mean that HQ was already working on a rescue plan. She doubted that Milo had any idea that several of his hostages were secretly communicating with their spouses and were passing information back to Scanguards. She hoped it would remain that way. It gave them an advantage, and if Milo really had over forty vampires on his side, they needed any advantage they could get.

All of a sudden, there was some activity in the corner where Milo was talking to his men. Vanessa watched closely, when she noticed that Milo and three of his men were approaching. All whispers subsided instantly, and all hybrids watched the kidnappers approaching.

Milo stopped a few feet away from the corner where all sixteen hybrids were tied up and looked at each of them as if trying to choose one. He grunted, then pointed to Grayson.

"Well, look at you. So much like your father," Milo said, his voice calm and almost friendly, though the evil glint in his eyes betrayed his words. There was nothing friendly about him.

"What about it?" Grayson spit, rising to his feet.

Monique, his mate who was chained a few feet away from him, cast him a warning glance.

"You shouldn't even exist," Milo claimed. "Nor your siblings."

He pointed to Isabelle and Patrick, and it was clear that Milo had done his homework. Most likely he knew all his captives' names and whose sons and daughters they were.

Grayson didn't take the bait, and remained silent. Vanessa had to admit that she was surprised. The old Grayson would have started an argument that most likely would have gotten him killed right here and now. But the new Grayson, the man who'd blood-bonded with a vampire princess, was smarter and knew when to pick a fight, and when to hold back.

"I should have killed your mother myself, when I had the chance," Milo taunted.

Next to her, Vanessa felt Patrick tense up. She put her hands on his arm to stop him from doing something stupid. With a nod he acknowledged that he would remain calm like his older brother.

"I'm assuming you want something from my father," Grayson said in calm tones. "Milo, is it?"

"I see I haven't been forgotten," Milo answered with a smirk. "Even though I hear that Thomas moved on. Got himself a boy toy."

Surprised at Milo's comment, Vanessa wondered whether Milo was still pining for Thomas. Or was it just another remark to show his disdain with anybody connected to Samson and Scanguards?

"I'm really grateful to him. Thomas let me live, when he should have killed me. Ah, he was always too soft for his own good. Too weak." Milo shrugged, then his voice changed, turning icy in a second. "So here's how this is gonna go. I'll send my demands to Samson. He'll have one hour to comply, and for every hour that he doesn't, we'll kill one of you."

He pointed to one of his associates, who lifted a cell phone in the air so everybody could see it.

"And Clint here will send the video recording to him so he'll see that we're not bluffing." Milo chuckled. "And just to make it interesting, we won't tell him with whom we start. It could be you." He pointed to

Grayson. "Or you." He turned and pointed to Damian.

"Or you." He pointed to Vanessa, and her heart instantly began to pound into her throat, cutting off her airflow.

Milo let out a chuckle, and the three vampires next to him joined in. He cast a glance at Grayson.

"Now sit down, or I'll stake you just for fun."

Vanessa could see the tightness in Grayson's jaw as he suppressed an angry reaction, before he sat down without letting Milo bait him. She was surprised that Milo hadn't mentioned what his demands were, but she could guess. After having failed stealing Samson's millions thirty-seven years ago, he was giving it another try, this time with an army behind him. But would he also demand a life in exchange for his sister's? Even though Vanessa knew next to nothing about Milo, a look at him told her more than she ever wanted to know. Milo wanted more than just money. He wanted retribution.

38

Cole jumped out of the taxi he'd taken to Scanguards' headquarters building and hurried into the foyer.

The receptionist waved at him. "They're in the command center. They're expecting you."

He's never met the woman before, and could only assume that Gabriel had already sent word to her to expect him. With a quick word of acknowledgement, Cole hurried down the corridor, jumped into the elevator and headed to the floor where the command center was located.

He'd left his car opposite the alley the kidnappers had entered and gotten a quick lay of the land to determine in which building the kidnappers were holding the hostages, before hailing a taxi to take him to HQ.

When he entered the command center, the room was chock-full of vampires, some of whom he hadn't seen at the meeting a few hours earlier. Gabriel waved him to approach, and Cole paved his way through the crowd to join him at the computer console where he and Samson stood.

On the monitors behind him, a multitude of live feeds without sounds were showing scenes. One he recognized instantly. It was a video feed from his cell phone, which he'd affixed inside the passenger window in a way so it was pointed directly at the alley. It would alert them if any of the vampires were leaving, or if more of them were arriving.

Gabriel put a hand on his shoulder. "I can't even tell you how grateful we all are. Without you, we would have no idea where Milo took our kids."

Samson squeezed Cole's shoulder for a moment, then pointed to three young women. Cole looked at them. He recognized Scarlet immediately, but had never seen the two blond women before.

"Naomi, Scarlet, and Anita are communicating with their blood-bonded mates telepathically. But it appears that all hybrids were blindfolded," Samson said, "and therefore couldn't give us any information as to their whereabouts. So, thank you, Cole. You did good."

"We have the same goal. Get our loved ones back."

Cole let the words sink in, and even though he wanted to know why these three women could communicate telepathically with their husbands, he knew there was no time for long explanations now. They had to mount a rescue operation.

"Did any of the vans leave?" Cole asked.

"No, they're all still in the building," Gabriel replied.

The curvy woman with the long blonde curls tapped on a microphone, sending a crackling sound through the loudspeakers in the room, silencing the murmurs and hushed conversations.

"Damian is reporting that there are at least forty-five vampires working for Milo. And they're pretty sure that there are no hybrids among them."

"Thanks, Naomi," Samson said, and turned to the others. "Then our plan might work. Thomas, where are the drones?"

Thomas moved from one computer to another, and tapped on something. Several of the camera feeds became smaller to make room for another projection. This was an aerial shot, flying over the rooftops of San Francisco.

"We have three drones in the air, each one of them covering a slightly different section." Thomas looked over his shoulder. "Cole, is that the building?"

Cole took a step closer to Thomas, and took Thomas's mouse to point to it. "That's it."

"Good," Thomas said and took the mouse again. "One of the drones is equipped with infrared cameras, so we can get an idea of where in the buildings the hybrids are held."

Thomas switched to the drone with the infrared camera, and a bunch of yellow, orange, and red dots appeared on the screen. Some of the dots were so close together that it was impossible to see how many people were huddled together, because they became a continuous warm area.

"From previous tests with our infrared cameras, we know that hybrids and pureblood vampires show up with slightly different heat signatures and—"

Thomas was interrupted, when a beeping sound suddenly came from the computer console in front of Samson. Everybody seemed to hold their breath, as did Cole, while he watched Samson press a button.

"Milo, I was expecting your call," Samson said, his jaw tightening.

"And I was expecting you to catch on a little earlier." Milo's voice came through the loudspeakers in the command center for everybody to hear. "Frankly, I'm a little disappointed in your IT staff that they didn't figure out earlier that the incels were just a diversion."

"What do you want?"

"Oh, right down to business? No reminiscing about the past? No *where have you been all these years*? Well, all right then." Milo blew out an audible breath. "Here it goes. Wire all cash in Scanguards', as well as your personal accounts, to a Swiss bank. I'll text you the details. And don't cheat me. I know down to the penny how much you have in all your accounts. You have one hour to complete the transaction. If the money isn't in my account by then, I'll kill the first hybrid. I'll pick one at random. Maybe it'll be your son, or your daughter, or one of Amaury's sons."

Cole could see the tension in Samson's face, but his voice remained calm as he replied, "Send the account information."

"What? No haggling? No threats? Wow, having children really made you soft."

A chuckle echoed through the loudspeaker, and Cole felt as if a snake slithered down his spine.

"Why waste time? We know you have the upper hand. And I'm not stupid enough to underestimate you."

"That's good to know. Oh, and now the second part of my demand."

Cole watched as the vampires in the room exchanged surprised looks.

"Go on," Samson demanded.

"When the money is in my account, I'll send you a location. I want Amaury."

"What do you want with him?"

"Isn't that obvious? You said it yourself back then: Amaury staked Ilona. So, it's only fair that I take his life for hers. Or would you rather I chose you?"

Samson exchanged a look with Amaury, who now lifted his hand to stop Samson from replying. Instead, Amaury raised his voice. "I can't wait to do to you what I did to your sister."

"Still the same bravado as always. You really haven't changed, Amaury. You know, I never liked you."

"The feeling is mutual."

"Whatever." Then Milo's voice changed. "Oh, and Thomas, if you're trying to trace this call, good luck, but I've learned a thing or two since you and I were an item. Not even you will be able to follow the signal. Samson, you've got one hour."

There was a click, and Milo was gone. Another ping sounded, and one of the screens showed the banking information Milo had promised. On the screen next to it, a clock started counting backwards.

Samson turned to the assembled vampires. "Everybody, down to the supply rooms. Let's get suited up. Thomas, you know what to do here."

Thomas shook his head and put his hand on Eddie's arm. "Eddie will run things from here. I'm coming with you."

Thomas rose from his chair.

"Thomas, you don't need to—"

"Samson, I have to. It's my fault. I'll put it right. Milo will die today, even if it's the last thing I'll ever do."

Cole watched as Thomas and Eddie exchanged a long look, but neither said another word. It was as if they understood each other without words. Or could they, too, communicate telepathically?

"What can I do?" Cole asked, his gaze ping-ponging between Samson and Gabriel.

"I suppose I won't be able to convince you to stay here with Eddie?" Gabriel said, grimacing.

"No. Vanessa is with that madman. There's no way I'll stay here twiddling my thumbs."

"Figured." Gabriel waved him to follow, then looked at Samson. "Guess we'll have to arm him."

Samson nodded. "Just as well that Luther got us a large supply of guns from the prison."

"Guns?" Cole asked. "But I thought vampires could only be killed with stakes?"

Gabriel put his hand on Cole's shoulder. "I'll explain on the way."

39

Twenty-five minutes after Milo's phone call, Cole sat in the back of one of the blackout vans. Gabriel, who sat next to him, shoved his cell phone back into his pocket.

"The police have blocked off the streets around the building, advising motorists and pedestrians that there's a dangerous gas leak. No civilians are allowed in the area. Press helicopters are also banned."

"But what if the vampires in the building notice that there's suddenly no traffic going by?" Cole asked. "Won't they get suspicious?"

"No, because there will be traffic. We've dispatched a couple dozen of our Vüber drivers to drive back and forth on these streets instead. And I've arranged for a little distraction," Gabriel promised.

Cole was surprised at how quickly Scanguards had gotten ready to come to the hybrids' aid. Two dozen vampires, women and men, had put on full-body Kevlar suits that covered every inch of their body, then added a large helmet that made sure their head wouldn't be exposed to the rays of the sun. In their gloved hands, the vampires carried guns. When Cole had seen them the first time, he'd assumed they were toy guns, because they looked like they were made of black plastic. But according to Gabriel they were deadly to a vampire.

"Are you sure those guns will kill the vampires?" Cole asked, pointing at the weapon in Gabriel's hand.

"Trust me, the UV-rays they emit will turn any unprotected vampire to dust in seconds." He pointed to one of the other vampires in the van. "Isn't that right, Luther?"

Luther nodded. "We use the same guns at the vampire prison in Grass Valley, though I recently made a little adjustment to the ones Scanguards has." He winked. "They have a little more power behind them, but they need to be recharged more often."

"You mean they're gonna run out of juice in the middle of the fight?" Cole asked, alarmed.

"Doubt it," Luther claimed.

"Team one and two, to the front entrance. Team three and four, to the alley." Samson's voice came through the earpiece everybody wore, even Cole.

He was also wearing a bullet-proof vest, but no helmet. There hadn't been enough equipment to dress him in the same fashion as the vampires. Cole didn't mind. The

Kevlar suits looked heavy, and would make it hard for him to move. The vampires didn't seem to be worried about the weight of their uniform. Gabriel and Luther put the visors of their helmets down, as did the other two vampires in the van. One of them slid the side door open, and one by one, they exited the van.

Gabriel's team was assigned to the alley entrance of the building. From the blueprints they'd studied before leaving HQ, they knew that the building the hybrids were held in also had exits to the main street, but on that side, there was no garage door, meaning if Milo's men wanted to escape during daytime, they could only do so from the alley side, leaving in one of their vans.

Scarlet, Naomi, and Anita were in one of the other vans, making sure that the hybrids knew when to expect the rescue team, and informing the rescue team of the goings-on in the building. The drones were still in the air, but wouldn't be much help once the Scanguards teams entered the building.

"Cole, stay behind us at all times," Gabriel cautioned.

With a nod, Cole acknowledged the demand and followed the six vampires who crossed the street, looking like a military special ops team. He glanced at the cars on the street, and noticed that they stopped without complaining to let them cross unimpeded. In their windshields, he noticed a red V sticker. This had to be the Vüber drivers Gabriel had mentioned, and he now realized what they were: a driving service for vampires.

Arriving at the entrance to the alley, onto which the van carrying Vanessa had disappeared, Cole's heart was pounding out of control. Despite the fact that Scanguards was clearly experienced in operations like this, he was worried. Too much could go wrong.

Vanessa listened for any sounds coming from the outside of the building. She knew from Ryder that Scanguards was on their way, but there hadn't been occasion to talk in detail about what they were planning, because some of Milo's henchmen were too close to the chained hybrids, and could overhear their conversations. They couldn't risk tipping them off. Everything depended on the element of surprise.

She wasn't sure how much time had passed since Milo had made his demand. Everybody on the ground floor had heard him speak to Samson. Was the hour nearly up? She felt her heart beat faster. While they were all chained to the big iron rings on the floor, they were sitting ducks. Their kidnappers were carrying weapons, and she was sure that they were loaded with silver bullets.

Vanessa's ears suddenly perked up. She

heard a sound of metal scratching against something. The sound was coming from somewhere near the doors to the alley. Her gaze snapped to the two vampires who were guarding the hybrids, and she realized that they had heard something too. Fuck! She couldn't allow them to go to the door and investigate the sound.

Making a spit-second decision, she lifted her hands and rose. "Excuse me, hey," she said loudly, addressing the two vampires.

Both snapped their heads in her direction, instantly alert, raising their weapons slightly.

"Sit down!" one of them ground out.

"I'm sorry, really sorry," Vanessa continued. "But I have to pee." She crossed her legs to pretend that it was urgent. "There must be a restroom somewhere in here. Please."

"You're gonna have to hold it!"

The other vampire let his fangs extend and snarled in her direction. She pretended to feel frightened and gasped loudly, drowning out the scratching sound from the door. She was certain now that somebody was picking the lock.

"I'm sorry," she added, just as loudly, and raised her arms in surrender. "It's just that I drank a lot of coffee this morning."

"Fucking hybrids!" the vampire griped. "Serves you right for eating human food!"

"Now sit down!" the other guard added.

Slowly, Vanessa dropped down next to Patrick, exchanging a brief look with him. A second later, there was a sound of a siren approaching. It came from the front of the building that was abutting the main road.

Several of the vampires ran in that direction, calling commands out to each other, when someone from the stairs that led up to the second floor called out, "It's a fire truck."

Milo came running and headed to the stairs, while the siren was still wailing outside. "What's it doing?"

A second passed, before the answer came. "It stopped on the other side of the street. Looks like there's smoke coming from the building across."

Vanessa exchanged a clandestine glance with Ryder, who nodded confidently. This was the diversion. She felt her body tense. It was time.

The door was pushed open an instant later, and all hell broke loose. A man in a full-body Kevlar suit entered, his head hidden behind a helmet with a reflecting visor. From the gun in his hand, a strong ray of light was emitted. It hit the vampire closest to the hybrids with full blast, vaporizing him in less than a second. Behind the Kevlar-clad men, others swarmed the building. The next ray of the UV-gun turned the second guard into dust. The kidnappers were screaming, running for cover and reaching for their weapons.

When she saw a movement in the corner of her eye, Vanessa's gaze shot to the stairs.

She caught sight of Milo who, instead of running upstairs, went around the staircase to the area where the vans were parked. He disappeared behind them, and she lost sight of him.

Following the first team of Scanguards rescuers, who now moved deeper into the building, several other figures also clad in Kevlar, came running, carrying shields. Vanessa recognized them as the kind of shields the police used for crowd control.

The vampires entering with the shields rushed to the area where the hybrids were tied up and shielded them to protect them from the kidnappers in case they could get off a shot to hurt or kill one of the hostages.

Vanessa let her gaze roam, and noticed that more Kevlar-clad rescuers were entering from the front of the building where the firetruck was still parked and making noise. They too were armed with UV-ray guns and now attacked the kidnappers from the other side, herding them into a corner where Milo's men managed to hide behind old machinery. There was no escape from that corner. Even though Milo's henchmen shot at the Scanguards staff, their bullets didn't penetrate the Kevlar suits.

Meanwhile, two more Kevlar-clad vampires entered, both of them equipped with bolt cutters, blocking her view of the goings-on in the building. As fast as they could, they cut through the hybrids' chains and handcuffs. Vanessa was one of the first to be freed. She rose to her feet, when she saw Cole. He wore a bullet-proof vest, but no other protection, though he had a handgun in his hand.

"Cole!" she called out to him, running toward him.

Before she reached him, her gaze fell onto the stairs again, and she was reminded of the vampires that were hiding on the second floor.

"Dad! Orlando! Amaury!" she yelled in the direction of the biggest vampires. When two of them turned their heads to her, she pointed to the stairs. "There are more of them upstairs."

With a quick nod, three of them now rushed toward the stairs, while two others hurried to the stairs at the other side of the building. Relieved, Vanessa turned to Cole. He was only a couple of feet away from her, and now pulled her into his arms.

"I was so worried," he said and squeezed her to him.

"It's too dangerous for you here." Vanessa freed herself from his embrace and grabbed him by his arm. "You need to get out of here. There are more vampires upstairs."

She pulled him with her as she headed for the door. From the corner of her eye, she noticed that her Kevlar-clad colleagues were still firing UV-rays at the remaining vampires who had barricaded themselves behind some machinery and were firing wildly in the direction of their enemies.

When a bullet whizzed past her, hitting one of the blacked-out windows overlooking the alley, she pushed Cole down toward the ground, guessing that more bullets were coming. As she covered Cole and raised her head to see which way was safest to escape, she saw somebody's legs between the parked vans. She recognized the tacky purple cowboy boots instantly: Milo.

"Shit!"

"You hurt?" Cole asked, turning his head to cast her a worried glance.

"No." She pointed in the direction of the vans. "Milo is trying to escape."

"Fuck!" Cole cursed. "We've gotta stop him."

Vanessa let her eyes roam to assess the situation. The vampires who'd come in with the police shields were already ushering the unarmed hybrids out of the building, because without weapons and protective clothing, they could still become a casualty to the remaining rogues who were still fighting. Several members of Scanguards' rescue team were on the second floor, and by the sounds coming from there, they were fighting with Milo's men who'd tried to hide upstairs.

The vans in between which Milo was hiding, were cutting off Vanessa's direct line of sight to the corner from where several of Milo's men were shooting at the Scanguards staff. They wouldn't hear her now, the noise too loud.

"Cole, give me your gun," Vanessa demanded. "I'll stop Milo. You stay here."

"Fat chance," Cole protested. "I'm wearing a bullet-proof vest. You're not. I'll get him."

Cole already rushed toward the vans.

"Fuck!" she cursed and went after him. As she ran, she saw a wooden stake on the ground, lying amid ash, the remains of one of the rogue vampires. She picked it up quickly. She reached Cole where he was pressing himself to the back of one of the vans, his gun raised, trying to look past it to see where Milo was. Vanessa gritted through her teeth, "Stubborn idiot!"

"Yeah, well, get used to it." Cole bridged the distance between this van and the next, then stopped there, while Vanessa followed him. Again, he cast a glance past the corner of the van. "Fuck!"

Cole didn't have to tell her why he cursed, because Vanessa saw it too. The engine of the van next to the one they were hiding behind was running. The brake lights were illuminated. Milo was already in the van.

"Shoot the tires," Vanessa advised.

"Good idea." Cole shot the left back tire, then aimed for the front one, deflating this one too.

Vanessa heard a sound coming from the van. Somebody was opening the door, but it wasn't the driver's door.

"He's trying to get out the passenger

side," she whispered to Cole. "I'll go around the back."

"Wait, you're not armed."

She lifted her hand, showing him the wooden stake. She could see Cole's displeasure.

"Damn it. You'll have to get too close to him to use that."

"Distract him." Without waiting for his reply, she peered around the corner of the van Milo had just left. The passenger door was still open, but Milo was nowhere to be seen. "Fuck!"

Her eyes shot to the front of the van, when she saw movement there. She saw the muzzle of a handgun, and ducked, when she heard a sound to her left. The side door of the van slid open loudly. In her crouching position, she took a split second too long to whirl around and rise. Milo jumped onto her, the impact making her lose her stake, her back slamming against the other van. A shot rang out, and the window of the van shattered into a thousand pieces, but Cole's bullet had missed its target.

She caught Cole's horrified look as he aimed again, but didn't shoot. She knew why: she and Milo were moving too fast, trading blows and punches. One hard strike sent her reeling, while Milo's gun went off, before it dropped to the ground. She blinked, and realized that Cole wasn't at the front of the van anymore. Had the bullet hit him? Panic surged through her as she lost her balance. Before she could crash to the ground, and Milo could pick up his gun, somebody pushed her out of the way.

In the next instant, she saw Cole. He pulled her back toward the protection of the other van, while a Kevlar-clad vampire squeezed past her, his UV-ray gun pointed at Milo. She saw him pull the trigger, but no UV-light ray fired at Milo.

"Fuck!" He tossed the UV-ray gun to the ground, and reached into a pocket.

Milo fired his gun, and while he hit his

Kevlar-clad opponent, the bullet didn't penetrate the suit. Vanessa saw the wooden stake in her colleague's hand. Milo fired again, and shrank back, but the open passenger door prevented his escape.

"I should have killed you thirty-seven years ago." She recognized Thomas's voice now. "Better late than never." He lifted his arm and plunged the stake into Milo's heart.

A second later, ash rained onto the ground, and Milo's gun and several metal items hit the floor. Thomas turned around and lifted his visor. At the same time, Vanessa realized that it had gotten quiet in the building.

"It's over," Thomas said, his voice flat.

"You saved my life, Thomas. Thank you." Vanessa let out a sigh of relief, and turned to look at Cole, who was crouching on the floor with her. She squeezed him. "Are you hurt?"

He shrugged. "Just a few bruises. Nothing your blood won't heal."

For the first time in hours, Vanessa smiled. "You scared me. You should have stayed at HQ."

"That's what your father said too. And I wasn't afraid of displeasing him either," Cole claimed. "So, guess what. I'm not afraid of you punishing me for disobeying your orders." He smirked. "In fact, I'm looking forward to it."

She boxed him gently in his shoulder. "You're such an idiot."

"Yeah, but you love me nevertheless."

"Can't argue with that." She brought her lips to his and kissed him. "Let's go home."

40

Cole looked at the couples on the dance floor in the V lounge, a large room in the Scanguards headquarters building that was reserved for vampires and their families. The reason for it was what the bar served here: blood on tap. And not just one type of human blood but all of them, and it was free. However, not all vampires and hybrids partook of it, because the vampires who were blood-bonded to humans could only drink their mates' blood.

The assembled vampires, hybrids, and

their families looked relaxed and carefree as if the ordeal they'd all been through earlier in the day had simply washed off them like rain cleared the air. It had been a little harder for him to rid himself of the fear and the worry he'd felt when he'd found out that Vanessa had been captured. He never wanted to feel those feelings again, but he knew somehow that putting themselves in danger was par for the course for any Scanguards employee. He knew that he had a snowball's chance in hell of convincing Vanessa to quit her job. What she did was a part of her, and she wouldn't be the woman he loved if he tried to change her.

Since the rescue earlier in the day, he and Vanessa hadn't had any time alone. They'd been surrounded by her colleagues, friends, and family. Vanessa had introduced him to everyone he hadn't met yet, and he felt at home among the preternatural creatures who seemed so human in their interactions. He felt at home for the first time in the many years since he'd lost his father. At the thought of him, he felt pain in his heart. His father would have been accepted by these people. They could have been his family. And he could have found love among them. He knew this pain would always be within him, though he also knew that the rest of his heart would be filled with love. The love of a good woman. The love of a family. The love of this preternatural community.

Gabriel approached and put a hand on his shoulder. "You all right, Cole? Still a little shaken?"

"I'm calmer now. But I've been thinking about my dad." He gestured to the happy crowd. "He would have been at home here."

"And we would have welcomed him with open arms," Gabriel replied. There was a moment's pause, then he added, "Cole, wanna join me and Samson for a quick word?"

"Sure." Cole set his glass of whiskey on a

nearby table and followed him, as they made their way to the fireplace, where Samson stood.

"Samson." Cole extended his hand.

Samson shook it. "Cole, it's good to see you."

"Likewise."

Samson and Gabriel exchanged a look, before Samson began, "I wanted to speak to you because you turned out to be an integral part of the rescue operation today—"

"You've already thanked me for that earlier," Cole interrupted.

"It's not about that. It's about an offer I have for you."

Cole raised his eyebrows. "Yes?"

"We would like you to join us here at Scanguards. I understand that you have your own company, and maybe you don't have the time or the interest—"

"The company runs itself," Cole said quickly. He wasn't really needed for the day-to-day. And if he was honest, what he'd done today had been exciting despite the danger they'd all been in. The thought of being part of Scanguards definitely piqued his interest.

Gabriel grinned, and Samson continued, "While I would love for you to use your skills by working in logistics, there's something we require from all of our team members before that can happen."

Curious, Cole looked at Samson. Was he asking him if he wanted to be turned into a vampire? "Samson, if it means for me to become a—"

"A bodyguard," Samson interrupted.

"A bodyguard?" Cole let out a relieved laugh. "Fuck, yeah, sure. I thought you wanted me to become a vampire, but I don't want that..."

He caught Samson's and Gabriel's glances. Had he just insulted them? That wasn't his intention. "Not that I wouldn't be honored," he added quickly.

Gabriel stopped him with a hand on his

shoulder. "My daughter would stake me personally if we turned you into a vampire."

"I would do it, really, if it was the only way to be with Vanessa," Cole assured him, "but she mentioned that a vampire's mate can live just as long..."

Gabriel smirked. "I'm glad she explained that to you. And I'm sure you know that she enjoys drinking your blood. I have no intention of robbing her of that if that's also what you want."

"She told you that?" He felt a little embarrassed to be talking about this with his future father-in-law.

"She doesn't have to. I can see it."

Cole acknowledged Gabriel's words with a nod.

Samson grinned. "But we would like you to undergo our bodyguard training."

"You would do that?" Cole asked, excited. "I would love to learn skills that can help me protect her."

"Protect me?" Vanessa's soft voice came

from behind him. She put her arm around his waist and stepped next to him. There was a sparkle in her eyes when she looked at him. "I thought I was the one meant to protect *you*."

"I believe today I was the one protecting you," he said meeting her gaze with a smirk. "Not that I'm looking for a thank you or anything."

Vanessa beamed at him, but before she could say anything, Gabriel interrupted. "I think that's our cue to leave these two alone, Samson."

"You're right about that," Samson replied. "So, we're in agreement?" He extended his hand to Cole, and he shook it without hesitation.

"Yes!"

"Welcome to the team, Cole."

"Thank you. Both of you."

As they disappeared in the crowd of Scanguards employees and family members, Cole turned to Vanessa. "How about a dance as a thank you for your rescuer?"

"Is that all you want?" Her eyelashes fluttered.

"That's all I want right here. All the other ways I've come up with for you to thank me... Well, I'd rather not have anybody watch, no matter how much I like your family and friends."

"I can't wait to find out what you've planned," she murmured seductively.

He led her to the dance floor and pulled her into his arms. Slow music came through the hidden loudspeakers in the ceiling, and they swayed to the rhythm of the music. It felt good to hold her, to know they were both safe here among their friends and her family.

Cole caught sight of Thomas and Eddie dancing, whispering to each other, gazing into each other's eyes. For a moment, he couldn't stop looking at them. Thomas had saved Vanessa's life, and killed Milo without a moment's hesitation. What was going through him now? After all, Milo had been his lover once.

"Is Thomas okay?" he asked, looking into Vanessa's face.

A soft smile played around Vanessa's lips. "He will be. He's a strong guy. And he's got Eddie. I'm sure it wasn't easy for Thomas. It's one thing to kill a bad guy you don't know, it's another to have to kill one that you once loved. Though in either case, it's not easy."

Her words reminded him of what Vanessa had done for him, when she'd staked the vampire who'd attacked him not far from his condo. "I'm sorry you had to kill for me."

"I would do it again in a heartbeat."

Cole stroked over her cheek. "I would do the same for you. I want you to know that."

She pressed her cheek into his palm. "And I hope that you'll never have to kill for me or for anybody else."

He slid his lips over hers and kissed her gently. "Would it be rude if we left the party early?"

"How early?"

"Right now."

"I don't think anybody will notice. Look around."

When he let his eyes roam, he realized that everybody only had eyes for their partners.

He smirked. "Then what are we still doing here?"

41

Vanessa stepped out of Cole's bathroom, wearing a sexy negligee she'd shoved into the travel bag she'd brought from her home. In a few days, she would move all her things into Cole's condo, but for the next few days she wouldn't need many clothes.

When she entered the bedroom, Cole sat on the bed, completely naked. Her gaze drifted to his groin, his twin erections greeting her. She hadn't expected anything less. Something unspoken lay between them. They both knew it; they didn't have to say what they both wanted: an unbreakable bond between them. A bond that would last for eternity.

"You're beautiful," he murmured, and their eyes met. "I don't know why I got so lucky."

"Nor I," she replied and cast a glance at his two cocks.

Cole chuckled in that husky tone that sank deep into her body and ignited a flame in her center. "I'm glad you like what you see."

He wrapped his hand around his lower cock and tugged on it, then did the same to his upper one, beckoning her to approach. She licked her lips and slid her knee onto the bed, crawling toward him.

"Do I get to taste them?" she whispered, bending over his groin.

"Just for a few seconds, or you're gonna make me come," he cautioned. "And I don't wanna come yet. Not tonight."

"Mmm," she hummed and wrapped her

lips around his upper cock, then slid down on him, her saliva making the descent smooth.

"Fuck!" Cole cursed.

A smile stole onto her lips. She liked how he reacted to her caress. She allowed his cock to slip from her mouth, then took his lower cock into her mouth and sucked him in a slow and steady rhythm, her hands on his thighs to steady herself. Cole gasped, his muscles tensing under her hands. Another second, and he placed his hands on her shoulders and pulled himself from her mouth.

"Fuck, baby! Have some mercy on this poor human," he demanded.

"Not just any human; my human." She looked into his eyes.

"Care to make it official?" As if trying to tempt her, he tilted his head to the side, offering his neck.

"Is that a proposal?"

"More of a demand," he admitted. "I'll

propose later when I've had a chance to buy you a ring."

His words warmed her heart and made it beat in an excited rhythm. "You don't need a ring to propose."

He shook his head. "I do. Because you, my love, deserve a real proposal, with me on my knees, a sparkling diamond ring for you. But since I haven't had any occasion to find the perfect ring for you, all I can offer you right now is my blood—" He stroked his hand over his carotid artery. "—and my heart."

Overwhelmed by his tender and heartfelt words, she moved over him, straddling him so his cocks were imprisoned between their bellies.

"That's all I really want. Your blood and your heart." She brushed her lips over his for a featherlight kiss. "And what can I offer you in exchange?" she asked, even though she already knew.

"Your heart. And your blood, so I can

stay young for you. Young and strong." He pressed her closer to him, so she could feel his hard-ons more intensely.

"Mmm. It looks like I get the better deal out of this. A heart, all the blood I could ever want, and two hard cocks to do with as I please."

"Then how about you show me what you want to do with them?"

Cole saw a golden shimmer in Vanessa's irises and saw his own love for her reflected in it. Not waiting for her to act upon his demand, he gripped the seam of her short negligee and pulled it over her head, revealing her perfect body. Her nipples were hard, and her skin glistened. He caressed her firm breasts, while he leaned in and captured her lips for the kiss he'd been craving ever since they'd left the party.

Vanessa's response to his kiss was

passionate, and he could feel her heat as if a fire was burning inside her. She raised herself onto her knees, and a moment later he felt her guide his lower erection to her pussy. With the tip of his shaft, he felt her arousal, her juices coating him instantly when she impaled herself on him in one swift move.

All air rushed from his lungs, her interior muscles gripping him so tightly that he thought he'd lose control right there and then. Vanessa released his lips, pressed him back into the sheets, and began to ride him.

He feasted his eyes on the gorgeous woman who rode his cock in an excruciatingly slow tempo, clearly intent on killing him with pleasure. But he wouldn't be the only one who'd die of pleasure tonight. Cole took hold of his upper cock and pressed it toward her, so that it rubbed over her clit with every descent and every withdrawal. Vanessa moaned and dropped her head back, her long dark hair swinging back and forth.

She looked like a goddess, like a creature from another world, from a world that he was now part of. A world that promised to give him the love and acceptance he'd craved all his life. A world where vampires were real, where loyalty protected, where love ruled.

"I love you, Vanessa," he murmured at her lips before recapturing them for a deep kiss. His hips moved in synch with each of her movements, while he continued to rub his second cock over her clit to drive her to ecstasy.

Soft moans and sighs bounced off the walls of his bedroom, and the sound echoed in his body, where his heart beat rapidly, and spears of pleasure pierced him to leave their mark on him.

When Vanessa suddenly ripped her lips from his, he noticed that her fangs were descending. It was time. His breath was ragged now, and the knowledge that she would bury her fangs in his neck and drink his blood, made his cocks even harder.

Fascinated, he watched as her fingers turned into razor-sharp claws, and she cut into the skin of her shoulder with it, making blood ooze from the small wound.

"I love you, Cole," she murmured.

He pulled her closer, until he could lick over the wound and lap up the blood. "Fuck!" Her blood tasted like pure paradise.

Before he could tell her what this meant to him, Vanessa lowered her mouth to his neck and pierced his skin with her sharp fangs. He jerked involuntarily, then felt the pull on his carotid artery, followed by pure and utter bliss.

Cole set his lips to the cut on Vanessa's shoulder and sucked on it, taking her blood into his body, drinking the lifegiving liquid that would make them one.

I'm yours now, he heard Vanessa's voice in his head. *And you're mine.*

Always, he replied, reveling in the knowledge that their life would be filled with love and passion, and the chance for a family he'd never had before. *I will never let you go*. And that was a promise he would do everything in the world to keep.

Reading Order Scanguards Vampires & Stealth Guardians

Scanguards Vampires

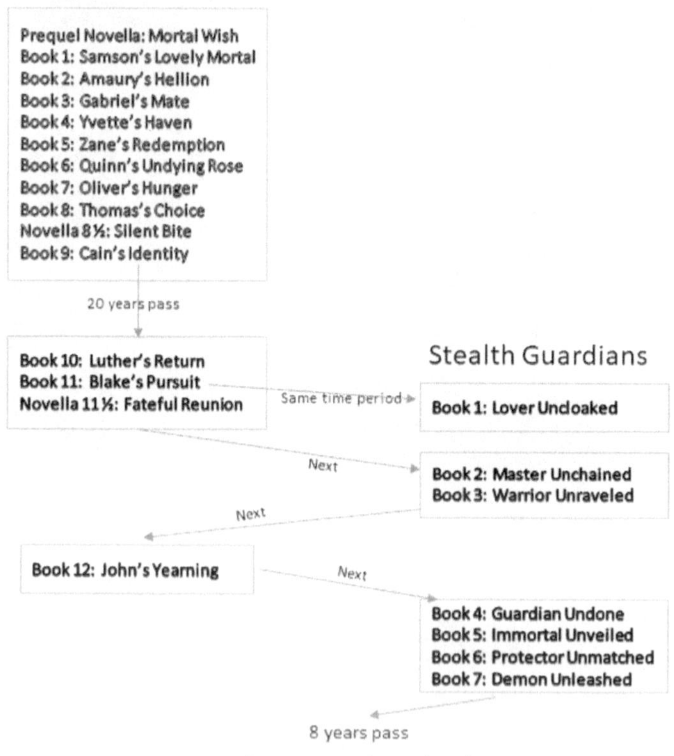

Scanguards Hybrids

The Scanguards Hybrids will also be numbered within the Scanguards
Vampires series (SV 13 = SH 1) to preserve continuity.

Book 1 (SV 13): Ryder's Storm
Book 2 (SV 14): Damian's Conquest
Book 3 (SV 15): Grayson's Challenge
Book 4 (SV 16): Isabelle's Forbidden Love
Book 5 (SV 17): Cooper's Passion
Book 6 (SV 18): Vanessa's Bravery
Book 7 (SV 19): Patrick's Seduction (2025)

About the Author

Tina Folsom was born in Germany and has been living in English speaking countries since 1991. Tina has always been a bit of a globe trotter. She lived in Munich, Lausanne, London, New York City, Los Angeles, San Francisco, and Sacramento. She has now made a beach town in Southern California her permanent home with her American husband and her dog.

She's written over 50 romance novels in English most of which are translated into German, French, Italian, and Spanish.

https://tinawritesromance.com
tina@tinawritesromance.com

facebook.com/TinaFolsomFans

instagram.com/authortinafolsom

www.ingramcontent.com/pod-product-compliance
Lightning Source LLC
Chambersburg PA
CBHW030330010826
48973CB00004B/947